DESIRE ME MORE

By Tiffany Clare

Desire Me More
Desire Me Now

DESIRE ME MORE

TIFFANY CLARE

AVONIMPULSE
An Imprint of HarperCollinsPublishers

Excerpt from *Desire Me Now* copyright © 2015 by Tiffany Clare.
Excerpt from *Close to Heart* copyright © 2015 by Tina Klinesmith.
Excerpt from *The Maddening Lord Montwood* copyright © 2015 by Vivienne Lorret.
Excerpt from *Chaos* copyright © 2015 by Jamie Shaw.
Excerpt from *The Bride Wore Denim* copyright © 2015 by Lizbeth Selvig.

EPub Edition AUGUST 2015 ISBN: 9780062380463

Print Edition ISBN: 9780062380456

AM 10 9 8 7 6 5 4 3 2 1

For Scott...

CHAPTER ONE

London, 1881

Amelia Somerset stretched out her arms only to find the immoveable force that was Nick lying next to her. Stifling a yawn, she spread her hands over his chest, molding every dip and plane of his body. *What a deliciously wicked way to wake up in the morning.*

Careful not to wake him, Amelia rolled away and grabbed Nick's pocket watch that had been set on her bedside table. Flipping it open, she was pleased to see that it was still early enough that she didn't have to get ready for the day but late enough to rouse Nick from his slumber. A grin tilted up her lips.

She knew that what they did wasn't something polite society would welcome. Women of any standing didn't carry on the way she and Nick were without the sanctity of marriage. She was also sure their intercourse wasn't precisely typical, or at least she never had imagined how many ways she could enjoy her lover. None of that seemed to matter since she was in love with Nick. Without him in her life, she was sure she would have found the past few weeks unbearable.

The man lying next to her had introduced her to an entirely new way of life and love, shown her things she never thought to see. Made her do things that had her blushing just thinking about them now.

Even though he had opened up her mind and her heart to a multitude of feelings she never thought she'd have for another, she was essentially his mistress.

His mistress...and his secretary.

Though she hoped no one yet guessed about the first.

She trailed her hand over his warm body, skimming his right bicep with just the tips of her fingers, making sure to trace every line of muscle as she explored him more thoroughly than she'd ever had the chance to do.

She could do this all day, but they only had an hour before he'd have to sneak back into his room and pretend they hadn't spent the night in delicious sin.

As she grew more daring, her hand lowered to his naval, her fingers circling his toned stomach. Should she caution her actions? Wake him up and get started on the one hundred and one duties that awaited them, or...

Or trail her fingers lower.

Curiosity decided her next course.

With a flick of her hand, she tossed the blanket off his chest and stared in awe at the perfection of his naked body. She loved the fact that he slept *au naturel*, as he was a sight to behold. Her gaze slid lower to see that he was aroused, and the sight had wetness slicking her thighs. She squeezed her legs together, wishing Nick's hand was buried there to ease the need building inside her.

Amelia brushed her fingers against his long, firm manhood. She could make out the dark vein running down the center of his shaft. The skin around the head was pulled back and the plum-colored head of his penis pointed right at her. Almost begging her to take it in her mouth.

His member moved, growing impossibly thicker as semen beaded at the tip. The sight fascinated her. Drew her closer. She had a sudden desire to touch that creamy drop of fluid...feel him like he often felt her. Taste him. She'd had the head of his penis in her mouth before, but she hadn't really known how to pleasure him.

Could she do so now?

Perhaps she could just lick him as he had licked through the folds of her sex. Would that draw more fluid from him?

Glancing up at Nick, she saw his eyes were closed, his breathing even. Turning her focus back to his penis, she lowered her hand enough to touch the wetness that had gathered at the tip. Her breath caught in her throat when his member jerked. She brushed her fingers against it again. Feeling more daring, she curled her hand around the head and squeezed it ever so slightly. Doing this excited her so much, she thought her heart might be pounding loudly enough to awaken him.

Suddenly, Nick wrapped his hand around hers. Her face burned with shame at being caught touching him while he was unaware, but under that shame there was a deep-seated desire, ready to be unleashed.

"You are awake," she said and loosened her hand, though it had nowhere to go with his grip tightening.

"Have been for a while." His voice was low and seductive, and a shiver of understanding shot straight to her core. He wanted to see how far she was willing to go.

Nick guided her hand low enough to cover the root just above his sac. He was so thick, her fingers barely curled around the base of him.

"Pull the skin forward and back." Nick's voice was hoarse.

He showed her how to increase the pressure of her hold. Watching him like this was strangely beautiful, raw, and without pretense. It was about the two of them pleasing each other and seeking their own pleasure, both at the same time. And it was about him giving in to her curiosity.

When she turned her face up to look at him, his eyes were heavy-lidded and lazily focused on her. Her heart skipped a beat and goose bumps rose along her arms. How could he undo her with one look?

He didn't release her from his gaze. He stared at her as though plotting to do very wicked things—and as if he would devour her any second.

She never wanted to get out of bed. She wanted to stay here until neither of them could move or talk and were too sore to even walk.

His breathing grew erratic as her hand stroked his hard length. She liked that he was letting his guard down, letting her see what her touch did to him. She grasped him tighter when his hand encouraged it.

Nick flipped her on her back and hovered over her before she could bring him to completion.

"How do you do this to me?" she asked, breathless.

He did not answer; his gaze locked on hers, his body hard and hot everywhere it pressed into hers. Absently, she stroked his arm, feeling the flex of muscle and the power he held just under the surface. She wanted to scratch her nails along his skin as he entered her but felt suddenly shy.

He leaned in and swept his tongue into her mouth, tasting her deeply. Her body grew heated and needy in a matter of seconds. She wanted him inside her, so in silent plea for more, she spread her legs as wide as her night rail would allow. She tilted her pelvis up, grinding herself against his thigh, trying to find some sort of release.

Nick pushed the material up and out of the way. He had her night rail off before she could offer to help. Her hands molding to the scars that crisscrossed his beautiful back. Every time she touched them she wanted to ask what had happened, who had hurt him, but the words stuck in her throat.

Nick held her hands above her head; then he positioned his body between her legs and worked his rigid penis inside her. Her whole body trembled with relief as he filled her, inch by tortuous inch.

When she tested his hold on her hands, he said, "Move them, and I'll tie you to the bed."

She bit her bottom lip. She almost wanted to dare him. Almost. Instead, she squeezed her thighs around his hips as he pulled out halfway before sliding back into her with a force that shook the bed frame.

Amelia arched her back off the bed, desperate to be closer, to feel him as deep as he could possibly go. Nick stilled once he was fully seated, his hand caressing the side of her face, brushing his fingers through the strands of hair that had come loose from her braid.

Mouth balanced above hers, his tongue swept gently across hers in a seductive dance with which she wanted to keep pace all day. But their morning would eventually end, and she'd make the most of the time they did have. Later, she'd think about the situation in which she kept placing herself and find the courage to ask him what he planned for them in the future.

Nick squeezed one of her nipples between his fingers, the pleasure drawing her attention away from her worries as she focused solely on him.

"I'm apparently not keeping you well enough occupied," he growled.

"It is thoughts of you tangling up my mind."

She kissed his chin and then his neck. Her tongue flicked along his pulse line before she settled against the mattress again.

"Then I will work harder to distract you from coherent thought." He pulled out of her and flipped her onto her knees. "Hold on to the top of the headboard."

Amelia curled her fingers around the cold metal frame. She waited in anticipation for him to slide back inside her. Instead, he kissed her shoulder, lightly at first, then openmouthed. His teeth bit carefully into her. Amelia's nipples peaked harder and harder with every scrape of his teeth. His hands ran up and down the sides of her ribs, skimming the undersides of her breasts with every pass.

"Nick..." She was panting, breathless from the way he teased her with so simple a touch.

Nick's chest brushed against her back, and the thick hardness of his penis lay demandingly against her backside.

"Hmmm." He moaned, as though she were a tasty treat.

Her head fell back, resting in the crook between his neck and shoulder. "I need you," she said.

"You have me."

"Please."

His hands smoothed over her ribs and waist. "Let me hear the words, Amelia."

"Touch me." She pressed her bottom against him. "I need your touch."

"Tell me where you need me." His hand tickled a seductive path over her hip. It was the barest of caresses as he slid that hand around to her stomach. Too low to touch her aching breasts and tweak with her nipples; too high to spread the juices flowing from her sex. "Or maybe you need me here?" His other hand slid over the front of one thigh and then into the vee of her legs but out of reach of her mound. She squeezed her legs together, wanting to hold him there. Wanting him to touch her more intimately and with more force.

Her breath caught as trembling sensations of arousal snaked through her, warming her and heightening every nerve ending in her body.

"Nick. Please…"

His hand wrenched her legs apart. A cool wash of air brushed over her wet thighs and had her moaning until finally—finally—he touched her clitoris. But the caress was nothing more than a fleeting tease…and not nearly enough. She thought she'd faint if he didn't touch her harder and fill her sheath.

"I want you inside me," she bravely said. "I need you, Nick. Don't deny me this."

"About time you asked," he growled in her ear before sucking her earlobe into his mouth.

Removing his hand from between her legs, he fisted it around his cock and pressed it to her entrance. His groan at the first touch of her wetness fueled her need to have him filling her.

One of his hands gripped the headboard beside her hand as he pressed forward. They both lost themselves in their joining, his chest hair abrading her back with the friction of their bodies as they grew slick with sweat.

His free hand squeezed her breast, and he rolled her nipple between his fingers, heightening her pleasure with the furious propulsion of his body in hers. She bit her bottom lip to keep from screaming out her pleasure, even though the racket they made could surely be heard by anyone on this floor of the house.

Lips hot against her neck, fingers still tweaking her nipples, he overloaded her with sensation, with feeling. Nick surrounded her, filled her, stamped himself on her.

Nick owned her.

Hand lowering, he flicked his finger over her sensitive clitoris, and she could no longer bite back the sounds she'd been holding at bay.

Giving her clit the same treatment he'd given her nipple, he squeezed it between his fingers, letting her grind against his hand as he worked himself inside her.

"Nick," she practically screamed. Her thighs were so slick, so wet, that her juices sluiced a wet path down her legs.

"I could fuck you like this all day," Nick growled in her ear.

She didn't know how to respond, other than to moan his name. Words were beyond her.

"You'd like that, wouldn't you." It wasn't a question. He knew that was exactly what she wanted.

How could one person have so much control over her? How could this man hold the reins of her heart so tightly that she would go anywhere he steered her and do anything he asked?

His words did nothing but inflame her desire further. Her body pushed back against his, needing more yet needing exactly what he was giving her.

"One of these days I'm going to show you what it truly means to be mine."

She shook her head, not able to think his words through. "I don't understand."

"You will…soon."

He grabbed both her hips and pumped into her so hard that the bed frame groaned and creaked with every one of their motions. They would be found out for sure. And while that should concern her, all she did was grasp on tighter, ensuring her hold wouldn't slip and that she stayed exactly where she was so Nick's penis hit her just the right way.

"I want you to come. I know how close you are." He punctuated every word with the movement of their bodies.

He grasped her braid in one hand and yanked it back, exposing her throat to his wicked mouth. "Come for me," he said, licking the sensitive spot between her neck and shoulder.

His legs were between hers, spreading them wide enough that she was sitting atop his lap.

She could feel the slap of his testicles every time she bounced off his lap. And before long, she did scream out. Her orgasm exploded through her. Her sheath gripped his cock so tightly that she felt every ridge of his hardness stroking in and out of her.

With a roar, Nick said, "Fuck."

With a final stroke his seed shot deep inside her, the semen pulsing out of him in a never-ending stream. The slick wetness between them only added to the friction of the short hairs on his sac rubbing and assaulting her clitoris, and she felt herself go off again. Her head fell forward to rest on the frame of the bed as she rotated in tight circles around his shaft, milking every bit of him as her body rode out her climax. Her breasts heaved with the violent breaths she took in and blew out. It was like she'd run a mile, and this was her first chance to pull air into her starved and deprived lungs.

Nick rubbed his hands all over her, as though it would calm her after the race she'd just run with him. Her body collapsed on his, though she couldn't help the slight rotation of her hips from time to time. He wasn't the least bit worn out, and she knew that because he was still hard.

When she finally had her breathing under control, she said, "You're insatiable."

"Only with you. I can never seem to get enough of you, Amelia."

"What if you should grow tired of me?"

"Impossible." He reached for her hands and loosened her grip from the bedpost. All the feeling rushed back into her hands, making them tingle.

Sitting in his lap, she had no desire to move. No desire to start their day. In fact, she would prefer to laze about in bed with Nick all day. That was an impossibility but still a nice dream.

She turned her head to the side to look him in the eyes. "We need to get dressed. If we didn't manage to already wake up the household with our antics, they will be up any minute."

"That makes me think you are trying to get rid of me."

She smiled. She couldn't help it. "I'll see you in the study."

Nick trailed one hand down her sternum and circled her breast. "Mmm, I still haven't had you on my desk."

She swallowed back a groan. Nick was forever trying to commit the wickedest of sins anywhere that wasn't one of their bedrooms, anywhere that they potentially could be caught. She enjoyed the danger of discovery associated with those scenarios, not that she would admit it aloud.

"You have appointments this morning, Nick. You already canceled dinner with Lord Murray last night. I am positive he will send a sour note before the day is through. And at some point you will have to continue working as though nothing has changed." Even though everything had changed since her brother, Jeremy, had tried to remove her from the safety of the house. Since Nick had been forced to take a stand against her brother.

"My priority is and will always be you."

With a heavy sigh, she pulled off his lap. It was pure torture, not being able to sink back down on his hard length. "As I said, we have a busy day."

Nick grabbed her hand before she escaped his reach. He held her at the edge of the bed. "If you want to talk business, then let me say this: I'm concerned your brother will make another appearance while I'm not here. Keeping you in bed seems like the best plan for keeping you safe until he crawls back to Berwick."

"You already have Huxley watching me," she reminded him. Even when she went down for lunch at midday, Huxley was never far behind. Sometimes she resented their close regard, but she understood the necessity.

Her brother had threatened to hurt her and every other servant in the house. He had told her that if she didn't pay him back the money she'd stolen from him, he'd torment the other women who lived here. He also told Amelia that she had to marry a man she despised. A man to whom her brother owed a great deal of money, including the family estate.

With her thoughts maudlin and her good mood taking a turn for the worse, she slipped her hand from Nick's grasp and pulled on her robe as she walked toward the washstand. The rustling of material behind her told her that Nick was donning his clothes too.

When her brother had tried to kidnap her, Nick had been there to stop Jeremy. Amelia would never forget the rage that had filled Nick's eyes as he punched and then threatened her brother if he dared try to get at Amelia again.

The incident had been seen by enough prominent members of society that word had spread of Nick's actions in less than a day. That had been a week ago. And while her brother hadn't come back to the house, she was afraid he would try to get at her again.

When she had run away from her childhood home, she'd promised she would no longer live in fear. But some things were hard to forget, some pasts never forgotten, and her brother hadn't spared her a kind moment in her whole life.

Being with Nick made her feel safe, and she wished she'd never have to leave his arms, but to admit such a thing would make Nick more protective. And really, how could she think that way when her feelings were torn by the fact that she knew so little about him?

She poured water over the linen in the bowl and wrung it out between her shaking hands.

"You're thinking about him again," Nick said, taking the cloth from her.

"It's difficult not to do. I don't know if he has given up his pursuit of me and gone back to Berwick. What if he is waiting for another chance to get me alone?"

Nick's arms wrapped around her as he wiped the cool cloth between her legs, washing away their mingled fluids. Amelia pressed her back against his warm body. She held back a moan, knowing that if she let it slip past her lips, they would end up right back in bed.

"If there's one thing I can promise with certainty, it's that your brother won't come here again."

"I want to believe you. I do. But my doubts have a tendency to consume me at times."

When his finger brushed over her swollen clit, she turned and wrapped her arms around his shoulders.

"I might not leave the house and give my brother a chance to catch me unawares, but he knows Devlin lives here and runs errands for everyone." Devlin was the housekeeper's son, and he'd had a confrontation with Amelia's brother that had resulted in a black eye for the poor boy. Amelia still felt immense guilt over that incident.

"Can you promise me that *everyone* is safe from Jeremy's wrath? I know what my brother is capable of. What lengths he will go to in the name of revenge. There is no decent bone in his body that would make me believe otherwise."

"And you don't know what I'm capable of."

"You're right. You know everything about me, and I know so little about you." She searched his eyes as she admitted this out loud. That very fact had been bothering her for the better part of a week.

Even through his short clipped beard, she could make out the tick high on his cheek. She ran her finger over the harsh line.

"I've promised to protect everyone in this house," he said, "and it's not a promise I make lightly, Amelia. He will never hurt you again."

She wanted to believe him. Trust only in him. And even though she'd confessed her love to him, she had to remind herself that she didn't *really* know much about Nicholas Riley.

She knew where his business interests lay, that he had a sister he doted upon, that his staff was devoted wholly to him. She knew she felt safe and loved when she was in his arms. She knew he'd had a difficult childhood and that he fought hard to reach the position he had in life. Beyond that, she didn't know anything about his past, or why he had the scars on his back. She wanted to know why he sometimes woke up in the grips of a nightmare, yelling incoherently, the words impossible to decipher. He was keeping the deeper parts of himself hidden. The parts that defined him as the man he was.

She trusted that he wouldn't hurt her, but she had more questions than answers where he was concerned.

She pulled Nick's face down to hers and kissed him full on the mouth. She didn't slip her tongue between his lips, even though she wanted to. It was a parting kiss for the morning.

When she let him go, she whispered against his mouth, "I'll meet you in the study once I'm dressed."

Before she could get away, he hugged her hard against his tightly muscled body. She pressed her head to his chest, comforted by the steady beat of his heart.

"I am reluctant to leave you when I know you're mulling over something that has upset you."

"I have so many questions and worries." She bit her lip to keep from saying more.

"About your brother?" He rubbed her back in languorous strokes, drawing a sigh from her.

"My questions are all about you."

"We are taking this one day at a time, Amelia. I have no intentions of letting you go."

But didn't all men grow tired of their mistresses? If that were to come to pass, where would that leave her?

She forced herself to take a step away from him. His gaze was searching.

"We really do have to ready ourselves," she said.

He placed his fingers under her chin and forced her to look at him. "This conversation is far from finished, Amelia."

"I know. And I'm glad for that. We have so much to discuss."

He placed a gentle kiss upon her lips. "You are giving too much thought to what's between us."

"How can you suggest that?"

"Isn't it enough that we are madly, deeply in love with one another?" The seriousness was gone from his tone, and his words held a sternness that took her by surprise.

"Yes and no." Shaking her head, she ushered him toward the door. "You have to leave. I refuse to be caught in a compromising position."

"I'm sure everyone already knows I have thoroughly compromised you."

She laughed as she darted away from his attempt to pull her back into his arms. "You're impossible."

"You like that about me."

"All right, I admit that to be true. Now, will you meet me in the study?"

Nick winked at her as he slipped out the door and closed it softly behind him. Amelia slumped against the wall, thinking about his parting words. Had he really just promised to tell her more about his past? About him? She needed to get dressed immediately so she could ask him all the questions burning in her mind.

CHAPTER TWO

The knocker sounded at the front door as Nick came down the stairs. Huxley emerged from the lower level of the house, but Nick waved him away since he was here anyway. His brows pinched as he opened the door and assessed the uniformed man who stared back at him.

The truncheon at his side and the chinstrap helmet tied just above his cleft chin identified him as a bobby. His coat was slightly rumpled and the buttons drew a crooked line down the center of his chest and tucked under a thick leather belt. The man looked as though he'd been up all night and was coming to the end of his shift.

Nick knew most of the local bobbies, as there was a higher rate of crime near his warehouses on the Thames, but this man was new to him. Nick crossed his arms over his chest. "How can I help you, Constable?"

"Inspector, actually. Inspector Laurie."

"Accept my apologies. What necessity has brought you to my door?" Nick really just wanted to ask what in hell the man was doing here but bit his tongue.

"I'm here about a murder. And you were seen in a precarious situation with this particular man only last week." The inspector produced a notebook from his jacket pocket and thumbed to an empty page. "Do you know the Earl of Berwick?"

Nick nodded. "Only in passing. We were not acquainted." This was perplexing...and disturbing that the inspector was asking Nick about his connection to Jeremy. "The earl is dead?"

"Found him floating in the Thames this morning." He scribbled something down that Nick couldn't make out. "Are you aware that he was residing in London?"

Nick leaned against the doorframe. "What exactly are you asking me, Inspector?"

"You were the last person reportedly seen with Lord Berwick."

Nick narrowed his eyes. "Are you accusing me of something? Because I can assure you I was here all evening. My man of affairs can confirm this if you'd like me to ring for him."

Nick had no intention of bringing Amelia into this. Huxley would vouch for his whereabouts. Though he'd still have to tell her the news about her brother.

How in hell had Jeremy ended up dead? That fool brother of Amelia's might have taken a beating by Nick's hand, but Nick left him breathing—as much as he hadn't wanted to. Did the inspector even have the right man? Something was off here. He needed to investigate this further on his own. Foremost in Nick's thoughts was that it had been a week since he'd seen Amelia's brother, and the inspector said no one had seen him since then. That didn't ring true.

"I'll check with my source again; see if you have been mistaken for someone else. I just needed to ask before I finished my shift."

"If you require some sort of statement from my man of affairs, I can send him over to your headquarters later this morning."

The inspector scratched the side of his jaw where a night's worth of stubble had grown. "No need. My apologies for disturbing you so early."

Nick didn't believe the man, for some reason. He stepped away from the door, ready to say his good-byes, but paused. "Who precisely saw me last night?"

"Unfortunately, I cannot divulge my source while we are actively investigating Lord Berwick's murder."

Nick furrowed his brow. "I see. Good day, Inspector Laurie."

The man assessed him for a moment before he nodded and bounded down the stairs, belying the tiredness that enveloped him.

When Nick closed the front door, a million questions came to mind. He headed to the lower level to find Huxley in the butler's pantry, a small room next to the housekeeper's office. Huxley's room was stacked with rows of wooden crates on every wall, most filled with wine and spirits. There was a desk tucked into one corner where Huxley often came to escape the noise of the house.

Nick closed the door behind him, drawing Huxley's attention away from the inventory ledger he was reviewing. Nick had known Huxley for the better part of a decade, and credited much of his success to their friendship over the years. Nick trusted no one as much as he trusted Huxley.

"Pretty early for visitors. What emergency had them calling so early in the morning?" Huxley asked.

"Lord Berwick was murdered. An inspector came by inquiring about it. He wanted confirmation on my whereabouts last night. Though I don't think it necessary, I said you might go down to his headquarters to say that we remained home last night."

"Berwick found himself some trouble, then."

Huxley didn't question where Nick had been or if he was responsible for any wrongdoing. That kind of trust came from their years of working together. Regardless, Nick had nothing to do with Amelia's brother's murder. But someone would know something, and Nick planned to get to the bottom of it.

"I'll head down to the docks in an hour or so," Huxley said. "I have to do the intake for a shipment transferred from Liverpool at the same time. Don't expect I'll be back before luncheon."

"That is fine. Be sure to talk to the man who watched Lord Berwick last night. He must have witnessed something peculiar."

"Already thinking that. Odd timing, considering you confronted him a week ago."

"I know. I plan to call on Landon this afternoon. If Lord Berwick was murdered, there will be rumors buzzing about Town and I want to know what everyone is saying."

Landon Price, the Earl of Burley, was a friend and business associate of Nick's. He raised sheep in Scotland and had the wool shipped through Nick's company to be sold in London. Landon was also one of the few people Nick trusted implicitly.

"I'll let Liam know we might both be out," Huxley said. "He can watch after the house." Liam, the footman, watched after the house whenever Nick and Huxley both had appointments to attend. "Can't say I'm sorry her brother is dead. Not after the way he treated her, and after the threats he uttered against this house."

"I couldn't agree more with that sentiment," Nick said. "Don't reveal anything about her brother to anyone. Amelia should be the first to know. But I can't tell her anything until I have more information."

Huxley grunted in response.

"I'll let you get on with your day. We can meet tonight before dinner."

"I'll be here," Huxley assured him.

Nick nodded and left the butler's pantry. There was a niggling voice in the back of his mind asking, who was he to keep this news from Amelia?

Nick scrubbed his hand over his face, wishing more than ever that he and Amelia had lazed about in bed all morning. While Amelia didn't profess to love her brother and insisted she never wanted him in her life, Berwick's murder would still wound her deeply. This put him in a moral quandary on keeping this secret from her at all, but his mind was made on the matter.

To Amelia's disappointment, Nick was not in the study when she finally made it downstairs. Perhaps he'd left the house to run errands after all. Although he was a pleasant diversion, she could do without his particular form of distraction for a few hours.

Gathering the letters that had piled up in the front foyer, she resigned herself to responding to Nick's correspondence, and then she would read through the purchase agreements of Lord Murray's lands. They had met with Murray on a few occasions to discuss the sale of his property in Highgate, and it was likely to be transferred to Nick's name over the next few weeks.

The housekeeper entered the study, drawing Amelia's attention away from her scribblings. "Good morning, Mrs. Coleman. How may I assist you?"

"Lord Murray is here with his secretary."

"Mr. Riley isn't here."

"Mr. Riley's occupied in Huxley's office. I told Lord Murray he wasn't available, but he refuses to leave without speaking to Mr. Riley."

Amelia briefly contemplated how best to handle the situation. "I would hate to be the cause of a misunderstanding or for Lord Murray to find someone else to purchase his property. This deal is important to Mr. Riley. Send Lord Murray in here, and let Mr. Riley know I am entertaining Lord Murray until he can join us."

Mrs. Coleman nodded and returned with one very irate-looking Lord Murray. His face was red, and his bushy brows were screwed together tightly in what looked like a permanent scowl. A tall, polished man entered the room with Lord Murray; Amelia assumed this was the secretary. He wore a decent tan coat with waistcoat and dark trousers. His blond hair was neatly parted and pomaded; his green eyes were sharp and focused on her.

Amelia stood to greet them, giving a slight curtsey when she stood before them. "Lord Murray. Shall I have tea brought up while you wait for Mr. Riley? He shouldn't be but a moment."

"That is not necessary," Lord Murray responded. Amelia motioned toward the leather chairs that flanked Nick's desk, but Lord Murray didn't seem inclined to sit.

Since Lord Murray didn't introduce the other man, Amelia took it upon herself to do so. "I'm sorry; we haven't been introduced. I'm Mr. Riley's secretary, Miss Grant."

"Mr. Shauley." His accent was thick, his eyes assessing as he looked her up and down as though she were…lacking. What an odd feeling to have on first meeting someone. "I preside over Lord Murray's business affairs."

Lord Murray didn't exactly have any business other than owning a few lots of land and sitting in the House of Lords.

"It's a pleasure to meet you, Mr. Shauley." She smiled, but he didn't return the gesture; if anything, a frown drew his eyes down and put creases along his forehead.

Mr. Shauley stepped closer to her—too close. Lord Murray was pacing the floor, ignoring them both as he flipped his pocketwatch open, only to snap it shut over and over again.

"What happened to Huxley?" Mr. Shauley inquired.

It was a question she should be used to. And though the question did not precisely bother her, it was the way in which Mr. Shauley said Huxley's name that had her hackles rising.

"Huxley takes care of Mr. Riley's businesses more directly now. I am responsible for the administrative tasks Mr. Riley has, keeping his appointments straight and such."

"I always thought Huxley was a man who could do it all," Mr. Shauley said.

"He most certainly is." She laughed a little, trying to lighten the mood. She didn't like the feeling of being cross-examined by a man she did not know.

"What is it you do, Mr. Shauley? I did not realize Lord Murray was a businessman."

"I manage his estates. And I have done everything in my power to advise against selling Highgate for such a disadvantageous price, but his mind is set."

"Oh?" She was genuinely curious.

"It is worth more. The land alone should be sold at double Riley's offer."

"Then why is Lord Murray selling Highgate?"

As Mr. Shauley took another step toward her, she decided that this particular man was no better than Jeremy, trying to use his presence and taller frame to intimidate her. She held her ground and looked him in the eye. She refused to be cowed by such a man.

Mr. Shauley's nostrils flared for the briefest moment and then he said, "Unfortunately, the house must be sold regardless of whether I agree with the price. Upkeep alone is more than the worth, so it's rotting and in ruins for the most part."

"I hadn't realized." She remembered Nick mentioning that he planned to restore the manor house. But if it was in such a poor state as Mr. Shauley indicated, why go to the trouble?

"Of course not, Miss Grant." He looked at her quizzically. "You're from significantly farther reaches of England. The north, I'd say."

Amelia swallowed back her sudden trepidation. Nick had once said something about her accent not being that of a Londoner, but she didn't think it was so obvious.

Before she could ask more questions of the odd man who was standing far too close, the study door opened, and Amelia couldn't have been happier to see Nick striding in. She looked at him apologetically, though she wasn't sure how she could have righted this situation. Nick's focus lay solely on Mr. Shauley, his gaze filled with something so dark she could only call it hatred.

Did the two men know each other? *Of course they do,* she thought. The negotiations with Lord Murray had been going on since long before she became Nick's secretary.

"Lord Murray." Nick broke the silence that had descended upon the room and turned his attention away from Mr. Shauley. "To what do I owe the pleasure of your company?"

"Cut the small talk, Riley. Did you think I would shrug off your slight?"

Amelia winced at the accusation in Lord Murray's tone. It had been her fault that Nick had canceled his dinner plans with Lord Murray last night.

Nick turned his attention to Amelia. "Miss Grant, would you please send up Huxley? I last saw him in the kitchens."

"Of course." She nodded toward Lord Murray and Shauley before she left, not sure if she was glad for the reprieve of Mr. Shauley's creepy regard or angry with Nick for sending her off as though she played no vital part in the purchase of the property.

Once Amelia left the room, Nick looked toward Lord Murray. "I had a family emergency that needed my attention this week, as the note I sent indicated. Really, Murray, you couldn't wait a few more nights to give me this high-and-mighty speech?"

"We were advised while sitting in the restaurant," Lord Murray responded. "I know what you are about, Riley. You are stringing me along, hoping to get the property for a fraction of its worth." He stood in front of Nick, his face crimson.

"A family emergency," Nick repeated. "It required my *full* attention. Stop acting like a bride jilted at the altar."

Lord Murray sputtered at the insult. "I'll not be treated like a second thought."

"And I will not be hounded in my own house. You forget that I make the rules in this venture of ours." Nick glanced in the direction of Shauley, who had yet to say a word. "I will contact you whenever I damn well please."

Shauley spoke then. "You can play this any way you like, Riley, but by all appearances you haven't come through on your word yet. You have delayed this sale by a month."

"You dare to come into my house and insult me on my word?" Nick sat on the edge of his desk, glaring at Shauley. No one told Nick what he should do, how he should act, or what exactly he was thinking, especially Shauley.

Huxley strolled into the study, and Nick was glad that Amelia was not behind him, though he would have to advise that she stay away from Shauley going forward.

"Good day, Lord Murray," Huxley said, not bothering to greet Shauley.

The tension that had built in the room dispelled with Huxley's arrival.

"It is clear we are of opposing minds," Nick said, "but our meeting has concluded. Miss Grant will advise you tomorrow where and when we will dine to go over any final particulars, Lord Murray. Huxley will show you to the door."

Nick didn't wait for Lord Murray's response as he walked around to the front of the desk and pulled out his chair. Huxley looked on with nothing short of amusement.

"I'll not forget this slight, Riley," Lord Murray said.

"If you want our arrangement to remain mutually beneficial you will guard your temper and leash your pet." Nick looked at Shauley with indifference, though that was the last thing he felt. "I don't need to tell you that my patience is thin when dealing with pompous lords like you. Even thinner for the scum you scraped off the street and dressed up as your man of affairs."

Lord Murray looked as if he was about to have a fit of apoplexy. Instead of another outburst, he turned on his heel and strode out of the study, anger radiating from him like a hive full of disturbed wasps.

Huxley followed Lord Murray out. Shauley, however, placed his hat atop his head and strode toward Nick's desk as though he had all the time in the world before he departed.

"Did I not make myself clear, Shauley?"

"You have certainly turned into a cold bastard over the years."

"If you think that our growing up across a shared laneway gives you any familiarity with me, let me advise you that you are mistaken."

"Now, Nick. You do wound my sensibilities."

Nick snorted, though he wasn't the least bit amused. "Do you have some asinine notion that we will renew our friendship because of my dealings with Lord Murray?"

"It would do you well to remember that I can be the worm in his lordship's ear and persuade him of another course of action."

"Then why let the manor go at all? I know how deeply attached you are to that pile of rubble. *Sentimentality* for your old way of life and all." The depravities of the man standing before him were extreme, and they reminded Nick of a time in his life that he wanted nothing more than to scrub from his brain.

Shauley pinched his lips together, though he didn't take the bait and storm out, as Nick had hoped. "It's no more *sentimentality* for me than it is for you."

It was a place they'd both lost whatever innocence they had as children. While Nick had risen from the ashes of his past, Shauley had smoldered and been molded into a man equally as vile as the vicar who had destroyed their childhood.

"It is mere coincidence that Highgate came up to be purchased at all," Nick explained, though Shauley deserved no reason for Nick's decisions. "I require a manor that has acreage close to the city. Highgate provides that."

Shauley grinned as though he had Nick's purpose figured out. What Shauley didn't realize, however, was Nick's plan to expose the vicar, who still resided in Highgate, as a way to wipe the slate clean from a past that still haunted Nick.

When Shauley didn't seem inclined to leave, Nick pushed out from his desk and stood, ready to throw the man out, if need be. Shauley took the hint but not before parting with, "Did the good old vicar break you after all? I thought you above the old man's machinations."

"Odd how the same cannot be said of you. Broken is the defining character for what you've become." The degeneracies of that vicar had seeped into Shauley long ago.

Shauley laughed shortly before he turned and left Nick's study. Huxley returned a short time later.

"I'd like to say I'm surprised to see them both here, but Shauley has been decidedly quiet since the negotiations were under way for Highgate," Nick mused aloud. Huxley crossed his arms over his chest and waited for Nick to elaborate. "If he comes around the house again, I want to be the first to know."

"Easily done," Huxley said. "Is he a danger to anyone?"

Nick immediately thought of Devlin and Amelia. "Yes. There's no telling who he will try to hurt if he wants to get to me."

"So we bury one problem with Lord Berwick's death, only to have another surface?"

"I'm not convinced the two are singular incidences." Nick pressed his thumbs into his temples. What was he missing that connected the two meetings this morning? "The inspector followed by Shauley's appearance cannot be coincidental, yet why should they be connected at all?"

Nick had never had dealings with Lord Berwick. Did Lord Berwick know Lord Murray? Had Lord Berwick known Shauley? Nick knew that Shauley was Lord Murray's secretary, but Shauley made a point of being scarce for any meetings or dealings directly with Nick. So after two months of avoiding a meeting with Nick, why come around today of all days?

"Where is Amelia?" He hadn't meant to be dismissive when he'd come into the study to find Shauley glaring at her like she was a rabbit set for the dinner plate.

"Said she would break her fast since she wasn't required in the study."

So he'd angered her. *Damn it, this day couldn't possibly get worse.*

CHAPTER THREE

Amelia heard the front door of the house open at nine. She smoothed her fingers over the satin bookmark dividing the pages of the book. She hadn't read more than three words before setting it on the table next to her. She'd waited in the library for Nick's return for nearly two hours now. She headed toward the adjoining study just as a lamp burned to life, chasing away the darkness of the room.

Nick had been gone for the better part of the day. Surprisingly, Huxley hadn't been his usual three feet away from her when Nick wasn't around. Had something happened during the meeting with Murray to take them away from the house? If that were the case, why hadn't Nick told her where he was going?

Had there been a development with her brother? With Huxley's absence, she wondered if Jeremy had gone home.

It wasn't lost on her that she'd had all day to think through her questions, but now that the opportunity presented itself…she didn't know how to ask any of the thoughts that had plagued her throughout day.

Nick was sitting in his chair with his head tilted back and one arm thrown over his eyes.

She broke the silence that had descended upon the room. "Good evening. I wasn't entirely sure we'd see each other tonight."

He removed his hand and looked right at her. The breath froze in her lungs. Just one look from him had the ability to render her speechless.

She looked toward the library, needing to break eye contact with him so she could at least think straight. "I was reading when I heard you come in. I didn't mean to interrupt your solitude."

"Amelia." Her name came out like a question, bidding her to meet his gaze again. Folding her hands in front of her so she wouldn't fidget, she raised her head to look at him. Nick pushed the chair out from his desk and patted one leg. "Will you sit with me for a while?"

Glancing at the door that led to the main corridor of the house, she noted it was slightly ajar. She shook her head. It was one thing for the household to know what they were up to, another thing entirely for the staff to witness their transgressions.

Nick must have noticed where her focus lay. "Close it." He patted his thigh again.

She swallowed and was too tempted not to do his bidding. She locked the door before returning to his side and sat carefully on one of his thighs.

He searched her eyes for a moment and then asked, "How was your day?"

"Fraught with worry."

He merely cocked one eyebrow at her questioningly. "Do elaborate."

She shook her head, not knowing how to voice any of her questions. She stuttered out a few I's and we's but couldn't formulate the words for how she was feeling. "My ability to express myself vanishes whenever we are in the same room."

The side of his mouth kicked up into a half grin. She never saw him smile for anyone but her, and that had her heart pounding to its own tempo in her chest.

"I'll take that as a compliment," he said, smoothing his finger over the creases between her brows. "Tell me what has you worried."

"Us. You. Your expectations of me. You ignoring me after the meeting with Lord Murray and Mr. Shauley this morning, after dismissing me from your company as though my presence was relegated to that of a dimwitted spouse."

Nick sighed heavily. "I regret my reaction to seeing Shauley and you in the same room, but my worry was for your safety. The less he can guess about what is happening between us, the easier it is for me to keep him at arm's length. I should have explained that before I left, but I wasn't thinking clearly."

Mr. Shauley might have seemed creepy, and there was no denying that his presence had made her uncomfortable, but… "Why do you have that opinion of Lord Murray's secretary?"

"I know Shauley more than I care to. We grew up together in St. Giles. Our mothers were in the same…profession. We had a falling out many years ago and have avoided each other since and for good reason. If he can hurt the people I love to get back at me, he will."

Amelia knew she had to pick her questions carefully, for Nick would change the topic and give her nothing of himself if she dug too deep. "Do you care to elaborate on your falling out?"

"He's a dangerous man, Amelia, and you need to avoid him. Trust me in this matter."

None of what he was saying was really an answer, but she would take him at his word. It sounded as though Mr. Shauley knew something more of Nick's past…more than to which she'd been privy. "Did you settle everything with Lord Murray?" she asked.

"He won't be going anywhere anytime soon. He needs my money more than he needs to keep the family lands. He can be as angry as he likes for the delays I've caused. I've been preoccupied by matters far more important to me." Nick ran his thumb over her chin, the move sensual and designed to make her forget the rest of her questions. "He's a concern for another day."

Her eyes slipped shut. Other things had been niggling at the back of her mind all day, but it was hard to recall those questions while he was touching her so innocently…yet so intimately.

She finally remembered. "And us?"

"My expectations?"

She nodded, as she stared at his lips.

"I would never ask for anything more than you are willing to give. You are your own person. What we have isn't shameful, not when we feel the way we do about each other."

"How can you call it anything but? I won't argue that with you, but the rest of the house cannot ever know how we carry on in the evenings."

"Neither of us is naïve enough to believe our time together is a secret to anyone. Least of all those living in this house." Nick placed his fingers under her chin to tilt it up.

He was right. Even though she knew they needed to set clear boundaries that would make everyone believe nothing sinful was happening between them, she found it hard to refuse him anything. What a conundrum she was in—her heart warring with her mind on the right course of action.

"I noticed Huxley's absence today," she said. "Has something happened?"

He curled his hand around hers, his larger size engulfing her, making her feel so small next to him. "I should have told you before I left, but I needed to see the truth for myself. It could have been a hoax, I kept telling myself; it was too easy to happen this way. And it still doesn't feel right."

"It's my brother, isn't it?"

"My sweet Amelia. I have bad news about your brother."

"Did you meet with him today? Is that why Huxley wasn't here?"

He nodded, hesitant.

"Just tell me what has happened."

"If I could shield you from this, I would. But you deserve the truth, as much as it pains me to relay it to you." He paused and entwined their hands. She looked at their fingers, tangled, his tanned skin in juxtaposition to her paleness. "A police inspector was here this morning. Just before Lord Murray's arrival. I'm sorry, Amelia, but…your brother is dead."

She heard a ringing in her ears, and her body suddenly felt numb. Her heart actually skipped a beat with her sudden inhalation. "Huxley said he was staying with a friend this past week. He was—" She swallowed against the nerves making it hard for her talk, and her lip trembled before she could temper the reaction. "I don't understand. How is this possible?"

"I intend to find out what happened." Nick watched her without saying more.

Was he expecting her to cry? There was no press of tears in the back of her eyes. Did that mean something was wrong with her? What kind of person did that make her? She felt nothing except…numb. Everything was numb. She stood from Nick's lap, disentangling their hands as she backed away from him. "This is *impossible*," she whispered.

"I went down to the city morgue myself to confirm what the inspector told me." Nick stood, following her every step.

"How?"

"He was murdered."

Her breath hitched in her lungs. Her hands shook so hard that she had to dig her nails into her palms to steady them. Denials built in her throat, but no sound or words came out.

How was someone supposed to digest the news of a blood relative being murdered?

Should she feel anger? She didn't. Should she feel elated that she didn't have to watch her back constantly? That felt wrong too.

She shook her head. "He's masterminded some sort of trick. He was always good at manipulating everyone around him. This isn't real. It can't be. I know my brother, Nick."

She heard the pleading in her own voice. This was wrong. It was all wrong.

"Amelia." Nick took another step toward her and reached for her arm. He pulled her close, tucking her head against his chest. The steady cadence of his heart in her ear helped even out her breathing, but it did not still the shaking that overtook her whole body.

"I'm sorry to be the bearer of bad news." His arms were strong and steady, and they were the only thing keeping her on her feet.

"This is not possible," she whispered into his shoulder. She felt as though she were in a terrible nightmare, one from which she was unable to wake.

Nick's hand smoothed over her hair, the gesture soothing but far from placating her emotions.

"I didn't believe it either. So I didn't tell you until I'd seen it with my own eyes."

She turned her head up at him. "I need to see him."

Nick looked back at her long and hard. "Foolish girl."

Amelia grasped his jacket at the sleeves. "I won't ever believe it if I don't see him."

"I won't lie to you, Amelia. He is far from resembling the brother you remember."

She appreciated that he didn't deny her this one request. "My brother has tormented me all my life, Nick. It was as though making me miserable was a sick game. I will never believe him gone unless I see him with my own eyes." Her lips trembled, and she took in a shaky breath. "I need closure if I am to move on and put my past behind me, once and for all."

"If that's what you want, I won't stop you. I will never take your choices away from you." He brushed back a stray curl of her hair and tucked it behind her ear. "I'll be right there for you if you need me."

"I wouldn't want anyone but you at my side."

Nick raised her hands to his mouth and pressed kisses to her knuckles.

"You said an inspector told you what had happened?"

He nodded, his gaze never leaving hers.

"Tell me what he said, Nick."

"That I was the last person seen with your brother."

She tried to pull her hands away. Surely he wasn't suspected of killing her brother. "But that was a week ago."

"I know. That's why I left so suddenly this morning. I had to find out who else had been in your brother's company. Huxley went down to see the inspector today and vouched for my whereabouts last night."

"Not…?" Why hadn't he asked her?

Nick rubbed his hands over her arms. "No. I won't ask you to do that."

"What did Huxley think of that?"

"I know he suspects what is happening between us, but he won't ask, and he won't say anything to anyone."

She breathed a small sigh of relief that Huxley would remain circumspect. Though knowing they were not pulling the wool over anyone's eyes should set her straight and make her want to stop their affair…she *couldn't*. Nick was as essential as the air she breathed; without him, she would slowly suffocate.

"We both saw my brother a week ago, as did a number of people outside this house when he accosted me. Surely he's been busy in gambling hells since then. Those places are rife with patrons."

"And prostitutes, criminals, and members of society who don't want to be found out." He kissed her forehead as though to apologize for the reality of that statement. "I know he was never kind to you. I know he made your life a living hell, but I also know how hard it is to lose someone who has been a constant in your life for as long as you can remember."

"I won't mourn him." She squared her shoulders, feeling calmer and more in power of her life now than she'd ever felt before.

"I am not suggesting you do. This once, I'll go along with whatever you tell me. I'm here for you, Amelia. Is that a deal?"

"How are you possible or even real?"

"I'm as real as you are."

"Thank you," she whispered and folded herself in Nick's arms, the place she felt safest.

True to his word, Nick accompanied her to the dead house. Amelia sat in the carriage and waited while Nick went inside to talk to the undertaker. The building looked like any ordinary chapel. Ivy grew along the fascia of the stone building and curled around the lead-paned windows, adding life to a place full of death.

There weren't any places like this in Berwick, so she had nothing to compare to it, but she hadn't expected the exterior to look quite so...pleasant and cheerful. So what had she expected? Some back-alley dungeon filled with rats and filth?

Nick stepped out of the building followed by a slender younger man, clean-shaven, with wheat-blond hair. She looked at him straight on from the carriage, though he was focused on Nick as they conversed.

The undertaker's shirt was rolled up at the sleeves. It had been washed and bleached so many times that it was a soft yellow instead of white. The top of his tan-colored waistcoat was visible under the stained brown leather apron that fell past his knees. The dark stains on the apron spoke to the type of job he performed and grotesquely reminded her of the butcher back home.

Amelia couldn't seem to look away from him. What kind of man would want to take on such a profession?

Banishing her troubling thoughts, she continued to study the bloodstains splashed across his midsection, as if that would prove that she could do this. If she couldn't face what this man did for a living, how would she ever make it past the threshold of the chapel?

As Nick strode toward her, she noted the undertaker's stance: firm, his posture reading irritated by the circumstance.

Well, that made the two of them, didn't it?

Nick held out his hand as he opened the door for her. "Ready then?"

She loved the fact that he didn't question her need to do this, or attempt to change her mind.

She took his hand without hesitation. When she stood before him, he added, "We can leave at any time; just say the words and we'll go. You don't have to prove yourself to anyone, Amelia. I mean that."

"I have to do this."

Threading her arm though Nick's, she walked toward the undertaker with determined steps. She was saved from having to introduce herself, for he turned on his heel and headed back inside. Surely women had visited this place before. Nick had to catch the door so it didn't shut behind the undertaker. The sick scent of death assaulted her senses and had her skin crawling the moment she crossed through the door. She wanted to scratch her arms to rid herself of the feeling, but she soldiered on, refusing to show any weakness.

There would be no peace, no real belief that any of this had happened if she didn't continue on her current path. She had to see her brother one last time.

Amelia stepped into the dark chapel, her steps stalling long enough for her eyes to adjust to the dim lighting. Covering her mouth with her hand, she swallowed back the bile that had climbed up her throat and took in small breaths to acclimate to the strong odor, though she didn't think she'd ever get used to the smell.

Nick leaned in close to her ear. "Just say the words and we can leave."

She shook her head, refusing to give in as she continued deeper into a place fouled right down to the shale foundation with the stench of death. Now that her eyes were adjusted to the dim room, she lowered her hand from her mouth and held her head high as she followed the undertaker.

They walked down a narrow hallway, closer to the stench fouling the air. Nick produced a handkerchief, which she took and pressed over her nose and mouth.

"Watch where you step," the undertaker said as he disappeared into a room just ahead.

Not knowing what to expect, she braved her fears and followed immediately upon his heels, eyes focused on the floor to see her footing. Nick had her elbow and she knew he wouldn't let her walk in the wrong direction.

In a room that's sole purpose appeared to be housing the dead, it was hard not to notice the stone floor covered in filth and other things she never wanted to identify. Lifting her skirts, she took in the rest of her surroundings. Wall sconces kept the room well lit, so she could see altogether too much of what was amassed in the small room.

Half a dozen large slate tables were lined up in two neat rows and spaced evenly in the central part of the room. Half were in use, with unmoving forms atop them but covered with dark sheets of burlap and cloth. Her eyes didn't linger on any one form as she headed toward the table next to which the undertaker hovered.

He gave her a measuring yet solemn look. "You understand he won't be as you remember?" he asked.

In fear that she'd lose the last of her nerves—and her breakfast that now sat heavily in the pit of her stomach—she nodded in answer. Nick was at her back, a solid and reassuring presence. Amelia took a small step back so she was pressed fully along the length of him, taking in the strength he offered by merely being here for her.

Without any further warning, the undertaker pulled back the thin material that covered the lifeless body, revealing her brother's beaten face and bare shoulders.

The undertaker hadn't exaggerated; Jeremy's motionless form didn't resemble the man she'd grown up fearing. The man before her was broken. Lifeless. Not the monster from whom she had constantly cowered. She didn't want to shrink into the background now as she stared at his heavily bruised face. She couldn't seem to take her eyes off him as she studied every cleaned-out cut, every broken part of his body.

When her vision clouded, she turned into Nick's arms, resting her forehead against his chest and closing her eyes to gather any stitch of bravery she had left in her. She needed to collect her own strength, give herself a moment to bring it together in her head and adjust to the reality of her brother's death.

Because this moment was what made it all real.

And the image of her brother would be with her for the rest of her life.

"What happened to him?" she whispered. She didn't need an answer, though, and Nick didn't respond. Her real question was, who could do such a thing to another person, regardless of the circumstances, regardless of the vile man Jeremy was?

Nick's hand pressed against her lower back, holding her close, letting her breathe deeply of his clean scent in a desperate bid to wipe away the foul scent of the room.

Braving her fears, she stepped out of Nick's arms and looked him in the eye. "I would like a minute alone with my brother."

Nick merely nodded and jerked his head toward the exit, indicating to the undertaker that he should give her exactly what she needed. Nick turned at the door. "I'll be one step outside. Call out if you need me, Amelia."

"I will."

She turned away from Nick as tears filled her eyes again and trailed down her cheeks unbidden. She didn't try to stop them or wipe them away. They just were.

She took a step closer to her brother's body. The usual sinister smirk he wore whenever he faced her was absent. Now, he was nothing more than a harmless man, unable to dish out the cruelties he'd delivered over the years. He was a shell. A lifeless shell, and it made her wonder how he had ever wielded any power over her.

Braving herself, she pulled the covering right off him, revealing his full, weak form. The material caught at his booted feet, hanging in a macabre fashion, like he was a fallen flag-bearer who hadn't made it through the battle.

He was unclothed from the waist up, his breeches hanging low on his too-narrow hips. His skin had taken on a yellow-gray waxen tone wherever the miasma of deep red and purple bruises hadn't discolored him. Bruises spidered out over his form, covering his lower ribs and various spots around his slightly distended stomach. His shoulders were red and raw, as though he'd been dragged without a shirt through the streets.

"You've brought this fate upon yourself, brother." She brushed a dirty strand of hair back from his forehead, revealing a deep gash at the edge of his hairline. It had been cleaned out and appeared almost white around the cut, as though it had bled a great deal not so long ago.

Was that the blow that had killed him?

"Who did you cross this time, Jeremy?" No answer came, not that she expected one.

There was only silence.

She was in a room full of the dead; all she could hear was the beat of her own heart and the shallow breaths she took in and out so as not to take in the full odor of the place. She rubbed her hands along her arms, which did nothing to dispel the cold that chilled her to the bone.

"You could have amounted to so much more, but your evil infiltrated you so thoroughly that you're not even a fraction of the man Father was as he lay on his deathbed. Even after all you have done to me, all you've done to others...I pity you. I don't want to, but there you have it. I know that sentiment would anger you, so let me say it again, brother." She leaned in close to his face and whispered, "I pity you in your sad death."

Whoever had done this to her brother had but one intention: to see him gone from this world. There was no one to claim him from this place. Not even she would be stupid enough to tempt fate that way. His past might have caught up with him, but she wanted to remain free of the burdens her brother had placed on her.

Even though he deserved no kind words from her, she rested her hand over his cold chest, and the lack of a heartbeat raised goose bumps through her entire body. "Godspeed, Jeremy. Perhaps forgiveness will find you in your next life."

She reached for the sheet and covered him once again.

There was no love lost between them, and while she was sad, a smidgen of relief filled her at knowing he could never hurt her again. She turned away, her heart heavier than it had been since she'd found out about his death. He had been her last living relative. Her own flesh and blood.

Oddly, his death was at once a yoke about her shoulders and a snapping of the reins that had always kept her in line with her brother's ideals. The freedom that washed through her was sickening, and nothing had ever felt so wrong as this. Maybe that was because her freedom had come at the expense of his life.

True to his word, Nick was waiting just outside the door for her. He wrapped one arm around her shoulders and hugged her tightly to his chest. Her tears had dried, but she felt…empty.

"We have to leave him here, Nick. I can't risk being exposed in my new life by claiming his body for burial."

"I can make any arrangements you want. No one has to know."

She was shaking her head. "I ran away with good reason. And I will not risk being found by anyone. My brother might be the last of my family, but that doesn't make me feel free from his obligations. I still don't know what Lord Ashley has planned, if anything. My brother *should* have a proper burial and mourning period, but I just can't…"

Nick's arm was like a vise around her, holding her tight, making her feel safe. "He deserves less than you think."

"That might be true, but he is still my brother. And he was the last Earl of Berwick. Our family line is no longer extant."

"Then to whom does the estate go?"

"I know of no living relatives who could make a claim for it. Lord Ashley won the cottage in a silly gamble. The rest will revert back to the crown."

"Let's get you home," Nick said against the top of her head, his hand cupping her nape possessively as he turned them toward the exit.

Amelia didn't take a deep breath until they were next to their carriage. The clean air helped clear her senses and shake the icy cloak of death that had wrapped around her while she'd been in that building.

Nick thanked the undertaker and then assisted Amelia inside the carriage.

She took the blue velvet seat opposite him. "Is it wrong that I don't feel any guilt, walking away from my brother's cold, broken corpse?"

"It shows nothing but fortitude."

She looked directly at him as the horses jolted forward. His expression was open, kind. Inviting her to come closer. She switched sides and rested her head against his shoulder. "I feel so odd. Empty of emotion but at the same time, better that I saw him one final time."

Nick kissed the top of her head. "That's normal. Mourn for your brother, Amelia. You needn't think of anything but letting him go."

Amelia slipped her hand over his firm stomach. She was thankful to have him right now. There was no doubt in her mind that she would be lost without him.

"I think the constant threat of my brother precipitated our relationship. And now I wonder if everything between us happened too suddenly."

Nick covered her hand with his, not saying anything to indicate his thoughts on the matter.

"With the danger of my brother eliminated, I'm afraid of what will happen between us," she admitted. She'd been turning that thought over and over since Nick had revealed her brother's fate.

"Nothing will change, so put it out of your mind."

"I can't help that I feel this way. When I ran away from home, I assumed I'd be an aging spinster before any man would catch my attention. We were thrown together by circumstance."

Nick turned up her chin with his fingers so that their gazes were locked. "Do you want to know how I remember the change in our relationship?"

She sucked in her bottom lip and nodded for him to continue.

"I hired you on because I couldn't let you go. That was long before I knew any details about your brother or your past. When we met, I told you that you reminded me of someone."

"I recall but you never said whom."

"Her name was Lillie. She was important to me for the short time she was in my life. And before you believe it to be some grand love affair, you should know she was fifteen when she died. I couldn't have been much older than eleven."

"Why do I remind you of someone so young?"

"Young in age, not in life experience." He rubbed his thumb across her lips.

"Are you saying that you put me on a pedestal before you knew me?" Amelia wasn't sure how she felt about this revelation.

"*After* I met you," he corrected her. "You had the same look in your eyes she often had."

"Which was?"

"Fortitude. You looked ready to take on the world, even though you were at a tether's end with your luck."

Amelia would never forget the day they met, not for as long as she lived. While humiliation should have superseded any other feelings when recalling how she literally fell into his life, had her circumstances not been what they were that fateful day, their paths might never have crossed. She hated to think where that would have left her. Hated to think of a life without Nick in it.

"Do I still remind you of her?"

Nick shook his head. "Life has ways of surprising us. Whether we met because of your brother doesn't change how we feel about each other now. I cannot deny that you make me crazy with need. And while what's between us doesn't scare me, I sometimes worry how far I'll make you go. How far I'll push you before you want to run."

Amelia curled her fingers around his and inched close enough that their mouths were scant inches from touching and their breaths mingled.

"The only thing I fear right now is myself and what I feel for you, Nick."

A dark look came over him, and he was as unreadable as the first time they had met.

CHAPTER FOUR

If Amelia knew what Nick was thinking, she might change her mind and think carefully about putting that much trust in him. He spanned his hand over her cheek and watched her nibble and suck on her lower lip in tandem. She did that when she was contemplating a problem.

And when she was thinking about kissing him.

But the last thing he should want after their morning was her spread out beneath him, taking her hard and deep as he swallowed her pleasured screams. It didn't matter what time of the day it was, where they were, or how sated they'd been this morning. He wanted her. He always wanted her. Especially when she gave him her complete trust. Even the look in her eyes right now—full of hurt, innocence, wonder—made him want her. He was rock hard inside his trousers, and it took every ounce of control not to press her hand over his erection.

He stared at her mouth, wanting her all the same, no matter how many times he told himself she needed today to mourn her brother's death.

But it was increasingly difficult to feel bad when she had scooted over to his bench to be closer to him. He closed his eyes, trying to banish his thoughts, to clear that look of hope and innocence he saw in her eyes every time she looked at him. But when he closed his eyes, all he could picture was how she'd been spread out naked beneath him.

He was the worst kind of ass.

Still, he couldn't stop himself. He pressed his mouth against hers, wanting nothing more than a small taste of her before they went about the rest of their day. But their mouths didn't linger and stop with a simple kiss. The next he knew, he'd picked her up off the seat, and her soft body was pressed against the length of his as his tongue worked against hers, slicking around her mouth and tasting her deeply. His cock throbbed, needing to be buried deep inside her.

He jerked his head to the side. "Amelia." She was breathing as heavily as he was, telling him that she was just as lost in the moment. "I know I should give you time to grieve. You need time alone."

But hell. He didn't really want that. His need for her was constant, unrelenting.

"I don't need time to myself," she said with a sigh. He swore he could taste her arousal on the air.

Nick took a steadying breath—or at least he tried to; it didn't work. How could he say no to her? He wanted nothing more than to fulfill her request, but he had sent a card to Murray last night, advising him to be at his club for luncheon. They had to finalize their agreement so that Shauley would be forever away from Amelia. And besides, Nick needed Murray's lands *almost* as much as he needed to help Amelia through her grief.

"Help me forget, Nick."

With her breathless sigh, his mind was made. He pulled down the curtains on either side of the carriage windows. Nick slid off the bench so he was on his knees, pushing up her heavy skirts as he settled between her spread thighs.

"Put your feet up on the opposite bench."

She hastened to do his bidding, scooting down so her tailbone rested on the edge of the seat. Nick lifted one of her legs to spread her open. The motion opened up her knickers and brought her sweet cunt closer to his mouth. It was the prettiest sight he'd ever seen, and he wanted to devour her with a fierceness that robbed him momentarily of his breath.

He would help her forget anything she wanted, as long as she let him drink down the juices wetting the hairs of her cunny.

Amelia barely recognized this new brazen side of herself. But she hadn't been like her *old* self since the day she met Nick. The expression in his gaze couldn't be described as anything less than ravenous. She could hardly believe she was doing this—and in a carriage, of all places.

A blush stole over her cheeks when Nick slipped his hand into the slit of her drawers and spread her thighs wider as he breathed a cool stream of air over her mons. A strangled sound escaped her throat as her pelvis tilted toward him. She wanted this. To forget. But more than anything, to feel.

Nick's teeth scraped against her inner thigh, licking away the momentary pain of his nip before he sucked on her sensitive flesh again. But that wasn't where she wanted his mouth.

She wanted to pull his head closer to her sex, but then she'd have to release the layers of her dress that she was holding up. And she wanted to see the look clouding his eyes just as much as she wanted him to kiss her in a more intimate place.

"Nick…please."

"Please what? I can think of a hundred things I want to do in this moment, so be specific in what you want."

She didn't know how to voice her needs. When she didn't respond, he bit her other thigh, and this time she felt a rush of wetness coat her entrance.

She gave a breathless moan and wiggled so far down the seat, she wasn't sure how she didn't fall right into Nick's lap.

"I want your mouth on me," she said, her desperation thick in her request.

He gave her a deep chuckle. "It is on you, love."

"*On* me…"

She demonstrated what she wanted by curling one hand over his shoulder and pulling him deeper into the vee of her legs. While that made him edge a bit closer, it wasn't close enough to get his lips and mouth exactly where she wanted them.

"I want you inside me," she finally said in pure frustration, when all she got was a stream of hot breath along her slick center.

"Is that so? And what will you give me if I fulfill that desire?"

She shook her head. She couldn't think when she just wanted to feel him touching her. "I *need* you inside me."

His fingers thrust inside her before she even finished giving voice to her request. But he wasn't filling her the way she craved most.

She moved against Nick, needing more and less at the same time. Her pelvis undulated as though his hand was another part of his anatomy, and they were in the deepest throes of passion.

Still. Not. Enough.

She needed more. She wanted to be so lost to his touch that she couldn't think.

She loosened her hold on her skirts and squeezed both her thighs around his head. He was forced to pull his fingers from her, his hands slapping against the bench on either side of her hips.

She thought she screamed—mewled, some sound came out of her—loud enough to throw her into a frenzy as he sucked at her with the fervor of a man who'd never feasted at the banquet hall. His tongue wasted no time and slicked through her feminine folds. She felt the scrape of his teeth along the sensitive flesh, but it only had her thrashing harder against him.

When he roughly flicked his tongue against her clitoris, she lost the last of her control, and her body lost its will to hold back the release that had been building from the moment he'd tossed up her skirts. She screamed through her orgasm; Nick's hand covered her mouth to muffle the sounds she made with abandon. The moment stole all sanity from her, and before she could comprehend what was happening and what she was doing, she was straddled over Nick's thighs on the floor of the carriage.

The bench dug into her shoulder painfully, though she didn't mind, as it only heightened her pleasure when she felt so many sensations at once. Nick's hands moved between them, freeing himself from his trousers moments before she sank down on his steel-hard length.

A soft puff of air escaped her the moment she was fully seated atop him. Arms wrapped around his shoulders, she looked him straight in the eye, unable to speak, only able to feel what it was like to be taken by this man.

"Is this what you needed?" he asked, his voice hoarse with mutual desire.

Words were beyond her, so she nodded a second before his mouth stole her next breath in a deep, all-consuming kiss. His tongue was unrelenting as it tangled with hers.

She could taste herself on him, the cream that had spilled into his beard slicked against her tongue, the scent light and—to her surprise—pleasant. And why that fired her desires more she couldn't say. She just knew that the longer he kissed her, the deeper she tasted of him, sucking on his tongue, trying to steal a little of that strong essence of his that she craved, day in and day out.

So lost was she in his kiss, she'd stopped moving over him. His hands were firm as he held on to her thighs, rocking her over his solid manhood.

Her breathing came in pants, her knees grinding into the hard wooden floor where little pebbles cut into her silk stockings. Frantic was the only way to describe the erratic pace of her hips.

Her hands tangling in his hair, she slanted her mouth against his again as he rocked their bodies together in a primitive dance that elicited animalistic sounds from them both. As he promised, there were no thoughts, no niggling doubts. There was only need, reaching that culminating point where they would be lost in each other's arms so that everything else—except for them and this very moment—was drowned out.

With a bruising force, Nick's hands held on to her hips, guiding her every move. And while she was no longer a stranger to his body, she liked it when he took complete control. Craved it, even.

While their bodies grinded together, their tongues swirled and searched. They were breathing each other's air with every pant of pleasure that fell past their lips. The scrape of his beard against her face made her skin prickle with tenderness and her thighs clench around his hips as she remembered its roughness when he had buried his face in that private part of her.

The tingling awareness of her climax started where Nick was working deep inside her, the pounding of his member never ceasing as one of his hands released her hip so his thumb could rub around her clitoris. Her head fell back against the seat, and Nick's mouth sucked and licked at her neck with the same ferocity with which she'd taken his mouth moments ago.

Their coupling had been anything but gentle, so why she thought her climax should be shocked her to the core, when this time it crashed through her so hard she swore her heart actually stopped beating. She stilled altogether, fighting against Nick's movements as she felt liquid heat bubble through her veins a moment before she smashed through the barrier of her orgasm.

Nick shushed her cries with his mouth once again. His hands were around her hips, his body slamming up into her as he rode her through the high that stole any last bit of sense she had. She could do no more than hold on to him. Her arms wrapped tightly around his shoulders, her mouth sucked his tongue and muffled his grunts as he fucked harder and harder into her. The slap of their flesh was louder in her ears than the rut of the carriage along the cobbled road. And the thought that passers-by might hear them and know exactly what they were doing inflamed her need further.

She pulled away from his kiss, taking in a much-needed swallow of air, and she rode him, never wanting her orgasm to end.

"Don't stop. Don't stop. Don't. Stop," she said, panting over and over again, not sure her words even made sense.

Nick leaned her back on the bench, giving his knees leverage as he pounded into her in their awkward position. And it was worth every bit of discomfort as she slowly came down from her state of euphoria. His hand was tangled in her hair, pulling the pins that held her chignon in place. He took her like a man possessed, hell-bent on achieving one thing.

Their coupling was so intense that her core clenched hard around his shaft, milking him, squeezing him, almost as if begging him to join her in the bliss that had washed through her. And that was all it took, for she felt the hot jets of his semen pumping into her, filling her as his movements slowed, and they finally fell back to the floor, temporarily replete.

He nuzzled the side of her face, showering her with light kisses. Amelia closed her eyes and pressed her forehead to his shoulder. Despite being slightly uncomfortable, she didn't want to get up. Getting up would mean facing everything she was avoiding, being responsible, and focusing on the real world.

"I wish we could stay here forever," she said between breaths.

"A sentiment I couldn't agree with more."

His cock twitched inside her. She squirmed in his lap, a smile lifting her lips. "Thank you...for allowing me to forget."

"I can make you forget all night long if you want." Nick placed his hands on her cheeks, moving her head back so she was forced to look at him instead of hiding against his shoulder. "Is that what you really want, though?"

She bit her lip, wondering if it made her a bad person that she never wanted to think about her brother again. She nodded. "It hurts too much right now, when I can barely wrap my mind around everything that's happened in less than a day. Right now, I prefer to forget."

Nick lifted her from his lap, setting her back on the bench. Fixing his trousers and tidying up his rumpled waistcoat and jacket, he sat opposite her. He helped fix her hair and then knocked on the wall of the carriage. Once they slowed to a stop, Nick opened the door to give the driver instructions on where to take them.

When he sat opposite her once again, a wicked gleam sparked in his eyes, the usual calm gray roiling like a storm about to wash over her.

"What are you up to?"

"I have decided to change my plans for the day," Nick said.

"You can't. Murray will be livid. He may not agree to sell you his lands if you keep pushing him off. I know how much you want that house."

"He won't change his mind. I'll worry about him. You"— he grasped her knees and slid her to the edge of the bench so that their noses nearly touched—"need to focus on enjoying the rest of the day. Tomorrow, I won't let you off so easily, but today will be about just us."

She smiled. "I think I can agree to that."

"Perfect, because you're going to love what I have planned next." His words didn't match his tone, not that she brought that to his attention, but he seemed...oddly nervous.

"Where are we?" Amelia stared out the window, studying the busy street. There were layers of filth, garbage, and debris everywhere. The people, for the most part, looked poor and definitely couldn't rub two shillings between the group of them. Women with makeup painting their faces and their skirts hiked up to show their legs whistled and called over the men walking by. An old man sat against a derelict building, tipping a bottle to his lips. Children with dirty faces and tattered clothes ran through the streets, looking to be up to some sort of mischief.

"There's something I want to show you," Nick said. "It will help you focus your attention elsewhere. On better things."

She'd never seen so much poverty, and the sight outside the carriage tugged at her heart. How could she think better things when she saw nothing but broken lives as they drove past? "This place...What is it?"

"St. Giles."

Tearing her gaze away from the window, she gave Nick a questioning look.

"I won't let anything happen to you, Amelia. If there is one thing I can promise, it's that we are as safe here as walking the streets of Mayfair."

She hesitated only a moment before Nick took her hand to help her out of the carriage. He led her down a series of alleys and narrow streets too small for the carriage. After a short time, she was so turned around, she knew she wouldn't be able to find her way back to their carriage, should she attempt to locate it on her own.

There were so many people in one place. No one talked to them as Nick traversed the area as though he was intimately familiar with every nook and cranny. The deeper into the maze of houses they walked, the closer she tucked herself to Nick's side. None of what they saw seemed to shock Nick as they wound their way farther into the slums until they finally came to a less densely populated area.

They paused outside a flagstone wall that had to be four feet high and was topped with a wooden trellis that blocked the view of what lay beyond. Nick reached through a gap in the trellis to unlock a worn and muddy wooden gate from the inside. The noise of children playing met her ears, and she stepped forward, eager now to see what he wanted to show her.

They entered a stone courtyard, where at least a dozen and a half children ran around a lone sapling, chasing a ball. If she had to guess, she'd say they were all between seven and twelve years old, though one girl seemed much older, maybe fifteen or sixteen. She was talking to a young woman who Amelia guessed was in charge of the children.

Nick let go of her hand and shut the gate behind them. The kids kicked the ratty old ball in his direction. Amelia watched in awe and fascination as he joined their game without a moment's hesitation. His demeanor changed, as if a weight was lifted, as he laughed at their teasing taunts and kicked the ball back, only to accept it again from the children.

He didn't try to extricate himself, as many grown men would have. No, he engaged them, dared them to try and take the ball from him as he ran around the small courtyard, dodging this way and that to keep the ball in his possession.

He looked genuinely happy.

Watching him brought to light how little she really knew about him. That she'd given herself to a man of whom she hadn't even skimmed the depths. Not sure what she should do, she leaned against the courtyard wall. She actually was content to wait in the background and watch their game play out.

A woman who'd been standing at the back of the small house approached, holding out her hand. "How do you do? I'm Sera."

"Well." Amelia took Sera's hand, shaking it. "My name is Amelia." She didn't give her last name, as Sera hadn't, though she did add, "I work for Mr. Riley."

The woman had the same uncanny gray eyes as Nick. Was this woman a relative? Their similarities stopped at their identical eyes, though. Her hair was wheat-blonde, not black like Nick's. Her frame slight and fragile-seeming, and her face was perfectly oval.

"And what is your role?" Sera asked, turning to watch the game the children played with Nick.

"I am Mr. Riley's secretary." She didn't know what else to say, so she continued to watch Nick playing with the children.

"I never imagined Huxley would give up the position," Sera finally said.

It shouldn't surprise Amelia that Sera knew Huxley. "Are you Mr. Riley's sister?"

The woman gave Amelia a winning smile, nodding. "Half-brother, at any rate," Sera said. "The odds that we share a father are stacked against us, considering our mother's profession. Considering he's five years old than me, and Mum never had a man around for longer than a few months."

It occurred to Amelia that she hadn't known what Nick's mother's profession was until that moment. The realization was shocking and heartbreaking when she thought of how Nick would have grown up.

"Did my brother mention his reason for stopping by today? He usually comes at the end of the week."

"He didn't say," Amelia lied, not wanting to reveal her own difficulties. She turned back to Sera. "What is this place?"

"A school for the wayward. Nick sets one up in every slum where he amasses properties. It's a way to offer a lower rent to those struggling to work and keep their families going. We grew up in St. Giles, so we have a kinship with the people here."

"How long has the school been here?" Amelia asked.

"Four years now. Not all the kids can stay on for a full and proper education. They're often called away by their parents to work outside of London in the mines when they're of age. A lot of the girls go into the business by the time they hit their fourteenth birthday. Cece"—she nodded in the direction of the young lady wiping down a chalkboard inside the house with a wet rag—"was one of the lucky ones. Her dad works at the docks as a lighterman, and her mother does washing, so Cece's free to pursue her learnings."

"I never would have guessed Nick hid such an amazing thing."

Sera chuckled. "Oh, he's not hiding it. He just lets me manage it as I see fit. It's essentially my school. He supports it through financial means, of course, but I have full say on how this place operates."

How fascinating. "I taught for a short time."

"But now you're a secretary. That's an odd leap in professions, if you don't mind me saying."

"Not at all. I more or less fell into this role. I like the work as much as I liked teaching children."

"Perhaps I'll use you when I'm shorthanded."

It was a genuine offer that brought a smile to Amelia's face. Before she could respond, Nick was jogging toward them, sweat dotting his forehead and temples, which he wiped away with the handkerchief he pulled from the pocket of his waistcoat. She hadn't even seen him strip out of his jacket when she'd been talking with his sister. His shirtsleeves were rolled up and his strong forearms were bare to her hungry gaze. Just seeing him partially unclothed made her cheeks flame. She hoped no one noticed her reaction.

"What brought you by today?" Sera asked her brother as he leaned in and kissed her cheek in greeting.

"I wanted to introduce you to Miss Grant. Huxley," Nick went on, "is required for other duties, and she'll be taking over the day-to-day tasks he once handled. She'll be more than happy to assist with any of the schools, should you require anything."

Amelia didn't fail to notice the odd look his sister gave him, almost like surprise.

"I can offer you some tea, if you plan to stay for a while." Sera posed it as a question.

"We won't keep you long when your class is full," Nick responded. "How is Cece doing?" he asked as they headed through the open doors of the small house. It was set up as a classroom; benches and long tables were lined in three neat rows. There was a small desk at the front of the house, facing those benches. A chalkboard was on an easel, now freshly wiped down.

"Well enough. Her mother wants her to look for employment in one of the houses, but Cece would rather stay here and teach those less fortunate."

"Then draw up an amount for her annual salary, and we'll pay her enough to earn wages for herself and some extra coin so her mother doesn't struggle to make ends meet."

"I thought you'd say as much." Sera elbowed him lightly before she sat on the edge of her desk and faced them both. It was an action Amelia was so used to seeing Nick do that it struck her just how similar their mannerisms were. "You didn't come all this way to ask about Cece, though, did you?"

Nick crossed his arms. "You were always so perceptive."

"More like suspicious," she answered, humor dancing in her eyes. "I've known Huxley since I was a young girl, but you never brought him around while I was teaching."

Amelia watched the exchange and felt their love for each other so viscerally that it made her sad that she and her brother had never had this type of rapport or exchange.

"We might as well get straight to the issue, then, Sera. Miss Grant's role will vary from Huxley's. While she does the usual tasks as my secretary, I also want her to be involved with the rebuild of the old manor." Nick motioned his hand around the quaint little school. "You've outgrown this house faster than we imagined possible. You'll be taking on more children in the coming years, and you won't be able to do everything on your own."

Amelia didn't know what to say or make of that revelation, and she focused her attention on the school children slowly filing into the classroom.

"When the Highgate lands are redeveloped for our purpose, I'll post for teachers if we can't find them from around here," Sera said.

Now it all made sense. The Highgate lands were part of the deal with Lord Murray. His lordship was important because he owned a house close to the city but not so far away that children who attended the school there couldn't easily return to their parents a few days a week. Nick's determination to have that land was now clearer.

"I'll have my hands tied in so many tasks, I'm not sure how I'll keep everything straight," Sera said, looking at Amelia. "But I'm dying to dig in and get to work. Some assistance down the line would be most welcome. You're always thinking three steps ahead, aren't you, Nick?" Sera clapped her hands together and stood. "Now, will you be staying for the lessons? Because I need to get these children in line if we are going to get them back to their parents before supper."

"That's all I needed to tell you. We have to be on our way, as I have a busy night ahead." Nick affectionately embraced his sister and kissed her forehead before returning to Amelia's side. "Send a note or come by the house, should you need anything," he said in parting.

CHAPTER FIVE

Once they were home and settled into the relative privacy of Nick's study, Amelia turned to Nick and said, "I never imagined your intentions with Lord Murray's land would be building a school. I thought you wanted to set up a manor house so you could escape the busy core of the city once in a while." She looked at him sharply. "Does Lord Murray know what you plan?"

Nick pulled her into his arms before she could make it any farther into the adjoining library. His actions were so fast that she collided into his chest, and it left her momentarily breathless. His hands were on her hips, holding her close.

"He won't care what I do with the lands, as long as he has a fat pocket and one less financial burden to keep him up at night."

"How can you be so sure?" She was doing her damnedest to ignore the feeling she got from his closeness. It was so tempting to lose herself in his arms, as she had in the carriage earlier. "Men in his position hate the thought of people talking poorly of them. Like it or not, that's exactly what the residents of Highgate will do when they find out that a school for less-fortunate children will be set up in the manor house. While I think your goals noble and perfectly suited to land not being utilized to its potential, I also know the gentry to be prejudiced against anything that affects their perceived quality of life."

Nick backed her into the library, leading them toward the sofa.

"I could not care less what they think, Amelia. What is right isn't always what people want. And once I own the lands, there's nothing they can do to stop me from accomplishing my goal."

"I don't doubt that for one moment. What you are doing is nothing short of admirable. In fact, I agree wholeheartedly with your plan." She traced her finger over his bearded jawline. "Thank you for today and for giving me something else on which to focus. Most of all, thank you for introducing me to your sister. It means a lot to me."

"You asked to forget about your brother. And I hope you did, for at least a short while. Sera can be a friend, Amelia. Someone you can confide in, if needed. And she is a bit of a mad genius at running the school. Her dream to teach goes back as far as I can remember."

"I'm glad she could make that dream real."

"Our mother always told us to wish for the stars and be content if we only managed to skim the skyline."

"That's beautiful and rather poetic. Your mother sounds like a wonderful woman."

"She was a dreamer. And she allowed herself to be lowered by the men in her life." Nick's mood turned darker with that admission.

She frowned. Had she said something wrong? "No matter your mother's profession, it's obvious how much she loved you."

Nick studied her drawn brows before he said, "Don't you worry about my mother, Amelia. Her greatest accomplishment was ensuring that Sera and I could fend for ourselves. And we eventually did."

"She still sounds like a marvel."

Nick kissed her hard on the mouth. When he pulled away, he said, "I will require your assistance once the acquisition is finalized with Lord Murray. We need to hire architects and builders to make the manor house into a school. It requires extensive work, both inside and out. While all that happens, Sera still needs to run the school. She runs her classes Mondays through Thursdays. You're free to spend time at the school. For friendship, if you desire. Or to assist in teaching, if you miss it."

She recalled her first job as a governess. That calling had been short-lived after her employer had tried to rape her. "While I do love children, I'll leave teaching to those far more capable than I was. What your sister has built in a community that so obviously struggles day to day…it's nothing short of amazing. I respect what she has done and what you help her do."

Nick's hands cupped her face. His mouth was inches from hers. "No less amazing than you."

"Flattery may get you everywhere." She wrapped her arms around his shoulders, her fingers drawing lazy circles over the back of his head, tangling in his slightly longer than fashionable hair. "But in all honesty, today meant more to me than you can possibly imagine."

They broke apart as the echo of footsteps grew louder outside the study. Amelia immediately headed toward her desk, smoothing her hair and then her dress to ensure everything was in place.

"Lord Murray sent a post just now; had it delivered directly to my attention," came Huxley's voice from the study.

Amelia sat in her chair and busied herself with opening the mail, though she kept one ear trained on the study to hear what was discussed.

"When does he want to meet?"

"Says he's found another buyer if you're not interested. He's listed an address where you can find him."

She could hear the rustle of paper. Nick must be reading the missive himself.

"No one else is going to buy that land. This is Shauley's doing."

"It doesn't surprise me," Huxley said. "It was likely to get dirty at some point when he wasn't getting the results he thought he should get."

"Bloody prig." Something thumped down on the desk. "I should let him stew for a while, but the school means too much to my sister, and Landon won't be happy if he finds out I've affected his chances of taking over the town leases."

Amelia listened without saying a word. Now that she better understood why Nick wanted the land, she sympathized with his anger. If there was one thing she'd learned in the weeks living here, it was that Nick hated to be in a position where his hand was forced. Though, she supposed, no one liked to be in a situation where others told one how to act.

She couldn't help but feel as though this was partially her fault. The reason he'd brushed off Lord Murray time and again was because he didn't want to leave her side.

Setting her letter opener down, she made her way into the next room. Huxley stood as she entered.

"I will cancel our dinner reservations at the Langtry with Mr. Hart," Amelia announced.

Nick looked at her as he put on his jacket. "Let Hart know I have business matters that are getting in the way of leisure." Mr. Hart—though she still wasn't sure if Hart was his first name or last, as no one had corrected her as of yet—was a friend of Nick's. She'd only met him on a couple of occasions, but he was a pleasant and kind man.

"Should I be more specific?" she asked.

"That should suffice."

She nodded.

Huxley picked up the crumpled paper from the desk and handed it to Nick. "You'll need this if you're to pay his lordship a visit."

Amelia faced both men, not sure what was going on, but they were looking at each other as if they were both in on a secret, and she wasn't privy to it. "Would you like me to complete anything else while you're out? It's been a bit odd of a day…"

She wasn't quite sure how to occupy her time, and she needed to do something to keep her mind from going to darker, unwanted places. She wasn't comfortable admitting that in front of Huxley, though.

"I should be back in an hour. You can read through the agreement my solicitor drafted for the purchase of the lands.

I expect we will offer less than I was originally willing to part with."

"But..." She was not sure why she should disagree with that stance. It seemed cocky and too sure. What if Lord Murray decided not to sell? That would break his sister's heart. Amelia had to wonder where the school would expand if the Highgate deal fell through.

Nick walked toward her, all dominating, his presence larger than life. She found herself backing up a step, feeling breathless and hot all at once. The second she realized what she'd done, she corrected herself and stepped forward. Nick stopped a foot away from her, respecting her boundaries when Huxley was half listening, half looking like he wanted to find the first excuse he could to escape.

"I think you'll enjoy this process." That could be interpreted so many ways. And his grin said he knew she wasn't thinking about the Highgate deal.

Trying to keep the subject focused, she said, "I've never been much for taking unnecessary risks."

Not when her brother had a knack for losing all their money and their possessions, gambling in games of chance. No, she'd never been one to wager. Money should be saved and used wisely, never spent lavishly or rashly.

"This is a necessary risk, one that will work in our favor." Nick turned and left before she could respond.

She exhaled and stared at Huxley. What should she say to him? Had he noticed Nick's behavior with her? More familiar than an employer should act toward his secretary. These worrying thoughts would be the end of her if she didn't get them under control.

The facts were this: Huxley was intimately aware of the trouble Jeremy had caused. Huxley had been there on the day her brother had tried to drag her off to God-knows-where. He hadn't said anything to her about the incident, so she hadn't brought it up. Did he know her brother was dead? Surely he did, as he hadn't stayed behind yesterday as an additional presence in the house.

"Are you glad you don't have to watch me at all hours of the day when Mr. Riley leaves?"

The scowl lines deepened on Huxley's face. "I didn't so much mind it as you think. My loyalties have always been with Nick, and you're now part of this household, Miss Grant. While that didn't seem to matter where you came from, it means something here."

"Thank you, Huxley." Caught off guard by his honest response, she was suddenly teary-eyed. It was a ridiculous reaction, but she couldn't help it. "I have to get back to my correspondence."

She turned and headed back to the library, not sure what else to say. She busied herself answering letters and invitations, canceling more than she accepted, as that was what her mood called for.

Nick tossed down the letter Lord Murray had the audacity to pen. "You're not in a position to threaten me, Murray."

"How dare you come to my club and speak to me as if you were my better." Lord Murray stood, though his height left something to be desired, as he was a good half foot shorter than Nick.

Nick crossed his arms over his chest and stared down at him. "This afternoon could not be avoided. I have a dozen businesses and more than thirty lots of land to my name in this city. It's guaranteed that I'll miss a few appointments here and there when something comes up that requires my immediate attention."

"I don't give a damn what issues arose today. Our meeting should have taken precedence, had you thought to show me you were serious about purchasing Caldon Manor. I'm more inclined to hold on to it and let it fall to a far worse state of disrepair on principle alone."

Nick curled one hand around the top edge of the wooden chair tucked beneath the table. He could play dirty too, if that was what Lord Murray wanted.

"I do not take lightly to threats, my lord. If your piece-of-shit secretary put you up to this, it's a game you are about to lose. Perhaps you should see where his loyalties lie. I'll agree to two-thirds of the original price being negotiated. *That* is my final offer." Nick turned to leave.

"Wait," Lord Murray said, his voice hushed, defeated.

"Give me one reason," Nick said without turning. They both knew Lord Murray had no choice but to sell one of his properties. The one in Highgate was the better option, as no one could live in the house the way it stood. And until now, the offer on the table had been for a more-than-decent sum, as Nick was anxious to close it for any price, as long as it was his in the end.

Murray was visibly defeated. His shoulders slumped, his usual bearing beaten down. "I need your word the deal will go through before the end of the month."

Nick smiled but hid his reaction before turning to face his foe. Lord Murray was merely a means to an end. "Why should I agree? You think threatening me will make me buy it quicker? I don't know what kind of man you think I am, but you're sorely underqualified in making a deal with me."

"Don't forget that it was you who initially approached me, Riley. Not the other way around."

True, and he regretted his eagerness in the beginning when he'd found out Lord Murray was in financial trouble. It was a mistake he wouldn't repeat. "What you don't understand is that there's no skin off my back if I walk away from the original deal. You, on the other hand…"

The rest didn't need to be said. Perhaps Lord Murray now realized the mistake he'd made in sending that note.

The man visibly paled and sat heavily in his chair. "Heddie wanted the deal done." Heddie was Lord Murray's mistress and a woman of many stage talents. It surprised Nick that the woman hadn't moved on the second she realized his lordship couldn't provide the lavish lifestyle in which she was known to indulge.

As much as Nick wanted to walk away from this deal, he knew he couldn't. But he didn't have to let Lord Murray in on that fact. "Give me one reason not to walk away."

Lord Murray rubbed his hands roughly over his face and then looked Nick straight in the eye. "I know you're after more than the lands. At first, I couldn't figure out why you wanted it or that decrepit house. But I get it now. Your man Huxley's been seen about Highgate. Hard to miss that ugly bastard. He's been watching the locals, questioning the business owners. What I'm interested to know is what you think to find. I have owned that house for thirty years, and there is nothing that goes on at Highgate that I don't know."

Nick knew Lord Murray was pulling at straws. And probably from something Shauley had told him. *When a dog starts sniffing you out, you give it a bone to chew on.* He would not address the reason for Huxley's presence. "I planned on setting up a boarding school for the wayward. But that doesn't need to happen in Highgate."

It was half the truth—and a gamble telling Lord Murray that much.

Lord Murray narrowed his eyes, disbelief and curiosity warring in his expression. "A bloody school?" he sputtered, obviously not expecting that revelation.

Nick turned again, not willing to spend another moment with his lordship, knowing he had to play hard if he was going to succeed in getting what he wanted.

"Where in hell are you going, Riley?"

"To investigate other options."

"So you're no longer interested in Caldon Manor?" Lord Murray followed him out the door, not bothering with his jacket, even though the wind was cutting.

"That is not what I said." Nick gave the older man a bland look. Lord Murray seemed worried he'd lost this deal, but Nick wouldn't give the man any hope. Tomorrow, he planned to see his solicitor about a lower offer for the lands. That should sufficiently anger Shauley, and that thought brought on a smile. Nick would eventually have to deal with Shauley...after the purchase of the lands.

"You can't just leave," Lord Murray called after him.

Nick looked at the man one last time. "Yet that is exactly what I'm doing."

And he left. He needed to stop at Landon's. Landon was Nick's business partner and friend. They were going into this deal together, and they'd have to stand firm on this gamble if they were going to succeed in getting exactly what they wanted in the end. Nicked needed to ensure this deal succeeded. And just maybe Lord Murray would sack Shauley for suggesting they play a harder hand.

Patience, Nick counseled himself. He'd waited nearly twenty years for this opportunity, and he well knew Lord Murray was desperate, for he needed the money and could not afford this deal falling through.

CHAPTER SIX

Amelia woke with a start, not sure what had dragged her from the sweet tangle of limbs that had filled her dreams. Movement beside her had her rolling over to find Nick, who was usually wrapped around her, keeping her warm through the night. The only thing she could make out in the dark of Nick's room was his body twisted in the light blanket that normally was folded at the end of the bed.

Tentatively, she reached out to him. "Nick," she whispered, her voice croaking, still full of sleep. He mumbled something she couldn't make out the words to.

"Nick," she said louder. When he didn't wake, she curled her hand around his bicep, shaking him lightly.

He didn't respond, not that she'd expected it to be so easy to wake him.

She wished she knew why these nightmares gripped him so tightly. This was the third time she'd woken like this in the past week, as though something had triggered the increased frequency. When he was like this, he was unresponsive and sometimes violent, all while he slept. These nightmares frightened her, not for her sake but for his.

Sitting up in the bed, she pressed her hand harder into his chest—he usually woke if she talked for a while. "Nick, you need to wake up. Come back to me. Please…"

She shook him with both hands, feeling desperate to pull him from the nightmare and desperate to protect their privacy. If Huxley heard Nick, as he often did, he'd be in here soon enough. And that was the last thing she wanted.

Leaning over him, she shook him more forcefully. Now that her eyes had adjusted to the darkness, she could see the pained expression that morphed his beautiful face. To see such a strong man made helpless terrified her beyond measure.

She was sprawled over him, doing her damnedest to shake him out of his dream state, but he wasn't responding to her touch or her voice like he usually did. She didn't know what to do. Any minute, Huxley would be here. They'd be found out. And while she knew she couldn't be discovered in here, she would not leave Nick in his current state.

Making a quick decision, she bolted out of Nick's bed and ran to the door to lock it. When she was back on the bed, shaking Nick again, she heard the turn of the latch.

She gazed back at the door. It shook.

Straddling Nick's waist, she squeezed her thighs around his hips. Her voice low and careful as she heard the force of Huxley's shoulder meet the door.

"Please, Nick. Please. You have to get up. I don't know what to do."

When his eyes snapped open, a huge sigh of relief whooshed from her lungs. A second later, their positions were reversed, and his hand was around her throat. Madness lingered in his eyes as he stared back at her without actually seeing her.

"Nick." Her voice was a rasp as his grip tightened. "Nick." She coughed, trying to catch a deep breath as she attempted to yank his hands away from her throat. He eased up, but he didn't let her go, not completely.

A sob escaped her, not so much of fear for herself but of the situation in which they found themselves. Nick would never forgive himself if he hurt her, but she didn't know how to snap him out of what now appeared to be a waking nightmare.

There was a knock at the door, but Nick didn't acknowledge it. She wasn't sure he even heard it. Was he still dreaming? "Please see me," she managed to croak. "Nick. Come back to me."

Huxley's rough voice came through the door. "Nick, answer me if you're awake."

The thud of Huxley's body hitting the door had her heart racing faster and faster as the seconds ticked by. She was running out of time.

Amelia searched Nick's eyes. There was no recognition in the black gaze that stared down at her in the darkness. Tears trailed down the side of her face as she forced herself to remain calm.

Think, Amelia.

While his hand hadn't tightened anymore, it was a little difficult to breath, and she suspected that if she tried to slide out from beneath him, his grip would intensify.

She opened her legs to him, letting him settle in the cradle of her thighs. She tangled her hands in his hair, gripping tightly at the base of his neck.

"Wake up," she demanded. There was no fear left in her voice. *Think, Amelia. Think.*

Straining against his hand, she did the last thing she could think of. She closed her eyes and strained her neck enough that she could kiss him.

The press of their lips was fleeting, as his restraint on her gave her limited mobility. She couldn't move another inch without hurting herself in the process. So she kissed the next best thing she could reach: his lower lip, his chin, the strong cut of his jawline. Between each gentle caress of her lips, she asked Nick to wake up over and over again.

The thickening of his member was almost instantaneous, the heavy weight of it wedged hard between the folds of her sex where their bodies were crushed together. Every muscle in Nick's body grew taut, as though he were preparing for a fight. Amelia continued to kiss him, hoping he awoke before Huxley broke through the door.

The pained look that had taken hold of Nick's expression gradually loosened. Where his eyes had been empty of life, the first flicker of awareness now met her head-on. She breathed a sigh of relief as he released his grip on her throat and tucked his head into her shoulder, as though he needed to catch his breath. Comprehension must have washed through Nick because he cursed a second before he rubbed his lips back and forth over the erratic pulse at her neck.

Her mouth parted on a silent moan, and her knees spread wider, as she tried to wedge the thick hardness of his shaft tighter against her sex. The heavy thud of Huxley ramming into the door brought her back to the reality of their situation.

"I'm fine!" Nick barked, his body stiffening as he held his weight from her. "Go back to bed, Huxley."

There was silence on the other side of the door for long moments before they heard the wood-plank floors creak with Huxley's retreat.

Amelia closed her eyes. "What happened?" she whispered into the dark.

Nick hauled himself off her and went into the plunge bath that was attached to his room. Candlelight flickered, one stub at a time.

She could hear the water running in the sink, but Nick didn't speak to her. She sat at the edge of the bed and waited for him to come back...but he didn't. Was he hiding from her? Did he not want to talk about what had happened? When he didn't return to the bed after five minutes, she reached for her robe on the floor, slipped into the cool silky material, and cinched it at her waist before she followed Nick into the bathing chamber.

Nick's scarred back faced her as she entered the room. His dark head was bowed, and his hands curled over the edge of the white porcelain sink. She approached him slowly, letting him hear every step she took as she walked across the tiled floor.

When she was close enough to touch him, she didn't lay her head against his back and wrap her arms around him, even though that was what she most wanted. She stood tall and firm behind him, knowing she would have to be direct if she wanted answers about what had happened. Answers about how to stop the dreams that tormented him too frequently.

"Nick?"

"Not now, Amelia." His voice was soft, tired.

"Don't shut me out."

"I can't have this conversation right now." His head was shaking back and forth. His body clearly saying no, no, no.

"Can I draw a bath for you?" she offered, refusing to back down.

"Go back to bed. I'll join you soon."

"I'm not leaving you like this, Nick. Help me understand what happened."

He abruptly turned and had her backed up against the cold glass-tiled wall. The look in his eyes was broken. She reached her hand up and pressed her palm to the side of his face, the rough friction of his beard grounding her to the moment. She would not give in so easily to his demands.

"I won't leave because you matter to me. And I cannot help you if I don't understand what happened."

"Stop. Just stop, Amelia. There are things you don't know—can't know. Let it be." His eyes focused on her neck a second before he caressed the back of his hand over her. "I hurt you. I'll never forgive myself for that. I can barely live with myself right now after the way I woke up."

She grasped his hand with her own and lowered it. "What were you dreaming about?"

He yanked himself away from her so fast, she nearly tumbled to the floor.

"You can trust me with your secrets, just as I have trusted you with mine." Her voice was barely above a whisper. If he didn't open himself up to her, how would they ever get beyond this point? "If you shut me out now, I will be forced to believe you do not seek a relationship with me, only someone to warm your bed."

It hurt her to admit that, but if that was the truth, she might as well know sooner rather than later.

"That's not what you are to me." He paced the floor in front of her, looking lost and angry. His hands were buried in his hair and periodically scrubbed over his face, as though he was still trying to shake remnants of the nightmare from his mind.

She walked toward him. How could she give up on him when she could clearly read the torment that hung over him, like a weight that wouldn't let up?

It was obvious that she wasn't going to get the answers she wanted right now. The one thing within her ability to offer was comfort.

Reaching for him, she threaded her fingers through his and led him back into his bedroom. He didn't fight her to leave him be, for which she was thankful, because she wasn't sure what she would have done, had that been the case.

Sitting on the edge of the bed, she tried to pull him down next to her. But he held firm; his expression, hovering on the edge of want and worry, told her he was torn in what to do. She wrapped her arms around his waist and pressed her head against the hard ridges of his stomach. Eventually, he loosened his stance, his hand petting her hair, his penis growing thicker with need between them.

Amelia pressed small kisses against his belly, trailing through the dark hairs that drew a line down to his heavy manhood. He stopped her with his finger under her chin before she could take his member into her mouth.

He shook his head, his expression no longer lost, just…needful. "I don't trust myself right now."

"I know you won't hurt me."

"So sweet and innocent." He brushed the back of his knuckles over her neck and then over her chin. "What I want *is* to hurt you. But not the way I did earlier. In a different way."

Her breath caught in her lungs. His words were a warning that she would be well advised to take to heart, but she wanted to know more.

"Show me what you want, Nick. I trust you."

Instead of answering her, he grasped the braid at the base of her head. "Are you sure you want this?"

She nodded, licking her lips.

"Suck my cock." His voice was gravelly, his need taking over the tormented look that lingered in his eyes.

She would do anything to banish that look completely.

Her fist around the base of his penis, she sucked the head of him into her mouth, her tongue playing with the slit at the top, lapping up the precome before swirling fully around the silky head.

Nick's hand guided her head, making her draw him deeper into her mouth. His hips pumped forward and back, driving him deeper, deeper than she expected she could take him. It was too deep. Her throat closed around him, and she gagged when he pressed too far. Nick eased off, pulling out of her completely, the head of his cock drawing a wet line over her lips, waiting for her to take him again.

"Relax your throat, and you'll be able to take all of me. Go slower this time."

She looked up at his hard expression. Hunger and desire fired his gray eyes, and in place of the haunting dream, something darker was there, darker than she'd ever seen before. She had no words to describe it and recalled his words: "*What I want is to hurt you.*" She suspected what he meant, and the thought only made her yearn for more.

With her eyes locked on his, she opened her mouth and let him slide between her lips. She rubbed the flat of her tongue over the thick vein that ran along the bottom of his manhood and took him deeply. Deeper than she had before. And then he started to rock into her mouth like he did her sheath. Spit dribbled out the side of her mouth, but she didn't care. His hand tightened in her hair again, his body strung taut as he held himself back from taking her harder. He was too big for her to take all of him, the head of his cock already touching the back of her throat with each motion of his hips.

Nick stayed in control of the situation, not giving himself over to her fully. He was holding back. And knowing that hurt. His thrusts came faster, shallower, so he wouldn't cause her to gag again. And that control he held over the situation made her angry. Made it difficult for her to lose herself in pleasing him.

Pulling against his hand tangled in her hair, she dislodged his cock from her mouth and looked up at him. His hips were still moving, his need bobbing wetly against her chin.

"You are holding yourself back from me." The hurt was thick in her voice.

"I have to."

"What part of 'I trust you' did you disbelieve?"

With a groan, Nick's hand released her hair, and he hauled her up to her feet.

"You don't know what you're asking."

"I want to be the person you come to when you need to forget what haunts your thoughts. I'm asking you to give me all you have."

He yanked her robe down off her shoulders, trapping her arms at her sides. "The things I want will scare you." When she glared back at him, he pushed her roughly down on the bed, face forward, bottom in the air. His hands were urgent, almost desperate, as he pushed the silky robe off her legs, tearing it in his haste to expose her rear. His hands squeezed each cheek of her buttocks.

"I don't want to scare you," he said.

"And what gave you the impression that I was afraid? I want you to lose yourself in me. Make me lose myself in you," she mumbled against the blanket.

Would he believe her at her word?

He smacked one cheek of her rear hard and then rubbed over the sting. The sound that came out of her was half surprise, half desire.

"Are you sure you're ready for this?"

"Do it, Nick. Take me like you need to." She growled her frustration.

He spread the cheeks of her buttocks. The wetness there was surely visible to the naked eye. The slide of his finger at her entrance brought light to that fact, and he growled something under his breath and then said, "Wet from my rough handling. What will you do when I'm fucking your ass?"

She waited with bated breath for his next move, not able to respond to that question, not sure she was meant to respond or even how she should respond.

It seemed as though he stared and rubbed his finger through her slick folds for ages. She knew deeply that he was fighting with himself over what he should do next. How much of himself he could really give her. Oh, God, she wanted him so badly that she felt a pulse start deep inside her womb.

"I need you, Nick. Please...Give yourself over to me as I have to you."

Hands tight around her hips, he raised her rear higher in the air, placing her knees on the bed. His hard length pressed demandingly against the crease of her bottom. She moved against him, desperate to feel him breach her sheath hard and fast, but he wasn't ready to give her what she wanted. And she suspected he was planning something altogether different.

Releasing her hips, he reached around to her stomach and pulled the tie on the robe loose. She thought he'd pull it right off her, but instead he yanked the material the rest of the way down her arms, until was it was twisted tightly around her wrists, binding them, making sure she couldn't touch him.

His lips pressed against her nape and trailed hotly over her spine. Every touch was like a branding deep in her flesh as he worked his way lower and, skipping the place her hands were tied, over her tailbone.

Going lower yet, the scrape of his beard over her bottom sent a thrill of excitement right to her core and fired her body to an urgent boil. Her hips swayed and her knees spread slightly wider. Why wasn't he filling her? His teeth scraped along the rounded flesh, light at first and then biting her. The sensation only added to her building desire, her need. She needed him more than she ever had before. Her body was so eager to be filled that wetness seeped from her core to trail a path of want down her thighs.

She pulled her arms up, wanting nothing more than to free her hands so that she could pull Nick closer, so he couldn't deny her his body for another second. Nick's hands tightened around the material so she couldn't move from her current position.

"You want me to fill you up, to stuff my cock so deep in you that you feel me in your throat again."

Her nipples pebbled harder, the firm tips scraping along the soft blankets beneath her. The sensation made her pelvis thrust, rubbing them over the blanket, wishing Nick's fingers were plucking and pulling on them instead of her fulfilling her own desires.

When she didn't respond, he pulled away, and cold air washed over her body. She cried out in protest, frustration building in the back of her throat in the form of a growl.

"What do you say to that, Amelia? Do you want me to ride your pretty cunt, fuck you so hard you won't be able to get up from this bed?"

"Yes."

Her eyes slipped closed as he touched her, only this time he ran his finger down between the cheeks of her rear, exploring parts of her that had her heart pounding so hard in her chest that she could hear the thump, thump, thump loud in her ears.

She breathed easy again when his fingers found her slick center, and he slammed two fingers hard and deep. Her sheath tightened around the sweet intrusion. He pulled his fingers out only to repeat the process again and again until the slap of his palm against the skin between her entrance and her anus made wet noises. She was sure his whole hand was soaked with her juices, and she didn't care, didn't think to be embarrassed by her body's reaction. She just needed more.

Nick leaned over her, trapping her hands between their bodies as the heat of him enveloped her from his chest to her back. His mouth was next to her ear, his hard cock heavy between her thighs, but he didn't remove his fingers; if anything, he fucked them into her harder.

"I'm going to own every part of you," he whispered in her ear at the same moment his thumb breached her *other* hole.

Her instinctive reaction was to pull away, but Nick had his arm wrapped around her; she wasn't going anywhere if he didn't want her to.

She made a sound that was half protest and half shock as he worked the tip of his thumb in and out of her, the movement aided by the wetness coating his hand, fingers, and thumb.

"You like that, sweetheart. You want me to fuck this tight hole, don't you?"

She couldn't answer, lost in the euphoric feeling of his surrounding her and being everywhere in her. Desire built inside her like a storm about to rage out of control. She was panting—actually panting, like a cat in heat.

Nick bit at her earlobe, sucking it, his tongue playing with it. His breathing came hard and fast, and his hips were working almost as fast as his hand was stroking deep inside her. He was as affected by their actions as she.

The rigid length of his cock pressed against her thigh. She wanted to squeeze her legs together around that steely length, draw him closer, but she was completely trapped and helpless to his tormenting pleasure.

And she liked that she had no control over what he did. Liked being a slave to his desires, to hers. Powerless to stop him from doing the things that would have her shy away and pull back if she could.

Nick pulled his thumb out of her, and she cried at the loss, her body suddenly feeling too empty.

"Can't be without me, can you."

She shook her head. "I need you back inside me. I—"

He rammed his cock so hard into her sheath that her breath caught on her words, and she moaned instead of begging him to take her. His hips rotated, his rod twisting and gyrating as he took her so hard that her whole body was splayed to him. She felt him on every intimate part of her body, and the sensation was almost too much to process all at once.

"Oh, God. Nick. Nick..."

Her hands curled into fists. She wanted them free so she could give herself enough leverage to push back into him, to urge him to take her harder, even though this was the hardest he'd ever rode her. His hands grasped tightly around her hips, holding her in place as he pumped into her, working her toward that sweet precipice of release.

Amelia strained against her bonds, not sure whether or not she really wanted to be free. And just as quickly as Nick had taken her, he pulled away. She felt empty, needy. How could he stop and leave her wanting?

She looked over her shoulder at him, searching his eyes for the answers she wasn't sure she wanted, when the head of his steely length pressed against the tight puckered hole higher up. The hunger in his eyes nearly undid her. He didn't break his gaze as he pushed forward, breaching the tight hole he'd thumbed earlier.

Her mouth opened on a wordless sound as he stretched her with just the head of his penis, working it in and out of her slowly. Oh, so slowly that she wasn't sure if she was feeling pain or pleasure. It just felt different.

An alien noise rose in the back of her throat. The burn of him working his way in drew her body forward. She hesitated, not sure whether or not she wanted what he was offering. His hand came down hard on one cheek of her buttocks, stilling her.

"Tell me to go slower, if that's what you want, but don't pull away from me, Amelia. I'll own this part of you as much as I own every other part. Is that understood?"

Her face flamed red, knowing she shouldn't want any such thing; she was, after all, her own person. But the truth of the matter was this: she wanted exactly that.

What they were doing felt so far beyond forbidden that she pulled forward another inch and buried her head into the bedding to hide her deep blush. Only the very tip of him remained inside, stretching the tight hole of her bottom. Indecision had her frozen to the spot, unable to move or able to speak.

"Talk to me, Amelia. You said you wanted all of me. Are you still sure you want that?"

She nodded.

"I need to possess every part of you. It's like an obsession, eating me up inside."

"Why?" It was the only word she could form.

"Because I need to own you." His answer came easily, truthfully. But the better question was, did she want that? To be completely controlled by this man?

Yes, she wanted that, but deep down, she felt that was not something she should ever want from anyone. Nick made her feel and think differently. She was losing herself in him, and that scared her more than anything.

"What you're doing feels so…" *Wrong? Strange? Foreign?* "Different."

Nick leaned over her, his beard scraping along her shoulder as he kissed and nibbled her overheated skin. The motion drew him further inside her.

"I can do this all day, my sweet darling." His teeth scraped along her skin, making her shiver.

Reaching around to her front, his fingers slicked through the wet folds of her sex. "Even fucking you this way has cream coating you. I want to lap it all up like a cat, suck it all away 'til I've feasted myself full, but I know you'll only cream more for me if I do that."

She closed her eyes, her breathing shaky as she rolled his words around in her mind. Every dirty word he uttered fired her desire higher. When one of his fingers flicked against her clitoris, there was but one thing on her mind. And that was *more*. She pressed her bottom back into him, needing to pull all of him into her. Needing him completely.

"That's it, Amelia. I'll have you begging for my cock fucking deep inside the tight hole of your rear."

He was relentless with his words, his body. His fingers still rotated around her swollen bud, the sensations blasting through her body and making her pelvis and hips undulate, lodging him deeper until finally it felt like his penis stretched her wide open. There was a slight burn, but it receded the longer he held motionless inside her.

Nick pulled his fingers away seconds before she found her release. She cried out at the loss of his touch, but was filled with an altogether different feeling as he pushed carefully forward, filling her, inch by agonizing inch. Her breath caught, stopped in its tracks, and ended as he slid fully inside. She waited for what felt like forever as his steely length remained still, and her body adjusted to his heavy girth.

"Shh," he whispered next to her ear, sucking her earlobe between his teeth. "The pain will ebb. I promise."

"It doesn't hurt...not really. It's...I can't describe it."

His lips trailed over her shoulder, across her back, and stopped at the little bone at the base of her neck. "Relax."

Lost in the way his lips trailed over her, she was left breathless when he pulled out, only to push back inside her, his pace careful but no less titillating. The slowness was soon a torture in and of itself, and she had to move with him, against him, forward and back. Nick let her move with abandon until her body couldn't keep up with what her heart wanted; her actions grew jerky and erratic. Nick was on his knees behind her, grasping her hips tight, sliding her along his hard length.

Setting a steady pace, he slipped one hand between the folds of her sex again and rubbed her clitoris in hard, even strokes. She unfurled her hands, pressing one palm against his lower abdomen with each plunge forward. His fingers were like magic, building a firestorm in her so high that she was sure she would combust at any moment.

The way he hit her inside only heightened each sensation, drawing her closer to a finale she knew would trump anything she'd ever felt. Her heart skittered and raced; each of his propulsions forward had moans slipping past her lips. His fingers drew on her harder, pulling at the swollen nub between the lips of her sex.

And she begged. "Nick, don't stop. Don't stop. Please. I need to finish. I need you so badly. Please. Please..."

"My minx likes to beg when I'm so close to giving her what she wants."

"I need this."

"And I will give it to you."

He scissored his fingers, sliding them around her clitoris. She cried out his name once more as she flew over the edge and straight into pure ecstasy. She felt impossibly tight, impossibly good. Impossibly free. As her body clenched and released, her cream ran down her thighs with each movement of his hand, each propulsion of his cock in that forbidden place.

Nick shouted, and a second later she felt the pump of his seed deep inside her. He felt so different this way. It was as though she could feel more of him, every twitch, every slide like a thousand hands running over her body in unison. Nick's movements slowed, his body collapsed on top of hers, his hardness diminishing only slightly.

They didn't say anything for some minutes. When their breathing evened out, Amelia spoke first. "The way you make me feel...that scares me about us."

Nick's hand came down to rest near her head. The motion brought him completely out of her bottom, and she exhaled a small sound of relief but felt a twinge of regret at the same time. How could she want *that?*

"Hearing that makes me feel like a monster."

"I don't mean it that way. I just…I don't know who I am without you anymore. Untie me, Nick. Please. I need to touch you."

He sat up on his knees and unwound the material binding her wrists together. Her hands throbbed when they fell forward. Nick flipped her onto her back and rubbed her wrists between his hands.

"Forgive me," he said quietly.

Placing one hand along his jaw, she waited for him to focus on her eyes. "I trust you, Nick. I just need to take this slow. You make me feel things that cause me a great deal of guilt."

"There is nothing wrong with anything we do. Nothing to feel guilty about."

"You'll think me a ninny, but I want to see you and look in your eyes when you want something new. I want to touch you. I feel bereft, having that sense taken away from me."

His thumb lazily circled one of her wrists, drawing the numbness out. "I'll never bind you again."

Amelia buried both her hands in his thick, black hair. "That's not what I want."

"What do you want, then, Amelia? Don't you know I'll give you anything you ask?"

She bit her bottom lip. "I want to do everything with you. But I need to take this one step at a time. We are still learning about each other. The things you want, I would never have dreamed possible. I want to give you complete control, but I also want you to be honest with me. I want you to talk to me and reveal yourself to me, as I've shared myself with you. There's nothing you don't know about me. Nothing."

Nick's thumb brushed back and forth over her lips.

"I won't taint you with my past." One of his hands caressed the side of her face, and he kissed her tenderly on the mouth.

Neither closed their eyes; they watched each other, even as their lips brushed back and forth in a lazy loving.

"Not all of your past is dark…" She was fishing for anything that would chase away the remnants of his dream, of his guilt for taking her in a way that she didn't think many indulged. And to her surprise, she'd do it a hundred times more. For the pleasure and to hand him the reins of control, if that was what he needed to pull back from the darkness.

He pushed off the bed and padded across the floor toward the bathing room, and for the second time that night, she followed him. The water in the tub was running as she entered. Nick retrieved a linen cloth from a cabinet and ran it under the water of the washing stand before wiping himself off. He was still hard, and his member bobbed when he released it and tossed the cloth over the porcelain sink.

The man was insatiable. She blushed and turned away.

"Cat got your tongue now?"

"You are changing the subject."

"It's three in the morning, Amelia. The last thing I want to do is talk about my dreams when you're standing naked, like a feast yet to be tasted. Get in the bath."

She crossed her arms over her middle, the motion plumping up her breasts. "And if I say no?"

"Then I'll happily assist. You're going to be sore. The hot water will help ease any lingering tenseness in your muscles."

She already was feeling a little bruised, not that she'd admit that. "It's going to be difficult to bathe with you here to distract me."

He smiled, and there was nothing innocent about the look her gave her. "I promise only to keep you company."

She gave him a suspicious look and then finally dunked her toes into the hot water. It took her a while to ease in, but when she did, Nick pulled a stool over and washed her hair as she lazed in the water, feeling her muscles loosen the longer she soaked. It didn't escape her that Nick was still closing himself off from her. He couldn't continue doing so. Whatever they had between them wouldn't work if he couldn't he honest with her.

CHAPTER SEVEN

Amelia tapped her fingers along the edge of the velvet bench. Her hired carriage jostled along the uneven road, hitting quite a few bumps that required her to hold on to her seat intermittently.

She couldn't keep her mind from repeatedly wandering back to Nick and the fact that he hadn't roused her this morning so she could sneak back into her room undetected. It did not matter who had guessed they were sleeping in the same bed; what mattered was respecting her wishes that their relationship appear to be no more than professional.

After spending her morning feeling frustrated and ignored by Nick, she knew she needed to get out of the house for a while and focus on anything but matters of the heart. But here she was, thinking about him…again.

Amelia pulled the curtain aside to peek outside. The clouds rolling in promised quite a storm later this afternoon. She hoped to make it to Sera's before the skies opened up.

While Nick had invited Amelia to befriend his sister, she suspected he would not approve of what Amelia had in mind right now. Sera could provide information on Nick's past. Give Amelia the insight into what haunted him so thoroughly that he refused to open up to her. Desperation to understand why he was avoiding her drove her to do this, but it wasn't her sole reason for meeting Sera. She did miss having a friend in whom she could confide. And she had told Sera she wished to discuss the building of the new school.

After only twenty minutes of fretting, the carriage slowed and pulled up in front of a quaint two-story blond-brick townhouse. The front door was painted sage and had an oval section of stained glass in the upper half. Clay flowerpots lined the windows on either side of the door. The pots were empty, though, a testament to the coming winter season.

Amelia stepped out of the carriage, mustering her courage with a deep breath. The street on which Sera lived was quiet. Few people strolled by, but the appearance of those who did seemed to indicate this was a working-class neighborhood.

Before she could change her mind, Amelia tapped the knocker against the wood door. A rotund woman, an apron wrapped around her and a small mobcap covering her hair, opened the door.

"Good day, miss."

"I have an appointment with Miss Riley. She's expecting me at four, but I'm afraid the carriage ride was quicker than anticipated."

"Bella," rang Sera's voice from inside. "Escort Miss Grant into the parlor."

The housekeeper stood to the side so Amelia could enter. Amelia removed her gloves and shawl, which Bella took before leading her into a cozy room just off the front entrance.

Sera stood on seeing Amelia and approached to take her hand in greeting. Sera didn't release Amelia's hand until she had led her over to a seating arrangement of red floral-chintz chairs.

The room was small but perfectly suited for two women catching up on news and gossip. There were four chairs that invited a guest to sink into them, with an ottoman sitting squarely between then. The walls were papered in a gold leaf and ivory-colored design all the way up to the wood-beamed ceiling.

"I apologize for arriving so early, but I had no idea where your address was in relation to Mr. Riley's residence. I thought I would be in the carriage a good deal longer."

"Nonsense. Your timing is impeccable. Bella just brought in the tea service."

Amelia breathed a sigh of relief on the casualness with which Sera handled the change of plans.

Sera placed two teacups on the trolley and filled them. "What do you take, Miss Grant?"

"I drink it black."

Sera handed Amelia the teacup and saucer.

Amelia inhaled the black tea and felt suddenly recharged. "Mr. Riley suggested I help with the school, once the purchase of Caldon Manor is settled. As my note this morning indicated, I am willing to assist in any capacity." Amelia sat in the chair closest to the fireplace, absorbing the warmth, feeling a bit silly for blurting out her plans.

Sera looked at her for a full minute, assessing her in the same uncanny way her brother did. "For some reason, I think you might have come for more than that reason alone."

Amelia tucked a stray curl behind her ear as she met Sera's gaze. "It's been a long time since I could confide in anyone, Miss

Riley." She hadn't really had anyone she could trust, other than Nick and her father, for more years that she cared to admit. "Truthfully, I took a chance coming to London. I do not know anyone here, and have no extended family to speak of. I haven't had tea with another woman since I was a young girl."

"If I might say so, coming to London on your own is an incredibly brave thing to do. I insist on being your first friend and companion."

"Thank you, Miss Riley," Amelia said, ducking her head as the warm infusion of a flush bloomed in her cheeks.

"And I insist that you address me by my Christian name."

A smile lifted Amelia's lips. "And vice versa."

"Absolutely, Amelia."

"If you don't mind my curiosity, I wonder about the origins of your name, as it is uncommon in spelling."

"It's short for Seraphina. My mother called me her little angel for the longest time. I asked her why she would call me that when I caused trouble, and she told me that I was the brightest thing to come into her life and that my name was a sacred order of angels for only the most special people."

"Whenever you and your brother mention your mother, it's with the highest regard and with the most beautiful of stories."

"She was a wonderful woman and an adoring mother. Now, tell me what brought you to my house today."

"In all honesty, I couldn't stop thinking about the school and its importance to the children who will use it. I want to be more involved, but I worry that the difficulties of the deal with Lord Murray will make that impossible. Mr. Riley and Lord Murray seem to see things differently."

"My brother has always made calculated risks during his purchases. I don't think he has ever lost out on a deal about which he was so passionate. And if there is one thing that I can promise, it is that Nick is passionate about this deal."

"He is; I won't argue you that. However, he immensely dislikes Lord Murray."

Sera laughed uproariously. "Amelia, I hope you don't mind my pointing this out, but your experience seems insular, considering the length of time you've been employed by my brother. I should make it clear that he abhors more people than he admires."

Amelia frowned at this revelation. Everyone she'd met, aside from Lord Murray and Shauley, seemed to be a friend of Nick's.

"Now you're thinking of anyone else he hates," Sera suggested. "That's easy—anyone from whom he buys property. As I said, his risks and business interactions are deliberate."

"What is his purpose, then?"

"Retribution. For my mother, for the life we lived when my mother died."

"What does Lord Murray have to do with Mr. Riley's past?"

"Not Lord Murray." Sera took a sip of her tea, watching Amelia curiously. Amelia felt as if she had asked too many questions. "He wants to crush Shauley, and the best way to do that is to make him look bad, to strip away the reputation he has built for himself."

Amelia recalled the tense moment when Nick had sent her away upon discovering Shauley standing in his study. Now it all made sense. "I thought there was unusual tension between Mr. Shauley and Mr. Riley. You know Mr. Shauley, too, don't you?"

"I do. Our mothers were in the same profession. A lane-way separated our homes."

"In St. Giles? Nick…" She'd been so caught up in the con-versation that she'd forgotten to keep up the front of merely playing the role of secretary. Clearing her throat, she hoped Sera hadn't noted the slip of tongue. "Mr. Riley mentioned growing up in St. Giles."

A smile played on Sera's lips, and Amelia wondered if she was thinking of the familiar way Amelia had addressed Nick. She must mind her tongue.

"If we are to be friends, Amelia, I would at least like the truth from you."

Sera's question caught her off guard, and she sputtered out her tea. "I'm sorry." She set the teacup down, not sure what to say. Not sure what kind of question Sera planned on asking and worrying her charade was up.

"You and my brother? I don't think I would have ever guessed, except he hired you without my having ever heard of you—and your familiarity. You realize what this means, don't you?"

"Please…" Amelia didn't know how to change the direc-tion of their conversation. And she doubted she could lie her way out of this. She'd been foolish to come here at all.

"Oh, you need say no more, Amelia. I will keep your secret."

"Your brother and I haven't exactly come to an under-standing, aside from the fact that I am his secretary and he my employer. Please don't make any more of my comments than that. The nature of your brother's ventures means that I work closely with him and sometimes at all hours of the day. I see why you would make an assumption."

"So he hasn't been honest with you."

"I'm not sure what you mean." Amelia put her shoulders back, wishing more than anything she could slink away like a scolded dog. There was no one to blame but herself for allowing her secrets to be so easily read.

"I've scared you. I promised I wouldn't say anything. I won't even bring up the topic with Nick."

"I did wish to discuss the school."

"My brother will get that land from Lord Murray. I know him; I have seen the games of chance he plays, but mark my words—my brother always wins."

"And when he does?"

Sera frowned into her teacup. "I haven't seen the manor house yet. My brother assures me it will have to be practically rebuilt from the bottom up, but he knows a good architect and advised me that I can meet with him just as soon as the deal is firm."

"When do you suppose you will teach from Caldon Manor?"

"It won't be for another two years. But I need to do a lot in the meantime."

"Is it something with which I can help? I genuinely want to be a part of this project."

"I'd be very happy to have you assist me. I know Landon plans to take over the leases, along one of the main strips. I think six or seven properties come with the house; they are only halfway through their lease terms, which I believe is ninety-nine years. Landon is good for finding tenants who want to make something of where they live and work."

"What do Lord Burley's buildings have to do with the manor?"

A wicked grin curved Sera's lips. "An incentive for families with a lot of children to move."

Now Amelia understood. If they couldn't convince parents to let their children attend school outside London center, they needed to entice them to move and build a new life, if they were willing.

Nearly three hours had passed before they realized how much of the afternoon they had used in talking about plans for the school and for their future. Amelia hadn't realized that Sera planned to move into the house that was going to be built for her and situated near Caldon Manor. It was admirable that Nick was giving his sister her lifelong dream.

Amelia learned nothing else about Nick, which was just as well, as she hated to shine another light on just how close she and Nick truly were.

When it came time to part, Sera walked her out to her carriage. Rain had already washed through the city, and everything was damp in the early evening hour. Sera took her hand. "I haven't had this much fun spending time with another in ages. I would love to make this a Friday habit, if we could."

"You honor me. I don't know if I will be able to get away every Friday, but we will make arrangements to see each other soon."

Amelia climbed up into the carriage. Before she could shut the door, Sera stuck her head in. "I see why my brother has taken a liking to you. You are a wonderful person with a big heart. And I have to say that Nick has needed someone like you for far too long."

Sera shut the door before Amelia could respond, and she was left with her thoughts, turning over the revelations during her conversation with Sera.

CHAPTER EIGHT

Nick slipped into Amelia's bedroom well after midnight. The thud of his shoes, no matter how quiet he was trying to be, always woke her. She cracked open her eyes, tiredness still holding her immobile, as Nick pulled his shirt over his head and tossed it on the floor.

The familiar crisscross of scars on his back illuminated by the moon was a constant reminder that he held himself back. She promised herself it wouldn't be long before she ferreted out his secrets. *Tomorrow*, she told herself, and she wouldn't back down until she was satisfied with his answers.

As he came into bed, she rolled over and tucked her back along his chest. His hand wrapped around her stomach and dipped lower.

"Didn't mean to wake you," he whispered in her ear.

"That's all right." She tilted her bottom back, allowing the hard ridge of his penis to lodge between her thighs.

Nick's hand slid lower, grazing the coarse hair covering her mons and sinking his fingers between the folds of her sex.

"You're wet." He kissed her shoulder, lingering there.

She turned her head and pressed a kiss against his mouth. "I think I was dreaming about you."

"Now I wish I'd come to bed earlier." He rolled her onto her back as he came over her, wedging himself between her open legs.

Curling his arm under her thigh, he entered her in one swift motion, eliciting a moan from her. Even though she was trapped beneath his welcome weight, her back arched to position her pelvis in just the right spot that allowed him to sink deeper inside.

He worked into her with long, even strokes. One of her legs curled over his shoulder. His free hand molded to her breast as his fingers played with her nipple, tweaking it, making it longer and firmer.

With his mouth against hers, he caught her moans as they grew in volume. He practically stole the breath from her lungs as their tongues swirled together.

Amelia tangled her hands in his hair, wanting to keep him close. He made a grunting noise with each thrust of their bodies. She cried at the loss of his mouth when he went up on his knees to give himself better leverage. One of his hands wrapped around the frame of her bed; the other grasped tight to her hip as he pounded into her sheath with a vigor that revealed just how desperate he was to claim her.

She gave herself over to him willingly, openly.

"Looking at you like this, I can barely keep control," he said. "Look at the way your breasts bounce, begging me to take hold of them."

He lowered his head and swiftly sucked one nipple into his mouth. She felt dazed when he released her with a pop.

"Pinch your nipples for me."

This was something he hadn't asked her to do before, but she wanted to please him, and she didn't want him to stop the breakneck pace of their pelvises moving together. She rolled her fingers around the firm peak, pulling it enough that the already distended tip grew longer. The sensation was pleasurable, but she needed more.

Nick's hand eventually pushed hers away to cup her and suck the tip of her breast into his mouth. Her whole body convulsed, and her sheath clenched with every pull of his mouth. Her hand curled around his arm, feeling the strength and his muscles flexing with every lunge into her body.

Amelia threw her head back as Nick's mouth trailed higher, biting and licking at the frantic pulse beating at her neck. Her orgasm crept up in her body, slowly at first, her sheath clasping him.

Her body convulsed and trembled. And while her orgasm had started off as a trickle, it now flooded through her at the pace of an exploding geyser. She screamed out his name as sensation upon sensation lashed deliciously against every nerve ending in her body. Her body strained against his, unable to move; the only thing she felt was the pulsating clench of her sheath, trying to milk Nick.

"Fuck, you're so tight right now," Nick muttered against her mouth before pushing his tongue against hers and sealing their mouths in an all-consuming kiss, as he pounded into her until he finally let go. He jerked hard against her, filling her with his seed, as their hearts pounded heavily where their chests were crushed together.

While their breathing evened out, Nick remained buried inside her, still hard, still in need.

My insatiable lover.

He looked down at her, his hand tracing a line along her face. "What I'd give to keep you in bed until we're too wrung out to even walk."

She couldn't help but smile. "While that sounds perfect, we do have appointments we cannot miss tomorrow." She wiggled against him, feeling the flex of his member. "You're always like this, after. Is that normal?"

"Only when I'm with you. I swear, Amelia, I could fuck you all night and still have a raging cockstand at the end of it. I think about throwing you down on my desk all day long. I think about taking you in the library, pressed against the windows. There is no end to my need. It's constant. And when I slide into bed at night and find you naked…" He shuddered, his cock saying what he wasn't as it grew impossibly harder inside her.

"Then don't stop," she said, cradling her legs around his hips.

One of his hands pushed beneath her bottom and titled her pelvis in such a way that he only had to rotate his hips to move inside her.

The way her body responded to him…

Whenever he was inside her, it was hard to care about anything except for this. Amelia grasped his shoulders, keeping herself where she needed to be as he stroked in and out of her body again. Their renewed lovemaking rekindled her desire, igniting a blazing fire of need that struck right through her heart until she was lost in the sensation of their bodies, finding release once again.

"I might just keep you up all night like this," he said.

"I think that plan is the best one I've heard all day." She nibbled on his chin and kissed his throat, allowing the short hair on his beard to abrade her tongue and prick at her skin.

Their lovemaking was slow and indulgent. And as Nick promised, he kept her up all night long.

They didn't talk, other than Nick saying all manner of dirty things that made her blush even to think about them. They just felt, touched, tasted. Tomorrow, Amelia vowed, they would talk. And she wasn't letting him leave her room until they had a few of their issues sorted out—namely, what their future held if he wanted to continue in an illicit matter.

Nick untangled himself from Amelia, hating that he had to leave her at all. But his dreams were escalating, and he couldn't do anything to stop them from stealing his body and mind once he was asleep. Not sleeping seemed like the best solution, though even that was starting to catch up with him.

Every night, he waited until Amelia was asleep before he retreated either to the study or to his room. If she was hurt by his absence, she didn't make it known. In fact, she seemed more and more understanding about his difficulty in talking about his past. She hadn't pushed him for answers, but he knew it was only a matter of time before her questions got the better of her. Before those questions started to affect their…relationship.

He watched Amelia sleep a while longer before pulling on his trousers and slipping his shirt over his head. With one last look at her, he left her room and headed for his. After dressing in something more decent than the rumpled suit from yesterday, he went down to the study.

Huxley was at Nick's desk, writing a note.

"To what do I owe the pleasure of your late-night company?" Nick asked.

"Figured you'd be down," Huxley said morosely. "You've been wandering the house at all hours of the night the whole week."

"It's that obvious." It wasn't a question; he'd just hoped to keep his sleeping difficulties to himself—though it was hard to get anything past Huxley.

"Yes. But I'm sure I'm the only one who's noticed. Keep it up, and the rest of the staff will see something amiss. You look like hell, Nick. Almost as bad as when I pulled you out of the fighting pits you favored."

The last thing Nick wanted to do was take a trip down memory lane.

"Had I not fought for money, I wouldn't be as successful today as I am." Nick plopped himself down in a leather chair and leaned his head back with a yawn. Tiredness and restlessness were a terrible combination. Even if he did try to sleep, his thoughts alone would keep him awake. "I will have it back under control before anyone is the wiser," Nick said, though it felt like an empty promise, even to his own ears. His demons were his own to fight. "What has *you* up so late?"

"Penning a note to my man in Highgate."

Nick sat up. "Didn't take you long to set up someone there."

"Not at all," Huxley gave him a strange look. "I know what's got your thoughts all twisted. And it won't do you no good running from it. Highgate is going to be in your possession soon. You have to decide how you want to handle the business with the vicar."

"This isn't up for debate, Huxley. I will handle him in my own way when the land is transferred to my name." And when he figured out just how he would deal with the vile man.

Huxley and Sera were the only people who knew about Nick's past, but no one really knew the whole of it. Except Shauley.

Huxley bent his head again and started scribbling out more words. "Does she know?"

"I can only assume you mean Amelia."

"Who else? She's been besotted with you from the moment she came here. Didn't think she'd be the type you'd pursue, but she's a good enough lass."

"I didn't come down here to discuss her either."

"Oh, I know. Just thought I'd mention you aren't exactly being circumspect. Neither of you is."

"And what makes you think I would want to be?"

"I don't much care what you do, Nick. We go back too many years to not see a difference in each other. Especially a difference like *her*. But you should tell her your real intentions with the Lord Murray deal. A lass such as she doesn't come by often."

The Lord Murray deal. The vicar. His dealings with Shauley, who had been such a significant part of his past that *that* was the reason sleep eluded him of late. The reason he paced the house with a million thoughts traipsing through his head, unable to shut them out. Thank God the deal was going to be done in the morning.

Nick stood. He couldn't sit here for the rest of the night, discussing the darker days of his life. "I'm going to catch a few hours of sleep before we meet with the solicitors in the morning."

"Probably wise."

"We'll leave at ten."

"Your secretary should attend in my stead."

He was right. But Nick didn't want Amelia anywhere near Shauley, who was sure to be there. He was a slimy bastard. And he suspected the man to be entrenched with Highgate's darker secrets...

Amelia had proven that she could handle herself in any number of situations. She wasn't a delicate flower he needed to shield from the world. And as much as he wanted to do just that, he knew his overprotectiveness might cause her to wither.

"You're right. Amelia will attend with me in the morning." He stood to leave, as he couldn't very well stay in here when he craved solitude. "Good night, Huxley."

Waking up alone again this morning shouldn't have been a surprise to Amelia, but after her resolve to talk to Nick last night, it stung. She'd been patient with him. But that patience was wearing thin. He couldn't continue avoiding her.

She dressed and went down to the kitchens for breakfast. Not everyone had made it down for the day, but Huxley was present, reading the paper as the twins, Jenny and Jessie, set the table.

"Good morning," Amelia said on entering the dining hall.

Huxley looked up and gave her his usual grunt. He was a man of few words unless he wanted to make a point. While he played the role of Nick's man of affairs, anyone could tell they were friends that had a deep appreciation for each other. Amelia guessed that came from knowing someone for so long.

"Morning," the twins said in unison.

"What's for breakfast today?" she asked of no one in particular. In the first household she'd worked in, she'd never had the camaraderie she had with these people. Misfits, every one of them, including her. Everyone one of them plucked from a bad situation and given a home with a decent job to support themselves.

Mrs. Coleman bustled into the room with a hot dish in her hands. She was like a mother hen to them all. "Kippers, ham, and hash."

"A hearty breakfast," Amelia mused aloud. "How's the weather, then?"

"Getting colder by the day," Mrs. Coleman responded.

Amelia went into the cooking area and said good morning to the cook. "What can I take into the dining hall, Joshua?"

The cook looked at her, his glass eye eerily unmoving. While the sight once had made Amelia uneasy, Joshua was the most jovial and one of the kindest people she'd ever met. "Good morning to you, too, child. Mrs. Coleman's got the breakfast platters taken care of. I'm just finishing up these tomatoes. But if you want to do something, prepare the tea set."

She gave him a smile and did as he asked. She'd never felt kinship with anyone who'd lived in her house when she was growing up, so being at the Riley residence was a relief in so many ways.

Carrying the tea service into the next room, she saw that everyone else was present. Lately, she'd been dining with Mr. Riley in the breakfast room on the second floor, but not these past few days. She missed his company, but was thankful for the friends she had made among the rest of the serving staff.

They remained informal in the dining hall, which helped lend to a welcoming atmosphere. Everyone milled about the table and piled food on their plates before taking a random seat. There was no order to station or position. Everyone was equal here.

Mrs. Coleman prepared Huxley's dish and set it down in front of him. "And what's the gossip today?" Mrs. Coleman asked Huxley.

"This and that. Nothing in particular that might affect this house," he responded.

"Well, that's not what I heard," Jenny said.

"What have you heard, then?" Olive, a young maid of only sixteen, piped in. "The butcher's son came by, he did; gave me a good earful."

"Rumors 'bout Mr. Riley killing a man," Jessie said.

Amelia's fork stopped halfway to her mouth. "Are you sure he meant Mr. Riley?"

"Yes, Miss Grant," said Huxley. "Been expecting it too. Heard it a week ago from my man about the docks and thought that was the end of it. He's got no reason to be killing off people that cross him, whether they're a relation to you or not."

"I never suspected him of being involved with my brother's death, Huxley. Why would Mr. Riley have reason or cause to harm anyone?" Amelia asked. Since the moment she'd arrived, Nick had been nothing but caring and generous, and despite what Sera had told her yesterday, she knew in her heart that Nick wouldn't harm someone to the point of causing death. "Surely none of you believes the rumors."

A chorus of no went around the table, and everyone focused on breakfast again. There were a few tidbits of gossip related to Nick's businesses, but Amelia paid none of it the attention she should. When the meal was finished, she helped clear the plates before she headed upstairs. Huxley wasn't far behind her.

"Is there something I might help you with?" Amelia asked.

"I have errands to run outside the house. Nick wants you present. You'll need to witness, as will Lord Murray's secretary."

"I'll make sure I'm ready before ten." She grabbed up the missives on the foyer table and then turned to call Huxley back. "Where is Mr. Riley this morning?"

"Went to meet Lord Burley at his club."

"Do you know how long it will be before Lord Burley takes over the leases in Highgate?"

Huxley eyed her suspiciously, probably wondering where she'd come by that information. She held her head high and waited for his response. Huxley would have to assume that Nick had told her about that particular arrangement.

"Best you ask Mr. Riley for further clarification. I wouldn't want to give you the wrong information. I've been out of the workings of this deal too long to recall all the details."

While Amelia had a great deal of respect for Huxley, he never let her in on much and often told her to discuss her questions directly with Nick. She supposed that was how he remained loyal to Nick, but it still irritated her to no end when a simple answer or revelation would suffice.

"I will ask him, thank you." Amelia nibbled on her lip as indecision stalled her. "Huxley?"

"Yes, Miss Grant." He folded his arms behind his back as he stood in front of her.

"The rumors about Mr. Riley... Why do you think anyone would believe him possible of killing my brother?"

"Mr. Riley was once a fighter. That was how he made his money, bloodying up other men's faces for high stakes. Anyone with a gambling mind and money in his pocket would remember that."

Her brother had been a gambling man, one without scruples. What would it take for another man to bet against someone being physically harmed? That thought sent revulsion though her whole body and made goose flesh form on her arms.

"Is someone trying to sabotage Mr. Riley's name?" she asked.

"Oh, you're something innocent at times, Miss Grant."

"I could do without the insults, Huxley," she snapped. "I can't learn anything if everyone keeps mum and if you try to coddle me. I'm Mr. Riley's secretary; these things are important to know if I'm to succeed in assisting him."

"They don't care about his name, though they'll enjoy trying to run that into the ground too. They want to frame him for your brother's death. Take him out of the race as a successful landowner and businessman. Let me ask you something, Miss Grant. Being a lady by birth and the daughter of an earl, would your father have considered Nick an equal?"

She mulled over her answer a moment. "My father was a good man, Huxley, and while I want to believe he would accept any man who worked hard as an equal, I can't say for certain if that would have been possible."

"So you see the dilemma with society. Nick is richer than most. He holds more property than they ever will and without the hindrance of being heavily taxed, as the gentry are when someone new successes a title. And while Nick's properties might not be in a desirable location, he holds all the cards on his businesses, and no one can interfere with the empire he's built over the last ten years."

"Except…"

"Men like us don't mingle as equals in any social circle, Miss Grant. We have to conquer and sometimes diminish those around us to get ahead."

"Doesn't every man anger someone on his path to success?"

"Not when you're born into the privilege of money *and* status. Those men are held to a different standard than the rest of the world."

Amelia frowned at this revelation. "I understand what you're saying, but that doesn't explain why anyone would think Mr. Riley capable of killing my brother."

"It's easier to point a finger at him, Miss Grant. That's how it is for men like us. We are a challenge to be crushed, to be diminished, so those with higher social standing can feel vindicated and worthy of their stations in life."

Huxley's words held merit, but that didn't make any of this situation right. Nor did it make it clear why they would want to blame her brother's death on Nick, when Jeremy was a wastrel of the worst sort. The bigger question was, who was trying to destroy Nick's credibility? Who wanted to see him lose everything? Lord Ashley, the man she was supposed to marry to clear her brother's debts? That didn't make sense and seemed unlikely, for she was sure that man was forever out of her life the moment her brother had died. So whom did that leave? How many enemies could Nick possibly have made?

"Thank you for your honesty, Huxley." Before she turned back toward the study, she said, "I plan on answering correspondence before heading out to see the solicitor. Will you be joining us?"

Huxley shook his head. "I'm off to the docks. I got a lead on the buyer who wharfinger's selling Mr. Riley's and Lord Burley's goods to."

A good portion of Nick's goods had gone missing en route to his docking company on the Thames. He brought in wool from Landon's sheep farm in the north of Scotland and consequently, those were the ledgers she had been reviewing for variances, as she had a good head for numbers.

She reached for Huxley's arm and squeezed it gently. "Be careful, Huxley. With everything that's happened over the past month, I want everyone to be vigilant."

"Don't you worry about me, miss. I've been through times more dangerous than this, if you catch what I'm saying." With that, he was off.

Amelia was surprised that Nick hadn't come back to the house before she'd finished her tasks, though he had sent a note advising her that a hired carriage would be waiting for her at half past nine. When she arrived at the solicitor's office—five minutes late, to her everlasting distress; she did hate to be even a minute late—Nick wasn't yet there. Lord Murray, however, was standing outside, his scowl in place.

"Lord Murray." She ducked her head as she approached. "I'm sorry if I kept you waiting. Mr. Riley was held back at his morning appointment. He sent me right away and said he would follow in a short while." She hated to lie, but to date, Lord Murray had been unimpressed with Nick, and she didn't want today to begin inauspiciously.

Mr. Shauley stood next to Lord Murray, watching her to the point that she felt uncomfortable, and she shifted under his scrutiny.

"I don't want to hear your excuses, Miss Grant. It shouldn't surprise me that we are ready to do our sign-offs, and he's nowhere in sight." Lord Murray's response was gruff, and while she was accustomed to his straightforwardness, she still cringed at his harsh words.

"I cannot apologize enough. The streets are overrun with carts and carriages alike. I could have walked here faster, had I the mind for some exercise."

Murray harrumphed but said nothing.

Trying to change the tone to something lighter, she decided to ask about the love of his life, a woman she'd had the pleasure of meeting a few weeks earlier over dinner. "How is Heddie? I did so enjoy our dinner conversation at the Langtry Hotel."

"Good enough. Happier when I unhand this land."

Apparently that left them with nothing else to discuss while they waited on Nick. She was beginning to understand why Nick disliked Lord Murray—he wasn't a great conversationalist, at least not without a never-ending supply of wine.

"Shall we?" Lord Murray said, opening the door to the solicitor's office, allowing her to enter the warmth first. She shivered a little when the heat of the room slapped her in the face but was thankful to get out of the wind. Lord Murray approached the man sitting behind the mahogany desk off to the side of the room.

"Ten o'clock with Mr. Cavendale." His voice boomed around the spacious room.

"Yes, of course, Lord Murray. Mr. Cavendale is just concluding his last appointment. May I offer you refreshment or a hot beverage?"

"We'll wait. Riley's running behind schedule as it is."

Amelia stripped off her gloves and warmed her hands near the burning coals; the red brick of the fireplace covered the whole of one wall. Lord Murray picked up a newspaper and flicked it open as he sat in one of the two dark leather chairs, ignoring both Amelia and Mr. Shauley.

"Mr. Shauley, how was your morning?" Amelia asked, not sure what they should discuss. An instinct told her not to trust this man, so the less personal their topics of conversations, the better—and that might have something to do with Sera's revelation in how far back Nick's acquaintance went with this man.

"How are you keeping as Nick's secretary?" he asked, making her feel more uncomfortable with his familiar use of Nick's name.

"Well." Amelia pulled her hands away from the coals and faced Shauley, determined not to let him frighten her.

"Only 'well'? Surely you can say more about the position than that. I haven't run into any women in this profession, so I am genuinely curious about you."

She couldn't help but feel as though Mr. Shauley was trying to obtain private details of her relationship with Nick. "It's been a great challenge, and Mr. Riley has been a kind employer. I'm still fairly new to the position and learning the role."

"Lady Luck must have been on your side to land such a lofty job after only just arriving in London."

Like the previous comment about her country accent, his familiarity with her sent a shiver of fear across her skin. "I hadn't realized Lord Murray knew of my situation."

Mr. Shauley inched closer, so close that Amelia felt her pulse kick up and goose flesh prickle her skin. "I assure you," he said, "his lordship remains blissfully ignorant."

To say Amelia felt uneasy was an understatement. "You are well informed of my circumstance, Mr. Shauley."

"I make it my business to know every *intimate* detail of anyone with whom Lord Murray has dealings."

While Amelia would have liked to take a step away from Shauley, she refused to be cowed by a man of his ilk. Head high, shoulders back, she faced him unflinchingly.

"I'm curious to know if you'll be staying in London, what with the estate sitting empty and alone in Berwick. All it needs is a male heir, and you are at the prime of your age." His eyes travelled the length of her body, lingering at her breasts and hips.

Amelia swallowed the disgust building low in her belly and forced herself to stand firm even though she wanted to shrink away.

"Did you know my brother?" She wasn't sure how she remained calm, asking that much, but now she understood why this man made her so uncomfortable. Not only did he seem to know an inordinate number of personal details, but she had to wonder how she knew of her brother's death. It wasn't information easily come by.

"Lord Berwick and I had a few dealings."

"Of what nature, Mr. Shauley?" She wished she could have bitten her tongue because she felt like she was borrowing trouble, trying to uncover what this man might know.

"Some mutual endeavors, Miss *Grant*."

If he knew she was using a false name, why not just end her charade? The door to the solicitor's office opened, and Nick made his entrance. A sigh of relief audibly passed Amelia's lips. He looked dashing and in command whenever he entered a room. At least he did to her.

Realizing she'd been staring at him, she made her way to his side. "Mr. Riley." She was a little breathless. Nick's gaze fell on hers and then caught on her lip where she nibbled it. She lowered her gaze. "We are waiting for Mr. Cavendale to conclude his previous appointment."

Nick addressed the men. "Lord Murray. Shauley." Amelia didn't miss the undercurrent of distaste as Nick said the secretary's name. When they finished their affairs here, she planned to ask him why he disliked Shauley as much as he did.

"Riley," Lord Murray said. "Only you would show up late to an important appointment."

"Couldn't be helped. Don't worry; we'll wash our hands of each other soon enough." Strangely, Nick was watching Shauley as he spoke.

They were ushered into the solicitor's office before more sentiments could be exchanged. Amelia also took note that the underlying animosity between Nick and Mr. Shauley didn't end in the waiting room. Their time with the solicitor went by quickly, and before she knew it, they were all standing in the street having concluded their business. Nick was studying her, as though he knew she had a hundred things she wanted to discuss with him, but not while they were in the company of others.

Shauley came within a foot of her as they walked to the edge of the pavement. She bumped into Nick as she tried to put distance between her and Shauley. When she caught Nick's eye, there must have been an expression on her face that indicated her feelings, for Nick said, "Wait here while I talk to Shauley a moment."

She bristled. "I should hear anything you have to say to him." Even though she wanted to be as far from Shauley as possible.

"I promise to tell you every word exchanged between us. For now, stay here by the carriage."

Amelia gave one succinct nod, not happy with being made to stand aside, no matter the situation, no matter the discussion Nick wanted to have with that man.

It took one look on Amelia's face to tell Nick everything he needed to know about what transpired while she'd been stranded with Lord Murray and Shauley.

Fear.

Nick cursed the hired carriage again that had caused his tardiness, when he'd had every intention of arriving prior to Amelia.

"Shauley," he called. As his nemesis turned toward him, Nick took a moment to address Murray. "Your lordship, do you mind if I have a word with Shauley?"

Lord Murray waved him off, indifferent, shouting his directions to the driver as he shut the carriage door.

"I don't have time for you right now," Shauley said. "You've just delayed my next appointment, Riley."

"Our conversation will be quick." Nick hovered so close to Shauley that the man took a step back. "Now that this deal is done with Lord Murray, I don't expect to see you again. And that means you will stay away from anyone who works in my household as well."

"Even your precious Miss Grant…or shall I address her as Lady Amelia Somerset?"

If Nick had hackles, they would have risen just then. And while he raged on the inside, he knew he needed to keep his expression free of reaction so as not to give away his feelings. "Miss Grant, as with anyone living in my house, will be offered the same protection from any potential threats."

"You always did have a sweet spot for the fairer sex."

"And you've always scared them away. I mean it, Shauley; any threat you pose against my household will be acted upon swiftly and without mercy."

Shauley chuckled low. "Should I be worried for my life? I find it odd that people end up floating in the Thames after a confrontation with you."

Nick considered this silently. Inspector Laurie must have used Shauley as a source for information. How else would he know of Lord Berwick and of Miss Grant's true identity? So how did Shauley tie into Lord Berwick's death? Because there was no question in Nick's mind that the two men were somehow tied together.

"Perhaps you should be worried that the last person who got on my bad side ended up dead."

Shauley's eyes lit up. "I have measures in place to deal with the likes of you, Riley. Men of your ilk have fallen down the social rabbit hole with little provocation."

These were all empty threats, meant to incite Nick to act rashly—and he knew it. "You have nothing on me, Shauley."

Nick walked back to Amelia's side and held out his arm for her. He didn't bother turning back to see Shauley's expression at being dismissed so abruptly. After his plans this afternoon concluded, he needed to have a conversation with Huxley. For now, he would reveal a little something about Shauley to Amelia, as she had to understand the danger that man represented.

CHAPTER NINE

"Tell me what you needed to discuss with Shauley," Amelia said to Nick as soon as they were seated in the carriage.

Nick looked at her a long moment before sighing and placing his top hat on the bench beside him.

"His given name is Michael. We grew up together in St. Giles."

"I know you were once neighbors. I visited your sister a few days ago, and we discussed Shauley to some extent."

A smile tilted up Nick's lips. "I shouldn't have expected anything less. We were once the best of friends. But some men grow stronger from mistreatment, while others change into something twisted and different…I could almost go so far as to call it sinister."

Amelia reached for his hand and clasped it. "We both know the monster my brother was, Nick. I know not all men are cut from the same cloth, no matter their upbringing."

"Michael is a year my junior. His mother was also a prostitute, though she didn't have a place like my mum set up. Michael and I were good friends at one point. We did everything together. My mother saw the attachment we'd formed, so she paid for him to attend school with me."

"What caused you to stop being friends?"

"The school."

"I don't understand."

"There were a handful of teachers there who liked young men." Nick pulled her glove off and massaged the wrist he held captured between his hands. "More specifically, they liked boys."

She still didn't comprehend.

"I wish I could pretend it was nothing but my adolescent imagination, that it was all a dream. I wish I didn't have to reveal any of this to you, but it's important you understand what Shauley is capable of, and why he's capable of it. But I can't lie about this. Not after everything you've been through with your brother. Not when I am starting to think Shauley had a hand in your brother's death…"

"What did he say to you, Nick?"

"Not enough to have a confession but enough to concern me of his involvement."

She'd thought as much—or had been close to that very conclusion. But for the life of her, she couldn't understand why Shauley would cause her brother any harm when she was sure neither knew the other.

"Tell me about the school, Nick."

"As there's no real way to word this delicately, I'm just going to have to spit it out. The teachers liked to rape young boys. The prettier the better. Willing, not willing. They didn't care. They ran a school to fulfill their own base desires." Nick's gaze didn't leave hers as he revealed this.

Amelia's hand flew up to her mouth. There was no covering the shocked sound that escaped her. Tears flooded her eyes. She didn't know what to say and stuttered out a few sounds before saying, "Did they…?"

Oh, God, she couldn't even put words to her questions. They'd hurt Nick; she knew it.

"I was kicked out after four months for stabbing the vicar who…" Even Nick couldn't utter that truth.

She didn't want him to and cleared her throat before redirecting their focus, "And Michael?"

"I visited his mother as she lay on her deathbed. She told me that it was a good thing Michael was able to learn the ins and outs of the business before she was gone."

"She *knew?*" Amelia couldn't temper the shock that flooded that question.

"I always assumed that Michael had told her. He stayed at the school after I left. Received a *scholarship*. We never talked again."

Amelia was sure she'd vomit. She asked Nick to have the carriage pulled over so she could step outside for fresh air. While the day had been cold and she'd found herself chilled to the bone, now she felt only heat and anger boiling in her blood and throughout her body. She took in great gulps of air. Nick stood close by as she paced the laneway they'd pulled into.

Sweat dotted her eyebrow and she swiped it away, agitated by this revelation and situation. As she saw it, there were two problems: the first was what Nick had revealed about his past. And that made her stomach twist again, so she paced faster, trying to ignore her discomfort.

The second: "You think Shauley was responsible for Jeremy's death. Why would he resort to murdering my brother when there are other people more important to you?" Nick's sister, for instance. Or Huxley, or even his old lover, Victoria. "He can't possibly know what we mean to each other."

"Are you so certain, considering the argument I had with your brother? Anyone who heard the threats I uttered toward your brother would know how much you mean to me."

Amelia stopped in front of Nick and studied him. Nick clasped his hands on either of her arms, keeping her from pacing. She'd had a bad feeling about her old employer, who nearly had raped her before she escaped. She'd felt uncomfortable around Shauley too. How poorly she judged men's characters—no, she gave them too much benefit over her doubt. Never again would she give any leeway to what she initially felt.

"Your brother nearly taking you was the end to my good grace, Amelia. I sent someone to watch Jeremy's comings and goings so he wouldn't get a second chance."

"I remember you telling me that." Amelia stepped closer to Nick. Suddenly, she needed to feel his warmth and the comfort of his embrace, and she didn't care that anyone could happen by. He opened his arms to her, inviting her closer.

"The kid I had following your brother came to me today and described a man resembling Shauley as one of your brother's constant companions. He hadn't thought much of it until the kid came by the house and saw Shauley leaving with Lord Murray."

"Why didn't he say something sooner?"

"Didn't think of it when he got caught up in his other tasks. It's not his fault, Amelia. He is but twelve."

Amelia would not fault a child. She pressed her forehead against Nick's chest and inhaled his amber-scented cologne. She could barely comprehend how any of this had happened or why it was happening.

"My brother is a continual nightmare, haunting me from his grave."

"I will ensure Shauley is crushed."

Tilting her head back to look at him, she saw that Nick's expression was resolute and as hard as stone. "I don't doubt you," she said. "But you have to be careful. If he killed my brother, he could harm you too. That's not a risk I'm willing to take, much as you aren't willing to risk my safety."

Nick brushed his thumb across her cheek until his hand stretched behind her nape. "I will always come back to you."

She hoped so, because she couldn't bear the thought of losing Nick.

They embraced a while longer before returning to the carriage. Amelia's thoughts rolled over in her mind. She felt great unease. And distress. How could she not remain in a constant state of uncertainty?

The hired carriage turned toward the shopping strip instead of the townhouse. "Where are we headed?" Amelia asked.

"I made arrangements earlier to spend the afternoon out of the house. I would cancel, except Landon and his wife are meeting us there."

"A day trip sounds like a wonderful plan. It might take our minds off everything else for a short while."

Nick didn't say much else on their ride; he just sat across from her in silent contemplation. Was he concerned he'd revealed too much about his past? She put her own worries from her mind, as she intended to enjoy her afternoon in Nick's company.

Amelia watched the scenery passing through the window as they wound their way through London's hectic midday streets. Finally, the carriage stopped in front of a row of unassuming two-story red brick buildings. There were only a few passers-by in the street; otherwise, it was an unusually quiet spot of London. Inside one of the storefronts, there were people sitting at tables that faced the overlarge windows.

Nick stepped out of the carriage and helped her down.

"It looks absolutely full for being the only shop with visible patrons," she commented.

"It's known for its Turkish coffee. Patrons are willing to go out of their way to come here for that delicacy."

Amelia screwed up her nose. She'd had one taste of coffee and didn't wish to repeat the experience. Nick chuckled at her expression.

"There are other delights aside from the coffee."

She exhaled in a rush. "Well, that's a relief."

"I will get you to like it yet."

"Unlikely. But if you insist on being disappointed by my dislike, by all means"—she motioned her hand in the direction of the entrance—"I will follow your lead."

The atmosphere when they entered was loud and far busier than she could have guessed possible when looking in from the outside. It was also unbearably hot.

Nick led them to a table near the window, tucked in a back corner of the shop. There was a sign that read *reserved*, holding the table empty.

Amelia looked at Nick. "You knew we were coming here all along and didn't think to tell me before you left this morning?"

His only response was a charming grin.

Looking around, she saw men wearing suits, some fine and elegant, some of the lower working class, as well as workmen with shirtsleeves carelessly rolled up their forearms as they sat at tables with their assorted hot beverages and sweets as they boisterously went about their conversation. No one, though, was as finely frocked as Nick. Some of the women wore hats with so many feathers, satin, and lace that they might be about to stroll through Hyde Park to attract a rich suitor. Other women wore the most beautiful walking dresses, the type Amelia expected to see only in the finest of shops around London and far nicer than the drab brown day dress she'd picked to attend the meeting at the solicitor's office.

She felt overwhelmed and less worthy of the man on her arm as she looked from one woman to the next, noticing their focus locked on Nick. The sudden insecurity caught her off guard. She didn't normally think like this, but she felt out of her element.

Nick checked the time on his watch. "We have more time than I thought we would have to ourselves."

"You make that sound as if it's a bad thing."

Nick's hand brushed over her arm as he removed her shawl and folded it over the back of a chair. When he pulled out a seat for her, he stood close enough that she felt the heat of his breath on her cheek, stirring wisps of her hair that curled over her temple. She wanted him to put his arms around her. She craved his touch outside their stolen evenings.

"You're very distracting," he said.

With that comment, he vanquished every one of her insecurities. Nick was so focused on her that he probably hadn't even noticed the other women in the coffee shop. She took her seat without responding, her hands twisting in her lap, her nerves suddenly on edge for an entirely different reason.

She was saved from having to say anything when a robust man approached their table carrying a silver tray with coffee cups and plates. She took the man to be a Turk, since he wore a fez atop his head—something, she was reminded, her brother used to wear in his smoking room. The man's beard rivaled Nick's in length and thickness. The hair on his upper lip was curled and moved as he spoke.

"Mr. Riley. I'll have a coffee service sent over," he said with an accented voice that held a smooth lilt that was almost musical in quality.

"Thank you for saving the table. I know how busy you are at this time of the day."

"It's no trouble for you, Mr. Riley. Now, can I get you something to eat while you wait for your companions?"

"Tea for my lady friend, Adnan. Though I promise to make her try the coffee."

Adnan put his hands together and bowed his head as he left them.

"You must come here often," she observed.

"I do. The patron base is mostly working class. Not too many highbrows come here, which isn't surprising, since it's surrounded by slums."

"I thought women weren't allowed in coffeehouses."

"A fine observation. Adnan is happily ruled by his wife's decisions. She once told me that if they cut off half of London by not allowing women here, they'd never have found success of this magnitude."

"I already adore her and all, without having met her."

Adnan came back carrying a two-tiered copper teapot. It was the oddest thing Amelia had ever seen. Setting it down in front of them, he addressed Nick. "My wife prepared some *lukom* for your lady friend."

A small porcelain dish was placed between them, with small cubes of jelly. She wasn't sure what *lukom* was, but it was dusted with a sugary powder. There were orange and yellow pieces, all similar in size.

"That is very generous, Adnan. She will love them. Thank your wife for her hospitality."

Amelia watched their exchange with interest. Nick seemed so at ease in this place. Normally, he held himself aloof, but just as he'd been in his sister's schoolyard, here he was more relaxed.

"For you, my friend, my wife set aside some *zerde* before it was gone. She garnishes it as we speak."

"Your wife is too kind to lavish me with special treatment."

"We can never be kind enough, Mr. Riley. Now, the tea must sit. I will be back to pour it for your friend." The proprietor turned to Amelia and gave her a smile and wink. "If you like sweets, I will bring you beet sugar too."

She only smiled since she wasn't sure what that was. He was gone again, and Nick was looking at her.

"Beet sugar? Dare I ask?"

"Adnan travels home three times a year and ships back large quantities of traditional items. Mostly teas, spices, and coffee beans. The sugar tastes the same, it's just processed differently."

"What about the squares of jelly?" She pointed at the plate with the dozen small cubes.

"You might know it as Turkish delight." He lifted one of the cubes and held it out to her.

"I do not know what that is. I'm afraid I lived too far north for any cultural variety in cuisine."

"Then you will be pleasantly surprised. Try it."

Amelia's eyes darted around the coffeehouse. "We'll be seen."

"And we won't be judged here. Try it, Amelia, because if you lick your lips one more time, I'm going to want to put my mouth on yours instead of feeding you this tiny morsel of heaven."

She tried to grab it from his hand, but he only tsked and pulled it away before she could snatch it up.

"That's not playing by the rules," he admonished.

"Those are your rules, Nick."

"In case you've forgotten"—he edged closer, his elbows on the table, his knees trapping hers under the small round table—"I like making all the rules."

She felt a blush warm her cheeks. "How could I forget?"

"Now, come here and take it."

She felt absolutely silly and awkward, but she leaned forward anyway because she wanted this flirting to be over. Well, not entirely—she just wished they had a private room at the very least. Nick didn't let it go when her lips touched the jelly; his thumb and finger brushed against her tongue before he slipped them out of her mouth, only to put them in his and suck the sugar clean off his fingers.

Amelia sat back in her chair, feeling suddenly breathless as she bit into the jelly cube. It had a distinct lemon flavor but under that was a flavor noticeably fragrant and floral.

"What's in it?" She picked up one of the orange ones and brought it to her nose. "It smells like roses." She bit into it, tasting a hint of orange zest and that floral scent again.

"Rosewater," Nick said. "Adnan has a lemonade he serves in the summer that has rosewater in it as well."

"Rosewater? Who would think to put that in food?"

"You don't like it?"

She popped another in her mouth, wishing she could steal the plate and eat all the tiny cubes. "I think I'm in love with it."

Nick smiled and leaned forward to brush his thumb over her lip. "You have a little powder here." There was a hunger for more than a mere touch in his eyes.

Her tongue darted out; she made sure there wasn't more sugar on her lips, fearing what she might do if he touched her so provocatively again. Her breath hitched, but before she could contemplate her reaction, Adnan was back, breaking the tension.

He set down a dish in front of Nick of yellow pudding with raisins and chopped nuts sprinkled on it. Holding a towel placed beneath the spout of the small copper pot, he poured Nick's coffee. It was darker than Amelia remembered and foamed at the top. Nick placed a cube of sugar in his cup and thanked Adnan.

The proprietor then placed a strangely shaped glass that looked like the rim had been dipped in gold. Its shape was thin through the middle and rounded on the top and bottom, like a corseted woman. Adnan separated the stacked teapots, pouring out the top one in the glass first. The color was nearly as dark as Nick's coffee.

"We steep the leaves in a small amount of boiled water first. You can dilute to your preference," he said. "We do not serve our tea with milk, like the English prefer, so you must tell me how strong you like it."

"I usually only take lemon and on occasion, sugar."

"Perfect," he lifted the other pot and poured out just as much of the clear boiled water as he had the dark concoction. The colors swirled together until they were a deep red instead of brown.

She inhaled some of the steam that came off the glass. "It smells like black tea."

"It is. Just brewed stronger." Setting the pots together, he bowed again. "I will come again when Lord Burley arrives."

"Thank you, Adnan. And thank your wife for the treats," Nick said.

"It is our pleasure."

Nick motioned toward her glass. "You're meant to drink it while it's hot enough to burn."

Amelia picked it up and tried the tea. It was bitter but still pleasant. She dropped a sugar cube in and stirred it with the small spoon Adnan had left for her.

Clearing her throat, she said, "There are some issues that stand between us that I would like to address."

"Now is not the time, Amelia," Nick said shortly.

"I'm beginning to think there will never be a time for that conversation." She sighed and ate another piece of Turkish delight. If the rest of their party didn't join them soon, she feared she'd eat the whole plate.

Nick took a sip of his coffee. Satisfied, he set it down and scooped up a spoonful of the pudding that sat between them.

"If you won't talk about why you're avoiding me, can you tell me why Lord Burley wasn't part of the deal with Lord Murray, if you are giving him the leases in Highgate?"

"He and Lord Murray go back some years. There was a feud between their fathers. On principle alone, Lord Murray would never have sold the land to Landon."

"But he knows you two are friends, that you do business together."

"Yes, so Shauley was quick to point out on more occasions than I care to recall."

Nick scooped up another spoonful of the pudding and held it out to her. She didn't think twice about taking it. When she realized what she'd done, she looked around her, and while the coffeehouse was brimming and bloated at the seams with business, no one seemed to pay them any mind.

"You shouldn't do that," she whispered.

"Why not?" He pushed his cup across the table. The strong smell of the coffee hit her nose pungently and had her pulling away. "Try it. It's different from the coffee you had at the hotel with me."

"Different how? It smells worse."

Nick laughed but still gave her a firm look. "Someone once told me you should try the things you dislike at least a dozen times before giving up altogether."

"I daresay, they could probably stomach a great deal more than I."

"Perhaps, but you'll never know if you don't sample it."

She nibbled at her lip, looking at the frothy cup of black coffee in front of her. He'd push if she refused. So she picked up the cup and took a small, tentative sip. Her mouth puckered as she swallowed it. "It's very bitter." She set the cup down and pushed it toward him again.

"I see you don't find it nearly as distasteful as you did the last time you tried coffee."

"Oh, I certainly do. I just don't want your friend Adnan to notice my dislike. He's been so generous since we arrived that I would hate to insult him or his wife."

Nick turned the cup where her lips had left a mark and lifted it to his lips. "But now, I can think of what your lips taste like when I'm enjoying my coffee."

His lips touched the cup where hers had just been. She couldn't understand why that felt…erotic, but it made her feel hotter than she currently was and as if Nick was feasting on her mouth instead of sipping his coffee.

"You have to stop doing this to me." Her voice was needy to her own ears. She pinched her lips shut, hating that he could so easily affect her this way.

He leaned forward, elbows on the table again, their faces but a handspan apart. His hand reached under the table and grasped her thigh. Her breath was frozen in her lungs as she stared back at him, feeling a familiar ache at the apex of her thighs.

How could she want him here and now? He'd turned her into a hedonist with only a few words. She was suddenly desperate for his kiss. Thank God the diameter of the table was wide enough that she couldn't accomplish that feat in their current position.

"Tell me something, Amelia. If I manage to get my hand under your skirts and between your legs, just how wet will I find you?"

"You're liable to make me embarrass myself. You need to refrain from such comments," she said, even though that was the last thing she wanted. God help her, she was addicted to this man.

"What if I should slide over to the next seat? My body would cover you enough that no one would guess where my hand is buried."

Amelia swallowed hard, picked up her tea, and took a larger swill than she should have with the temperature still burning. It did bring her back to her senses but did not diminish the ache she had for the things Nick promised.

"When is Lord Burley supposed to arrive?"

Nick's hand flexed over her knee, as though he were fighting whether to lift her skirts or let her be. She was torn on what she wanted too.

"Nick. Didn't think you'd arrive before us," came a masculine voice.

Amelia let out a shaky breath, and as she stood from the table, her chair knocked into the wall behind her. They were squished into a tiny table space, and she couldn't easily maneuver the seating arrangement. Lord Burley and his wife had either interrupted the most erotic tea break she'd ever had or perhaps saved her from committing a sin in public.

"Don't bother yourself, Miss Grant. My wife will sit next to you, if you don't mind."

"Not at all, Lord Burley," she said, ducking her head in greeting.

Lady Burley returned the gesture to those around the table. Amelia had met these friends of Nick's on one occasion, but they'd sat across from each other and hadn't had an opportunity to get to know each other through their last dinner.

"I've heard great things about you, Miss Grant." Lady Burley smoothed her hand over her skirts as she took the seat next to Amelia.

"You flatter me. But I hardly accomplish all that Huxley did, only a fraction of the tasks for which he no longer has time, as he is pulled away from the house constantly for business matters."

"Huxley is a hard man to replace, but from what I hear from my husband, you fill the role well. I'm fascinated by women who take on the workforce like a man would. It's admirable, and had I not married, I'd be tempted to do the very same."

"It was driven from necessity, not a desire to prove women are just as good as any man." Amelia did not explain that she'd gone the usual route and started as a governess, far more typical to women of gentle breeding.

"Let me be the judge. We are apt to spend a great deal of time together over the next few years. I'll be initiating raising funds for the school."

This announcement took Amelia by surprise. "I have spoken at length with Miss Riley and hadn't realized that we would be raising funds for the school."

"I only decided to commit to that recently. Why should all the money come out of my husband's and Mr. Riley's pocketbooks when there are plenty of purses that can be opened in society for such a charitable and community-building endeavor."

"You don't think the residents of Highgate will put up a front against the school?"

"The stores along the main center of the area have been mismanaged for years. Anything to help the local economy will be welcomed with open arms, once my husband turns over the leases on the less-than-desirable tenants."

"You're going to toss everyone out of their homes," Amelia said with alarm.

"Not at all, Miss Grant," interjected Lord Burley. "We are giving them an opportunity to make it a better place to live for everyone. The funds we raise will be used to build residences in the local township for the families of the children accepted into the school. With the integration of more people, more services will be required."

"Was this always your plan?" Amelia asked Nick.

He nodded and sipped his coffee. To think so far in advance of what you could do with a small lot of land with a dilapidated manor house…she admired Nick more and more throughout their conversation.

Adnan served more rounds of tea, coffee, and sweets through the afternoon. And Amelia's imagination was given no opportunity to stray, once she found out that Lady Burley was from Scotland and that they had visited a few of the same places. She also learned they needed to schedule a stay in Highgate this coming week.

Amelia allowed herself to be swept up into the extended friendship she had with Lord and Lady Burley and stuffed away all thoughts of her brother and Shauley for the remainder of the afternoon. Though she knew the escape from reality would be short-lived, she was thankful for a little bit of normalcy. All too soon their meeting came to an end, and they were off in their carriage toward home.

"I'll be dropping you off at the townhouse," Nick advised. "I have to meet Hart at his hotel and then make a few stops to inquire about the inspector who handled your brother's murder."

Just like that, their lovely afternoon was forgotten, and the reality of the past few weeks crashed through her good mood.

"When do you expect to be home?" Really, she wanted to know if she should wait up for Nick.

"Rather late. I'll come to your room when I get in." His focus wasn't on her as he said this; he was looking out the carriage window, staring at the passing scenery.

"Nick?"

When he looked at her, a whoosh of air emitted from her lungs. There was anger mixed with something indefinable as he stared back at her in quiet contemplation.

"What are you going to do to Shauley?"

"Nothing, until I have proof."

"Do you think he'll hurt anyone else?"

"I suspect he knows there is only one way to hurt me, and that's through you."

She did not want to believe that Shauley was capable of anything so sinister. That someone would want to hurt Nick so much that they were willing to commit murder. She wanted to believe that Nick was taking everything out of context, but the truth of the matter was... She trusted Nick's opinion, his belief. And that frightened her.

"Then why hasn't he already tried to hurt me?"

"Because he's playing a game, Amelia."

"Help me understand why."

The carriage slowed, and before he could answer her, he opened the door and helped her down.

"This conversation is far from over," she said, perturbed that he was shutting her out of his thoughts once again.

"I intend to find out a few of the answers myself, Amelia. For now, stay home, and do not leave for any reason."

CHAPTER TEN

Pacing the floor in Hart's office, Nick had one thing on his mind. And that was pummeling Shauley into the same grave that had been dug for Berwick. He felt helpless, and that was not an easy feeling for him.

He hadn't known where to start after leaving Amelia at the townhouse. He just knew he needed to do something, anything, that would have Shauley found out for the monster he truly was.

Hart entered, with a flurry of activity going on behind him in the main staff quarters. He was the same height as Nick, perhaps an inch taller. His frame was thinner but just as strong, and he could fight as lethally as Nick ever had in the ring. Hart looked like the perfect playboy, blond-haired, blue-eyed. Women generally fawned over him. Amelia, Nick remembered, hadn't given Hart a second look.

"I didn't think you'd be this busy," Nick said apologetically.

Hart walked over to the sideboard and poured two glasses of whiskey.

"We have the jewel gallery showing here next month and have to test our security measures after the art fiasco last year. Lewis at the front said it seemed urgent, so I left them to it."

After handing Nick a glass, Hart waved toward the chair arrangement in his office.

"Do you remember Shauley?" Nick asked.

"You mean the pompous bastard always following Lord Murray around like a lapdog?" Hart gave him a wry smile and swirled the contents of his glass around and around.

Nick had known Hart since his fighting days, not as a youth, so his friend would know nothing of Nick's past with Shauley. "The very one."

"Why do I have the feeling you're about to ask for a favor?"

"You have ears in high places."

"And so do you, my friend."

"Not in this case. I need a worm in Lord Murray's ear. Something to cause his trust in Shauley to cease." If it would have helped to go to Lord Murray himself, Nick would have done it, but they didn't see eye-to-eye.

"And what rumor do you want spread?"

So Nick told his friend a secret he'd long kept to himself. One that would not only threaten Shauley's job with Lord Murray but also have him arrested without delay. It was a distraction to keep Shauley off Nick's back as he tried to find evidence to tie the bastard to Berwick's murder.

"You play a hard game, Riley. Does this have anything to do with a certain secretary who's caught your eye?"

Nick downed his whiskey and pointed at Hart. "I'll ask you not to repeat that anywhere."

His friend wore a grin like a Cheshire cat. "Just stating the obvious."

After visiting a few more people who could help root out a few of Shauley's secrets, Nick arrived home after midnight.

He slipped into Amelia's room and climbed into bed behind her. Wrapping his arms around her and holding her close, he fell into the first deep sleep he'd had in weeks. But that sleep was short-lived, and he woke with a start, covered in sweat, sometime around two in the morning.

Sitting on the edge of the bed, he gathered his wits. He shouldn't have come to Amelia when his dreams were always just out of reach from his control. He wondered if they would ever subside. They were always the same. He was back in the school, waking up to the vicar over him.

He wasted no time in dressing, hating to leave Amelia's side at all, but he couldn't sleep now.

The soft click of her door woke her. When she turned over in her bed, it was to see that the covers were mussed where Nick had slept, but he was gone. Had his leaving awakened her? She threw off her blankets with a frustrated huff. This time, she would not be deterred from seeking the path toward which she and Nick had been heading. She was determined to follow him, no matter where he went to escape *them*. Because his sneaking away in the middle of the night needed to stop.

Bleary-eyed and tired, she crawled out of bed and cinched a corset around her waist before pulling on yesterday's dress. They couldn't ignore the problem that made it nearly impossible to move into another phase of their relationship—or whatever it was that they had. She was determined to have an answer to that today too. They'd come leaps and bounds yesterday, but today she would not allow him to close himself off again.

After finding Nick's bedchamber empty, she headed downstairs, only to find him in his study, pacing the floor. His hair was disheveled, his shirt only tucked in at the front. Seeing him thus caused a lot of the frustration building in her to vanish.

She shut the door and flicked over the lock behind her on entering the room. Nick stopped pacing immediately and scrubbed a hand over his face, scratching his beard as his eyes focused on her in the darkness. It broke her heart, seeing him so exhausted from too many sleepless nights.

"I didn't mean to wake you." He sounded genuinely concerned to have disturbed her rest, and that ebbed the rest of the anger that had built while she'd searched the house for him.

"And I didn't intend to let you sneak out of my room yet again."

He rubbed his face again. "I couldn't sleep."

"I could tell. As I have been able to tell every night for weeks, Nick. Please tell me what is going on."

He didn't say anything. Didn't confirm or deny her observation. With a sigh she thought she wasn't meant to hear, he went over to the sideboard and poured two decent-sized glasses of whiskey. He held one out for her to take and motioned toward the library. She didn't normally imbibe in liquor like this but took the glass anyway.

"Sit with me for a while," he said.

He was oddly unsure of himself. Not the Nick she'd grown to know and love since moving into this house. The

Nick who ruled over everything and everyone in his life like each layer was a finely oiled piece of machinery over which he had complete control.

Tumbler in hand, she preceded him into the adjoining room. She didn't sip the liquid fire, afraid it would cloud her thoughts when they needed to have a serious conversation. If she beat around the bush with this, it would give him reason to hide behind the carefully constructed wall he kept erected between her and his emotions.

If she couldn't find a door through that wall, she knew she had to find a way to climb over everything he was avoiding.

Before either of them could sit, she blurted out, "I think you've been avoiding me. Avoiding having another dream while in bed with me. And we need to discuss why." When she looked up, he appeared unperturbed by her questions, so she continued. "Help me understand what it is you're afraid of."

"What confessions do you think to garner from me? I've often been a night wanderer. This is nothing new, and it's unlikely to stop. Telling you what haunts my dreams will not end them."

"Then help me understand why you wander more than you have before. Haven't you noticed the strain it's causing between us? It makes me wonder if you regret what's happened between us. If I'm honest with myself, Nick, I don't think I can go back to being mere acquaintances. But if that's what you want…you have to tell me. My heart's too involved to have you slowly shrink away from me. I don't even know what you want from me. Am I your mistress? Am I your secretary? Do I even mean more to you than that? Because I feel that if I did mean more than that, you would open up to me."

Nick threw his tumbler at the fireplace so fast that a strangled sound caught in her throat at his sudden show of violence. The glass smashed into a thousand shards of glittering crystal that smeared across the brick.

"Nick," she whispered in her shock, fighting tears back.

Nick turned toward her, stalking her with all the grace of a lion eyeing a gazelle. She took a deep, steadying breath and braced herself. The only thing she was certain of was that he wouldn't hurt her.

He pointed at the fireplace. "That is what you do to me inside. That is how I feel. Broken, torn apart, afraid that if I lose you, there will be nothing left of me. I will be destroyed. Do you understand that?" His voice was low and dangerous.

"What do you want from me, Nick? Tell me what I am to you."

"Everything," he said with more force and conviction than she expected.

Amelia vowed to herself that if he wanted to end *them*, then she could handle the news. *Would* handle the news. Maybe. God, let it not be that.

She was sure she could be brave and stand up to Nick, no matter the decision he made. But now that the words she'd been itching to say to him for the past week were out, she wanted to take them all back. To pretend. To continue to love him because she'd been so happy until her brother had ruined it all. But to continue in the way they were, together but apart...it simply wasn't the way she wanted to live.

"Tell me what's wrong, Nick. It's just you and me here. No judgment, no theories. Just us."

"It'll pass. It always does," he said, as if that was the only answer she needed. It wasn't. It was so far from it.

"Stop lying to yourself. Every night that you pull away, I feel a little piece of my heart breaking. Whatever it is, you can trust me. Confide in me. Please. Before it's too late."

His hands braced either of her arms. "That I want you as my own will never change. Is that what you need to hear? That I won't let you go? That you are mine, whether or not you want to be?"

She shook her head and closed her eyes for just a moment—long enough that she could count to five so she didn't lash out at his nonanswer.

Opening her eyes again, she looked straight at him. "You're saying all this because you want to bury a past you think is so much worse than mine. It devastated me to have to tell you what my brother did, Nick. It made me feel half the woman I normally feel when I'm with you. I needed to be honest, and for the sake of our relationship, I let you in. I let you see me at my lowest. I let you see what broke me as a person. Why won't you do the same?"

Nick's forehead pressed against hers. His hands were warm where they covered her arms, looser now than the grip with which he'd originally held her.

"I can't and won't paint a pretty picture of my life growing up, Amelia. So much of it was filled with a darkness so black that it sometimes engulfed and decided my actions. I'm not diminishing what you felt in your situation, but there are some things better left unsaid. Better left in the dark, where they belong."

Tears filled her eyes. She couldn't help her reaction. This wasn't anything more than he'd told her before. None of what he said helped her understand what haunted him. "I can't begin to understand why this makes you the way it does if you won't explain it to me." Her frustrations were mounting, her anger brimming. She wanted to scream. Yell. Anything to make him understand that she could help him through his difficulties.

"I can't," was his answer.

"You won't."

"Trust me for now. Just let me get past this."

"Do you understand the position this puts me in? All I know is that you are pulling away from me. I can't even grasp at a reason. I just…" She dragged herself out of his embrace, not wanting his touch to soothe her. Distract her. "Perhaps we need time away from each other. Maybe I should go to the agency and find another job placement. Because the truth is…I can't live the way we are living. I can't *sin*, night after night, when you're heart isn't in it as much as mine."

Every word tore a new wound in her heart. But this was nothing more than the truth. Time apart might make him realize what he'd given up. Looking at the resolve set in his steely gaze and his unwillingness to talk about the invisible truths standing between them, she didn't think leaving would help them either. But she was out of options. She had no other way to approach this if he wanted to cut her off from his life.

Worse…he said nothing.

Not a damn thing.

His expression was unmoving.

Unable to look at him a moment longer, for she feared she'd completely break down, she turned and ran for the door.

Why hadn't she just stayed in bed? Instead, she'd set herself on an unknown path. One without Nick. Why? She hated this feeling that was ripping her apart from the inside out. It hurt so much and so deeply that she feared the wounds could never be healed.

Biting her bottom lip on a half-escaped sob, she violently wiped her tears away with the back of her hand. Nick caught her as she fumbled with the lock on the study door, spinning her around and wrapping his arms tightly around her, crushing her against his solid body.

She wanted to break down. To just let the tears overtake her. But she held strong.

"I have already told you I can't let you go. Stay, Amelia." His voice was so calm, just above a whisper. "I couldn't bear it if you left me. I can't let you leave. I won't."

Hearing him beg tugged at her heart painfully. Amelia's fists clenched where they were trapped between their bodies. There was only one thing she could do.

She pushed him away, hating that she was seconds away from breaking down. Hating that she knew she had to hold it together when every second in his arms chipped away at her control. "You are breaking my will every day. Making me lose myself in you. Don't ask this of me. Please, Nick. Let me go."

If she stayed, they would only end up back where they were. And she needed more than his physical comfort. He held her tighter against his chest, crushing her between him and the door as if he would *never* let her go.

"I told you I couldn't let you go. Don't try to leave. I warned you that you were mine the night I took your virginity."

Tilting her head back, she stared at him, eyes awash with tears she was helpless to stop from flowing over her cheeks. "Why are you doing this to me?"

The gray of his eyes was stormy, as though waiting to unleash a fury she'd never seen. "Because I can't let you go. Because I love you." His tone brooked no argument, so she said nothing to contradict him, just stared at him for another moment before pushing at his immovable body again. Nick's hand gently cradled her throat, his thumb forcing her head to lean against the door. "I've already told you that I wouldn't let you walk away. You belong to me."

Her lips parted on a half-exasperated groan at his declaration of ownership over her. "How could I belong to you when you close yourself off to me? I will not be controlled by you, no matter what I feel—"

Before she could get out the rest of her sentence, Nick's mouth took hers in an all-consuming kiss, his tongue robbing her of breath as it pushed past the barrier of her lips and tangled with her tongue in wordless need.

Hunger rose in her, but whether it was for physical desire or a need to draw as much of him into her as possible was hard to say. And she hated herself a little for not pushing him away again and again until she won this argument. Not now that she had a small piece of him all to herself. Even if it wouldn't be enough in the end.

Without a doubt in her mind, she'd never crave anything as badly as she craved Nick—his essence, his strength, *him*.

Her hands fisted around his shirtsleeves, holding him close. She didn't want to let go…of him or the moment.

His touch was like a branding iron as he tugged her dress from her shoulders, pulling down the front of the dress. The pull rent the delicate satin material as he pushed down her corset to free one breast. His hand squeezed her, the tips of his short nails digging into her flesh.

Their mouths didn't part once, almost as if Nick wanted to distract her from her original purpose. Keep her thinking of their kiss. The way their tongues slid knowingly against the other. The way he tasted like coffee and danger. Forbidden. Like the apple from the tree, he was a temptation she could not refuse.

His distraction was working.

And his hands were everywhere.

He pushed and pulled at the material of her underclothes, desperate to expose as much of her as he could. He wasn't gentle, and she hated that she loved that so much. That she wanted him to tear every inch of cloth from her body and expose her flesh.

She remained trapped between the solid warmth of Nick's body and the cold hard door at her back as he lifted her. She wrapped her legs around his hips, needing to be closer any way she could. It didn't escape her just how well they fit together. Nick's straining cock wedged powerfully between the folds of her sex, and he stopped kissing her to shove his hand between them, opening his trousers and shucking them impatiently down his hips. Their bodies were so tightly smashed together that his cock landed against her belly first. She moaned; she couldn't help it, and he followed suit when he seated himself deep inside her. Amelia curled her arms around his shoulders and neck to keep from sliding down the door.

This was a bad idea, but she was helpless to stop what was happening. She didn't think she could stop where this was going. She didn't want to. Not really. If this was the end of them, then she would take this memory with her. His complete need to own her body.

He tore his mouth from hers, his body grinding between her legs, building her need, her desire.

"Don't ever run from me." His voice was low, dangerous. And it was full of lust and a demand for complete control that she wanted to obey but knew she wouldn't.

Instead of responding, she pulled herself up higher on his hips, until her mouth was plastered against his again.

He swallowed that sound and ate at her mouth and sucked at her tongue, as if that alone would leave his mark on her. He hitched her hard against the door and fucked her like a man starved for feeling. The quick motions had her shoulders crashing against the wood behind her, causing her to hold on tighter as Nick found an angle that allowed him to drive ever harder and deeper.

He pulled away from their heated kiss and flattened his hands on the door next to her shoulders. Her head leaned back, the position arching her breasts up so Nick could bite and lick at the flesh he'd already exposed. Her hands tangled in his hair, pulling at it, needing to keep him close, needing him tighter inside her.

His cock was unrelenting as it beat into her like a sword, aiming true as it plunged deep. Like it was the only place it wanted to be. Her back was surely bruised; her body ached with a need so profound she could barely skim the surface of understanding just how she could allow this to happen when moments ago they'd been fighting.

Their bodies thrashed, pushed, and pulled. They both needed this.

Nick let her nipple go with a shout, his hands slapped tight around the globes of her buttocks to better grip her so he could pound inside her. She bit her lip and moaned. She'd never felt anything so intoxicating and overwhelming all at once.

"Fuck!" he shouted. "Fuck."

And then he took her harder—hard enough that her head smacked against the back of the door every time his body slapped into hers. He fucked her like a man possessed, bent on one thing: complete abandonment of their emotions.

She made breathless sounds of need as his seed shot inside her. His motions were strong and forceful as he emptied himself. She felt every heavy squirt of his throbbing member and felt her need for completion only grow.

Sated, he rested his forehead against her chest, his hot breath chilling her damp skin and teasing her firm, exposed nipple. She was still primed and ready. And it left her feeling empty.

He pulled out of her without saying a word.

Without looking at her.

Her body felt bruised and sore as her feet touched the floor one at a time. She felt his seed slide down the inside of her thighs and clenched her legs together as she righted her dress, tucking herself back into it and hiding her nakedness.

Nick tucked his penis away, still avoiding her gaze.

"I'm sorry," he said, as though that could explain what had just happened between them.

She hated herself in that moment. Hated that she'd allowed that to happen when it changed nothing between them.

"You have nothing to be sorry about." Only she could claim that.

Nick focused on her, his stormy expression freezing her to the spot, making her second-guess herself. His expression seemed lost, as though he couldn't figure out the next step to take.

Reaching behind her, she clicked over the lock. The sound was audible and undeniable in what it meant.

Was there really anything that could be said between them?

She needed time away from him—to reflect on what had happened and to think about what she'd threatened. She needed to make a decision on whether or not they could work out their differences and move past this hurdle, because she could not continue to be stagnant or carry on how they were. She realized she needed a commitment. But that commitment could only come with his complete honesty.

She turned and did the one thing he'd asked her not to do. She ran from the room—as fast and as far away from him as the house would allow.

"Fuck," Nick mumbled as he smacked the wall with the flat of his hand, hating himself for not holding back. For taking Amelia without a care for her needs. For using her body against her.

She was right; they couldn't carry on how they were. He was keeping his distance from her emotionally. But he wasn't

generally someone to confide in another. People either knew
about his past, having been there, or they could only guess.
But Amelia meant more to him than anyone he'd ever met.
He wanted to make her happy. Keep her happy. And what
was the harm in telling her the truth? She already knew that
he'd been defiled as a youth.

He paused on that thought.

She was innocent in so many ways that it was possible she
hadn't fully understood what he'd told her about his time in
school with Shauley.

If there was one thing he could give her, it was the truth.
Without that, he knew he would lose her. And he couldn't let
that happen.

CHAPTER ELEVEN

Was it possible to feel like she'd had too much to drink merely from crying all night long? Her eyes actually hurt and felt overly tired, and her head pounded as she slowly rolled over in her bed. The sun shining through her bedroom window enhanced the pain sitting behind her eyes.

She blinked a few times, trying to clear the haze and fog from view, but that didn't help, and she had to squint at her surroundings for some minutes.

When she could finally focus on her room, she noticed Nick sitting in the chair by her vanity. With elbows perched firmly on his knees, his head was in his hands, eyes toward the ground, so he hadn't yet noticed that she was awake.

She made a study of his rumpled shirt and disheveled appearance, the same way she'd found him last night in the study.

"Nick?" Her voice was soft, worn from crying through the night.

His head lifted. His eyes were red-rimmed and tired as they met hers. Had he been sitting here all night while she slept?

She sat up, pulling the blankets around her in the process. The less he saw, the less vulnerable she felt.

"I couldn't bear the thought of you leaving before I had a chance to explain myself," he said, his voice gravelly.

She waited for him to say more. When he didn't continue, she said, "Then you need to do just that, Nick." She rubbed her eyes, wishing she could go back to sleep. Wishing when she woke up that she could pretend last night hadn't happened.

"I never really explained how my mother supported Sera and me, growing up."

This was a peace offering. She knew it without having to ask.

Nick stood and walked over to the window. He threw the curtains to the side and pressed his hands against the frame as he looked outside. His breath fogged the glass. But she waited for him to continue, knowing she couldn't interrupt him now, or he might never open up to her.

"She was a lovely woman. An Irish immigrant. She came over during the potato famine in '47. The eldest daughter in a family of fourteen." He paused, letting her digest this revelation. "The youngest six didn't survive the famine, and the conditions of those times left my grandparents in poor health, poor enough that seeking work to support their family was impossible. My mother took up that torch, thinking that when she moved to London, as so many of those she knew were doing, she'd be able to send back enough food and money to keep her family going.

"Her first year here, she met more closed doors than anything for decent work. She eventually found herself without a roof over her head as she tried to get into a respectable house-hold. While she waited for the right opportunity to present itself...both her parents died. As did two more siblings. She said the rest had been displaced, and she never knew what became of them."

Nick paused, perhaps lost in his thoughts. Or thinking of how much more to reveal.

When he did nothing but stare outside, she said, "I'm sorry, Nick. No one should be put in such a position when her intentions are noble and her heart is in the right place."

"But it is the reality of this city or any great city. Where there is wealth to be found, there's also poverty that out-weighs it in sheer number."

Amelia stood from the bed, holding the blankets around her as she padded over to Nick and pressed her cheek to his back. He was tense and didn't want to be comforted, so she didn't wrap her arms around him even though she almost felt she needed to. "Go on," she encouraged him.

"I remember that my mother was very beautiful. I imag-ine over time that it grew more and more obvious as to what her options were if she wanted to stay out of the workhouses. She befriended another young woman. Both were smart, both wanted more, but they knew their options were limited. My mother would often joke that her only worth had been her chastity when she'd moved to London. Together, they worked on a plan to sell themselves to the highest bidders. It allowed them to make enough money to open their own place, where they took on patrons regularly."

Amelia swallowed against the lump building in her throat. She could imagine how easily a woman was forced to take on that profession and had been thankful that other options had been open to her. "I'm sorry she was forced to live that kind of life."

"It's the life many women lived when they came over from Ireland."

"Did you know your father?" She wasn't sure what made her ask. Something his sister had said.

"No. I never wanted to. I still don't want to know who he is. Though from my mother's accounts, he wasn't someone I would care to know. I was the product of a rape, an unwilling encounter my mother had with this particular man. Though many didn't paint him to be evil, considering the profession she was in."

Amelia covered her mouth, hoping she didn't give away her shock at that admission. "And your sister?"

"We do not share a father. Sera's father was someone my mother professed to love but who obviously did not return the sentiment, since he didn't stick around when my mother learned she was with child for a second time."

"Why are you telling me this now?"

He turned, pulling her into his arms, resting his chin on top of her head. His arms had found their way under her blanket, and his touch was hot against her back.

"Because I can't lose you, Amelia. When you said you would find other employment last night, something snapped inside me. Something ugly, and I felt like a beast for forcing myself on you when you were vulnerable. Perhaps I'm more like my father than I realize."

"Don't say that." She leaned back to look up at him. "You didn't force yourself. I wanted you just as desperately as you wanted me last night."

"Needed. Not mere want, Amelia. I needed you. Because the thought of losing you…"

His expression was firm and unmoving as he stared back at her. He looked tired. Worn out. She didn't think she was the cause of that, considering he'd been up at all hours of the night this past week.

"Have you slept at all?"

He shook his head. "Not since I was in bed with you last night."

She took his hand and led him toward the bed. Climbing onto the mattress, she carried the blankets with her. Nick paused at the threshold between taking the next step and leaving the room. She tugged him closer; it was a silent plea for him to join her. If he walked out this room right now…she didn't want to contemplate what that would mean. Nick had made one small step in the right direction this morning. Would he take that back from her by closing himself off now?

"We have a few hours before we need to get up. Sleep in here for a spell. I promise not to take advantage of you," she teased slightly. "Besides, my eyes feel like they've got sand in them. I could use more rest."

Nick pulled her hand closer, forcing her to walk over to him on her knees. "Promise me you'll stay, Amelia."

"Only if you promise not to shut me out." She wrapped her arms around his shoulders. Sometimes it seemed like he carried the weight of the world on them, and she didn't want to be a burden. She wanted to stand next to him and take some of that mass. "If you can't trust me, why do you want to be with me?"

"I don't trust anyone as much as I do you. But I've always been a private person."

"Well then, you'll have to consider that I'm in your life, for better or worse, Nick. But I can only remain that way if you share yourself fully with me. A relationship has to work two ways, and holding back your true thoughts and feelings from me makes me believe we want different things and have a different idea of what is between us."

After a light kiss on her lips that held only tenderness and no heat, he climbed onto the bed with her. She lay in the middle; Nick tucked himself tightly along the length of her body. Her head hurt a little less, knowing they had come to an agreement she could live with.

The most delicious feeling bloomed deep in Amelia's belly. She arched her back along Nick's body where it covered her in delightful warmth. Her buttocks tucked tight against the hardness jabbing against her backside. She stretched her arms over her head, wrapping them around his head, and pulled his lips closer to her neck. He scraped his teeth along the column of her throat, sending a shiver of need through her whole body.

"Does this mean we get to start this morning on a different note?" Her voice was barely above a whisper, still filled with tiredness but awakening to other things.

Nick's only response was to suck the skin of her neck into his mouth, making her heart rate pick up in speed with every flick of his tongue. His hand slipped down the front of her naked body, covering her mound. She wasn't sure when he'd taken her clothes off, but she was glad there was no barrier between them.

His fingers split the folds of her sex and slicked the rest of the way to her entrance.

"Already wet for me." He bit at her earlobe as he rolled her onto her back. She tilted her pelvis against his hand, needing him to rub her and fill her. Needing him inside her so badly, she actually ached.

Nick released her mound to push one of her knees out, opening her entrance to him. A cool rush of air hit her slick core, only to inflame her desires further. Where shame once filled her at being exposed this way, need was all she felt.

"I need you inside me," she said, her tone near to begging.

He gave her exactly what she asked, his manhood filling her before she could take her next breath. Her knee was hitched over his arm, her body stretched in a way she'd never been before.

His pace was unhurried, meant to titillate and tease. He was showing her he could be just as gentle as he had been rough. "Tell me you're mine." His demand was hoarse, with a thread of vulnerability.

There was no doubt in her mind that she belonged to this man alone.

"I'm yours, Nick. I'll always be yours." Amelia curled her fingers into the sheets for purchase as he fucked her harder and deeper, rubbing over a sensitive spot that had her toes curling and her hips rotating.

"I want to feel the tight clench of your cunt around my cock, milking me as your cream flows between us. I'm sorry I took that release away from you earlier."

She knew she was on the cusp of giving him just that but couldn't string any words together with their bodies entangled the way they were, with the dirty words he used to describe what he wanted. Even with the way he flicked his finger over her nipple, pulling it taut, and sending stabs of desire right to her womb.

All she could do was moan as their bodies came together, over and over again. His pace was no longer slow and easy. He twisted and rotated his hips and his cock with every plunge into her sheath.

She reached behind her, grabbed on to the metal rods of her headboard, and held on tight. She needed to anchor herself, to hold still for every slap of his body against hers. To keep her grounded in reality before she flew over the edge of release. She wanted this to last forever. To never end, to pretend the world didn't exist beyond this room, this bed.

Nick lowered his hand from her breasts and expertly flicked his thumb over her swollen clitoris. He didn't let up the sweet torture until she was writhing in his arms and desperate to find her own end.

She didn't just reach the threshold to the finale; she smashed right through the wall, her whole body clenching and throbbing simultaneously. She didn't just moan; she cried out so loudly she bit into Nick's shoulder to hush the sounds coming from her.

Nick didn't slow his pace once, and her orgasm continued until she thought she couldn't take it anymore.

"Nick," she said when she released him from her bite. "Nick." Her breathing was erratic, her voice hoarse and dry. She tried to push his hand away from her mound, to ease the pressure at her overly sensitized nub, but he was unrelenting, a man determined to break down every wall keeping her sane right now. Like he could erase what had happened earlier.

She thought she'd break apart if he didn't stop, thought she might never come down from the high of this feeling he filled her with.

Nick jerked in her one final time before stilling. It was as though they were completely in sync, pulsating and rippling together in unison. There were no thoughts, no words; their bodies told the whole story. Amelia could feel each throb of his cock as the seed pumped out of him, filling her, tingling along sensitive nerve endings inside her.

She wasn't sure when his hand had moved from the nub between her feminine folds, but he lazily rolled her nipple between his wet fingers, and the sensations he drew from her skated a thin line between pleasure and pain. His tortuous touch never quite let her desires dissipate, only fueled the fire still burning low in her belly.

"Let's stay in bed the rest of the day," he said.

She wanted nothing more than to say yes. But a voice of reason kicked her thoughts of lazing about aside. "You know very well we can't."

What would the rest of the staff think? What must they think now? Because judging by the light filling her room, it was midday, which meant they'd already overslept.

"Yes, we can." Nick's hand slipped over her hip, gripping her so he could work his still-thick cock in and out of her. His hold was unrelenting, bruising, but she didn't mind it in the least.

Not another word of protest made it past her lips as their motions went from lazy, with obvious intention, to more frantic, with need, in a heartbeat. Nick pulled out of her to reposition them, hoisting her up onto her knees so he could take her from behind.

Amelia steadied herself on her knees and pressed her shoulders to the mattress. She turned her head to the side as she focused on breathing, holding back the moans that wanted to flow freely from her throat. Her fingers curled into the counterpane. She was beginning to think this position let him hide from her.

She tried twisting in his hold, but Nick's hands tightened around her hips, practically lifting her knees from the mattress every time he pumped into her. His pace grew wild, and his motions robbed her of the remainder of her troubles.

Nick surrounded her, and sanity fled as they edged toward a second peak together. Nick leaned over her, covering her back like an animal in rut. His hand slid around her hip and over her stomach, inching those expert fingers of his closer to the folds of her sex. When he reached the bud, he flicked one finger over the sensitive nerve endings of her clitoris. Biting the blanket, Amelia moaned around that material stuffing her mouth.

Nick scissored his fingers around her clitoris, slicking through her folds with every shove of his pelvis against her backside. With a lazy awakening, her orgasm washed through her like waves slapping against the beach, subtler this time but not less powerful. As it ebbed, Nick slammed into her one last time and held deep, rotating and grinding against her core as he came. Every pulse of his cock was swallowed up by the clench and flex of her sheath.

Replete, he slumped over her, pulling them both to their sides, his cock slipping from her and leaving a wet trail along her thigh. His arms wrapped around her waist, one of his hands cupping her breast as he held her close to his chest.

She turned in his arms, putting one arm over his shoulder; the other she curled on the pillow and rested her head in the crook of her elbow.

"I refuse to lie in bed all day," she said to break the silence that descended once their breathing leveled out.

Without missing a beat or giving in to her, he responded, "Then we will stay here all *morning*."

She shook her head. "You know that is impossible… You know *why* we can't."

Mostly, she knew she'd ask him too many questions if she allowed herself to stay in his company for the day. Would he reject that curiosity, or reward it after all they'd been through in these past few days?

"Nick?"

Like a lion well fed, his eyes lazily focused on her. "Amelia."

"I mean it." She pushed playfully at his shoulder. "We don't need to give the members of this household more fodder for their whisperings of what's going on between us."

"I don't give a damn what anyone thinks."

Amelia pushed off the bed and started pulling out fresh clothes for the day. "Well, I do."

And Nick looked for all the world like he didn't give a damn. He lay on her bed, hands tucked behind his head, his nudity on full display. She'd be lying if she said it wasn't tempting to climb over him and straddle his thighs for a third round.

"Come back to bed."

"Absolutely not. They'll think me the whore of Babylon. Oh, hell. I can't believe I didn't think of it sooner. I've shamed myself."

Nick pulled himself up and sat on the edge of her bed, watching her in his contemplative way. He caught her arm and pulled her closer when she walked by him for the tenth time, trying to tie her corset. He turned her around and tightened the strings for her.

"Calm yourself, Amelia. Your first mistake is thinking anyone under this roof would judge what happens in private between us."

"You're a man; you can think that way. They won't care how you behave; you're the master of this house. I have to act above reproach if I want to be valued and respected."

After wrapping the long strings around her front and looping them in a bow at the back, Nick turned her around in the circle of his arms. "I don't agree. You have changed me for the better, Amelia. Everyone here will see that."

She placed her palms against his cheeks. "You haven't changed to me. You've let me into your life. Given me a part of yourself. I don't know any other Nick than the one sitting in front of me."

Her gaze dropped to his lap. He was still semi-erect. She breathed deeply and looked up at Nick's cocky expression before he turned serious again.

"You're the only person I've allowed this close."

"What about Victoria?" Why had she mentioned his ex-lover? She hated herself for having thrown that between them. Nick and Victoria had broken off a while ago, before Amelia had ever come across Nick. "I'm sorry. I don't have the right to ask that."

"That's where you are wrong. You want me to be honest, so I'll be as honest as I can. Victoria is my friend. And she knows nearly as much as you because she grew up in St. Giles, living the life my mother lived. Actually, she was a friend of Sera's growing up."

This revelation surprised Amelia, and she felt a twinge of sympathy toward the woman. "She's made a grand name for herself. Half the women in London would give anything to be in her shoes."

"That wasn't always the case."

Amelia reached around his shoulders, smoothing her fingers along the scars that marred his back. "Tell me how you got these."

He pulled her arms away and gathered her hands in his. "That's a story for another day."

Amelia pinched her lips together. "I'll be patient, but you'll have to tell how it happened. I'd like to wring the neck of whoever caused you so much pain."

"You're my little champion. But it happened a long time ago."

"And the person responsible?" Had he never been caught? Amelia suddenly had a hundred questions she wanted to ask. But they had to take this one step at a time.

"He will have his day of judgment, Amelia. It's not something you can fix. It's something I live with and will deal with in my own time."

"How old you were when it happened?"

"You're inquisitive this morning."

"I usually am when you're not busy avoiding having a real conversation with me."

Nick's mouth tilted up into the smallest of smiles. So small, she thought she was reading it wrong.

"I was eleven," he admitted, breaking her gaze as he did so.

Amelia felt her lips tremble and anchored her teeth into the lower one to still them. How could anyone do that to a child? She bit back a slew of curses building on her tongue. She would not ruin this moment. Nick had given her so much today.

Pulling out of his hold, she changed the topic to something neutral. "So what did we have planned for today?"

"Scheduling our trip to Highgate. As soon as the purchase closes, we'll be headed out there for a week or two; get a feel of the land and the tenants. We should be leaving by week's end."

"We? I hadn't thought Lady Burley was serious that we would all spend time in Highgate."

"I told you I wasn't letting you out of my sight. And we'll be gone at least a week; that's too long a time to be without you."

"And where will we stay?" There was an underlying implausibility about this proposal.

"There's an inn outside of Highgate. A mere horse's ride away. Have you been in the saddle before?"

"I have." Not since she was a child, but she'd cross that bridge when they got to it.

"Landon and his wife will be joining us. My sister will come out a few days later. She hasn't seen the house yet or the state of the land. I want to have a good look around before she arrives. Come up with a preliminary plan for construction."

"Shall I make everyone's arrangements at the inn when I send word of our arrival?"

She hoped Nick intended to reserve two rooms for them. In fact, she'd make those arrangements herself the moment they knew when they were going.

Amelia buckled the bustle around her waist, needing anything to distract her from where her thoughts were going. For anyone to discover what they were up to outside the house…she wasn't sure she was ready for that.

Nick stood behind her, naked and distracting. He lifted the skirts over her head and settled them around her waist to tie them in place. "You can work out those details with Landon's wife." His hands skimmed over her arms, and the warmth of his touch had her sighing and pressing back against him.

"You're wicked."

"Am I?" He kissed her earlobe and then worked his way down her neck. The scratch of his beard was sure to leave a mark, but she didn't care. She tilted her head to the side to give him free access. It was so tempting to fall back into bed with him.

"Very wicked."

"Tell me how to keep you here."

She cleared her throat, coming back to herself. She walked out of his embrace and picked up his pocketwatch from her vanity. "It's half eleven now. We can make luncheon if we hurry."

Turning to face him so she could ward him off, she pulled on the outer shell of her bodice. It buttoned in the front so she wasn't forced to ask for his assistance.

"Break your fast with me in the library," he said.

More time alone wasn't a good idea. They seemed to get into all kinds of naked trouble when there was no one else about.

"I don't think that's wise. Besides, there's plenty to do since we slept the morning away. I'm liable to have a stack of correspondence to go through, and Huxley's probably wondering where you've disappeared."

"He'll think I'm out on errands." He tugged the end of her braid, pulling her closer. "There's no one to interrupt us."

"You think no one will wonder where I'm hiding?" She laughed and drew her braid free from his grasp. Unwinding it, she pulled it back and twisted it into a chignon at her nape and pinned it in place, all the while having to stay out of Nick's reach. He seemed quite determined to get her back in bed.

"You're insatiable." She kissed him on the mouth and headed for the door, practically skipping to stay out of his hold. "I'll see you in the study."

She opened the door enough that she could slip out and so no one would see Nick in her room, standing naked as the day he was born, with his cock deliciously erect and ready for another tumble. Amelia ignored the twinge of regret at leaving him in that state. She also ignored the fact that her lower regions clenched with want. Nick was turning out to be a very bad influence.

CHAPTER TWELVE

Mrs. Coleman smiled at Amelia as she came down the stairs. Before they could offer good mornings, there was a summons at the front door. Amelia hurried into the study and busied herself with going through the correspondence. Perhaps she could make it look as though she'd been at this all morning—though she knew Mrs. Coleman and Huxley would have already been through this room. And she couldn't think up one good excuse for her absence.

Anything was worth a try, she supposed.

Amelia looked up when there was a knock on the study door. Mrs. Coleman came in, her face red and flustered.

"Miss Grant," the housekeeper said stiffly, "there's an inspector here to see you. Shall I show him to the parlor?"

"Yes, please," Amelia said loud enough that the visitor in the hall could hear her response. "Come back in here once that's done, please," she said in a softer tone, giving Mrs. Coleman a curious look. Mrs. Coleman shrugged her shoulders, just as baffled by the man's presence as Amelia.

Why would an inspector want to see her? It was obvious this had to do with her brother. Nick said an inspector had visited him the day before he'd told her of Jeremy's death. Amelia's hands shook, so she clasped them together and took a steadying breath. If this was the same inspector, why had he come back? Had he found news? Did he know who the murderer was?

Mrs. Coleman came back into the study, shutting the door behind her so they weren't heard. "I don't know this one, Amelia."

That comment caught her off guard. "Do you know many?"

"Nick deals with so many down at the docks and throughout St. Giles. Some are better than others. But I don't know this one, and he's specifically asked for you."

Amelia squeezed Mrs. Coleman's arm companionably. "Could you please find Mr. Riley? Let him know there is an inspector here?"

"Of course, Miss Grant."

Amelia released Mrs. Coleman and headed toward the parlor.

If her steps were slower than normal, it was because she had to prepare carefully what she would say. Surely he was here to see her because he knew of her association with Jeremy, knew they were brother and sister.

She shut down those thoughts the moment she stepped over the threshold of the parlor. The inspector was a tall man. His rounded hat sat firmly on his head, with the strap slung across his chin. His long black coat was neatly pressed and buttoned from his Adam's apple down to his knees.

Amelia folded her hands in front of her and dipped her head in greeting. "Good morning, Inspector. How may I assist you?"

"Inspector Laurie," he filled in. "Miss Grant, I presume?"

"I am Miss Grant. Mrs. Coleman said you asked to speak directly with me. With what may I assist you, Inspector Laurie?"

"This is about your brother, Miss Grant. Did you know that he was murdered?"

Amelia dug her nails into her palm. So the inspector knew of their relation. "I did. My brother had a lot of enemies, Inspector Laurie. Is this some sort of interrogation on where I was on a particular night in question? Or have you found the responsible party?"

"You're quick. I haven't found anything yet. But I do need to ask about the last time you saw your brother."

"It was more than a month ago. He…he wasn't well." She didn't dare give this man the particulars of that incident. Something about him seemed off. Untrustworthy. And unlike the last few times she'd ignored her discomfort toward certain men, she trusted her instincts on the inspector. The less he knew, the better.

"Why did he seek you out?"

Without missing a beat, she knew the truth would help her here. "He wanted money. I didn't have any to give him."

"Surely a man of Mr. Riley's status could assist."

She bit her tongue on giving him a million reasons why that couldn't be so. It was a crass suggestion, and the inspector knew it.

"It wouldn't have done my brother any good. And as Mr. Riley is my employer, I wasn't in a position to ask such a thing without risking my job. Jeremy had a habit of spending money on the wrong things." Amelia walked around the chairs and invited the inspector to sit. He waved her off, which meant he must not be planning to stay long. Perfect. "What information do you require from me, Inspector Laurie?"

"I'm simply trying to solve a crime that resulted in the Earl of Berwick's death." The inspector gave her pink day dress an up-and-down with his too-assessing eyes. "Considering you are his last relation and his sister, your lack of mourning brings a lot of questions to mind."

"My brother and I had been estranged for some time. We were not close, so while I admit I'm saddened to hear of his death, I have no desire to mourn his passing. If you are investigating me, Inspector, perhaps you should also look into Jeremy's past. You will not find clean ties anywhere. He had a habit of making more enemies than friends."

"I see. I'll keep that in mind. I still need to ask where you were one week after the incident in the street with your brother and Mr. Riley."

"That was a month ago, Inspector. I will have to check my diary."

"By all means." He motioned toward the door. "Why don't you fetch that schedule now."

Amelia tucked her hands behind her back and curled them into fists. This man was infuriating. What was the inspector hoping to find? She didn't have anything to do with her brother's death, and she couldn't even guess who would have killed him. It was exactly as she had said—he had a lot of enemies.

"Of course." Amelia held her head high as she faced the inspector she was fast disliking. "If you'll give me a few minutes, I can verify the schedule."

"If you don't mind, I'll go with you."

How could she say no? Wouldn't that look suspicious? "Yes, if you will follow me."

Amelia led the way to the study. Once there, she pulled out the book from the previous month. "For what day did you require information?"

"The last Thursday in October. If you could copy it out, I would appreciate it."

Amelia flipped through the pages, looking for the date. When she found it, she was almost relieved to see a list of places and appointments Nick had throughout the day, two of which she'd attended.

"This was the day Mr. Riley was finalizing the paperwork with his solicitor on a purchase he was making. Do you require the whole day's events? Or just a particular time?"

The inspector stood over her shoulder, reading off the ledger and taking notes on a small pad of paper he had pulled from his pocket. "I'll take what I need. Were you at this meeting?" He pointed to the line for two in the afternoon that indicated tea at the Langley with Hart and Nick. "I was."

"And after?"

"I was home by dinner, which is served at half six. After that, I spent time going through Mr. Riley's correspondence and preparing replies."

"And when did your day end?"

"I can't say for sure. I usually wait for Mr. Riley to get home, which is around eight or nine, depending on the next day's schedule."

He closed his notebook with a snap and straightened his shoulders. Something about his presence had her taking a step away from him.

"Thank you, Miss Grant…though I have one more question."

"Yes?" she asked, just wanting rid of him.

"Why did you change your name?"

She folded her hands in front of her. That was not an easy answer, and the closest she could come to the truth would be better. "Very few people would have hired Lady Amelia Somerset. I found the change of my name gave me a better opportunity at landing a job once I moved to London. A job that was more challenging than acting as a companion to an aged dowager."

And it gave me a clean slate, she thought, but she didn't say that out loud, knowing it would only bring forth new questions.

"You're a plucky woman, Miss *Grant*." He gave a slight bow. "I'll see myself out and let you know if I require further information."

"Inspector…" When he turned back toward her, she asked, "Have you found any leads or details on what happened to Lord Berwick?"

"I'm working off a tip that named you an accomplice. Just haven't found the kind of clues I like in this instance—or a motive, for that matter."

"Me? I had no reason to want my brother dead."

"And what of Mr. Riley?"

The inspector's reference was obvious. Nick had beaten her brother to a bloody pulp and threatened him in front of every man and woman on the street, shortly before he'd turned up dead. All Nick had been trying to do was protect her. To stop her brother from dragging her away to marry the man he'd sold her to in the name of making good on his debts.

"Mr. Riley didn't personally know my brother. And I can't imagine he'd want such an outcome for anyone."

"Perhaps. That still brings questions forth on his actions toward your brother the week before he was found dead and tossed in the Thames."

The image with which he filled her head had her pressing her lips together. Every bruise and cut on her brother's body was burned into her brain, but to have that small tidbit of information made her sick to her stomach and had bile burning the back of her throat.

"Unfortunately, I don't have those answers. I can only say that a gentleman seeing a woman hauled away against her will is likely to act any way he sees fit." She walked toward the door, hoping to usher him out quickly. She suddenly didn't want to be in his company. She wanted him gone from the house, though she had a feeling she wouldn't be so lucky as to not see him again.

As luck—or bad luck—would have it, Nick walked into the study just as they exited. The smile was suddenly wiped from his face. "Inspector," he said.

"Mr. Riley. A pleasure to see you again." The inspector's voice was anything but friendly, and his tone was cold enough that it stole the warmth from the room as the men eyed each other up and down.

"Mr. Riley." Amelia cut through the tension by walking ahead of both men. "I was just showing Inspector Laurie out."

"Why are you here?" Nick asked, completely ignoring Amelia. In fact, both men were still glaring at each other as if the person who stared longest would be the winner of some manly game.

"I had some questions on Miss *Grant's* whereabouts the night of her brother's murder."

"She's under my employ. You didn't think you should ask my permission to speak with her?"

"I like to get down to the truth of the matter. You're a tricky one, and something's not quite right about this whole scenario. I'll uncover the truth, find out that you killed Berwick, and have you hanged for murder."

"You dare come into my home and threaten me with false accusations? I could have your job for this, Inspector."

"Prove me wrong and it won't be a problem." The inspector gave a smug smile.

"Get out of my house, and don't come back without sending a card."

"My line of work doesn't require me to send word ahead of time. It's hard to catch a criminal in the act if I'm going to advise him of my arrival."

"I'll make sure to spell out my directions to Superintendent Jackson."

"Now who's threatening whom?" the man said before whipping past Amelia in a fury and slamming the door in his wake.

Amelia shrank against the wall, thinking she'd done something wrong. She wasn't sure how to explain what had happened between the two men.

Nick was watching her closely, visibly reining in his frustration at the encounter. "Come into the study."

She felt like a dog with her tail tucked between her legs as she crossed into the next room. Nick left the door open as he entered behind her and walked over to his desk, perching himself on the edge, as he usually did when he was about to interrogate someone.

"What questions did he ask you?"

"He wanted to know my whereabouts on the day Jeremy was murdered."

She looked at the swirling design of the floor rug, so unsure of what had happened and of how she'd handled the situation. There was something she'd missed in dealing with the inspector. Perhaps she should have sent him away without speaking to him.

Nick took a deep breath and rolled his shoulders. "If he comes around again, don't give him an opportunity to ask you any other questions. I will find another way to handle him."

"What do you mean?" She rushed toward him, at odds with whether she wanted to shake him so he explained himself clearly or hold him close and tell him it didn't matter. "Do you plan to handle this the same way you handled my last employer, who thought taking advantage of me was included in my job duties? You can't solve every problem with your fists, Nick. If you're angry with me, that's fine, but don't speak cryptically of your intentions, because it leaves me wondering…"

She didn't believe for one second that Nick had arranged for her brother's murder, but what would happen if the inspector turned up bloody and broken? Nick would find himself in trouble he might not be able to get out of.

"Wonder what? If I killed your brother? Is that what you're asking me?"

"No. Nick..."

"Are you afraid of me?"

She inhaled deeply. Wasn't it only this morning that they'd come to an understanding of where their relationship was headed, that they could work through his secrets one step at a time without her demanding more? Well, this time she *needed* more than his evasive answers.

"I'm not afraid." Her voice was firm. And left no room for interpretation. "Why do you push me away for something that relates to me?"

"Because right now, you are questioning whether or not I had a hand in your brother's death."

Her breath audibly caught. "That's not what I'm suggesting." She shook her head in denial. "Why would you think that?"

"Because you are looking at me with the same trepidation and fear that you gazed at me shortly after you came to live in this house. You were wondering if I had broken your last employer's jaw or if he'd found some other man's fist."

Amelia pressed her fingers against his mouth and tucked her head into his shoulder. "You dealt with Sir Ian the only way he could be dealt with. Any woman who'd just come out of the situation I had would have been wary. And while he deserved what he got, I didn't know you then. But I do now, and I trust you."

"Then why are you questioning me? Don't deny it. I see nothing but accusations in your eyes."

She pulled out of the circle of his arms and gave him a long, measured look. "Do you really think that? That I would think so little of you after everything you have done to help me?"

Nick lifted his hand and rubbed his thumb under her cheek. "It's my nature to assume the worst."

"Don't you know me better than that?"

"I like to think so. But you stand before me with too many questions of doubt." His hand curled around her hip and pulled her pelvis in tight to his.

"Then what do you know of my brother's death?"

"Nothing more than I've told you. I had eyes on your brother after he showed up to the house and tried to take you. Huxley set up a few trusted people to make sure he didn't come back for a second attempt. I thought he would try again; he didn't seem easily persuaded to a different course. Had he not met an unfortunate end, he may have still tried to take you away from me."

"But I'm here now. My brother is dead. And I know I said I didn't want to properly mourn him or do the things I should have for his burial, but it still matters that there's someone out there who killed him in cold blood. What did the boy say when you questioned him about my brother last night?"

"He'd gone on his usual nightly bender. Visited a gambling hell; went to a whorehouse. At the end of the night, he'd had so much to drink he was slurring his words and staggered his way halfway home before passing out. He pissed himself in an alley, woke himself up, and then headed back to the rooms he kept. That's how all his nights were spent. And I've thought it over a hundred times and questioned Brian at least twice that many times to see if there was anything that struck him as odd or different."

"Why didn't you tell the inspector that? Why leave him guessing when you are trying to work out the particulars on your own? What if you both have resources that can help solve the murder?"

Nick rubbed his thumb across her cheek, the motion soothing and speaking to the level of their familiarity with each other. "The inspector can't be trusted, Amelia. Word down at the docks is that he's easily bought."

"How..."

"Superintendent Jackson is a friend. I wasn't lying when I said I would talk to him about the inspector's behavior. The smug blighter is working with someone in the background. Perhaps the killer, or maybe he's working with Shauley. Either way, I promise that I will find out what happened."

"So he's trying to make it look like you did it? He said he more or less suspected me and that the only way to clear me of the crime was to verify my appointments that day."

Nick's hand tightened on her hip. "I'm going to keep Huxley back at the house when I can't be here."

"That's unnecessary, Nick. I doubt he'll come back, and I won't take callers while I'm here. You can't pull Huxley from his duties every time you're worried about me. Had I known..." She shook her head. She would have what?

"I won't argue about this," he said, as if that ended the matter.

"You're the only person arguing."

Nick gave her an exasperated sigh. "You should have stayed in bed with me."

She pushed him away lightly and moved out of his reach. "What would you have done, had my brother come after me again?"

"I would have stopped him."

"How?"

"I would never kill a man in cold blood, Amelia, but had your brother threatened your life, his would have been forfeited."

She flattened her shaking hands against her stomach and felt queasy with that admission. Because she couldn't fault him for the determination and promise in his words. What kind of person did that make her?

She sat on the arm of the leather chair, her head spinning with the events of the day. It seemed as if she had a hundred things to do. One of those things was having a lengthy conversation with Huxley but not while Nick was home. "You have some appointments; it would look odd if you didn't keep them, especially if the inspector is looking for us to slip up in some way. Why don't you visit this friend Jackson and have Huxley keep me company."

"A moment ago, you were eschewing the idea of his being here."

"Now I see the merits."

"What are you up to?" He eyed her suspiciously.

"Nothing. I have a lot to do today, and you've proven to be very distracting."

He didn't look like he believed her, but he didn't say so. "I'm heading down to the kitchens for something to eat. I have a tea scheduled with Victoria midafternoon. Would you like to join us?"

She knew Victoria was on the books, and had Amelia been thinking clearly this morning, she might have asked that they stay in bed all day, just so he wouldn't see his ex-lover.

"I think I might do just that. Tea at her shop sounds like the perfect distraction." Even if she was only present to keep that woman's claws out of Nick. They might be friends, but there was no mistaking the way that woman looked at Nick—she wanted him back in her life. And that was not something Amelia would allow.

Nick came at her, his intention to give her a kiss good-bye clear in his expression.

She shook her head. "You know where that will lead us?" She danced out of his reach.

"And I'll be in a foul mood if I can't taste you once more before I leave."

"Well, they say distance makes the heart grow fonder. Perhaps you should hurry to complete your errands and pick me up before tea with Victoria."

He tried once more to grab her, but she darted backward. "If I come home first, we won't be leaving again."

As tempting as that offer was, Victoria would find another way to see Nick if he didn't show up today. She shook her head and feigned a smile. "I'll meet you there at quarter to two."

He pointed at her. "I'll remember that you owe me a kiss."

"And I won't let you forget."

With a growl of frustration, he turned and strode from the room. Amelia took in a deep breath. She'd give Nick a half an hour to leave; then she'd hunt down Huxley.

Huxley, as it turned out, knew even less than Nick. Or at least he made it seem that way. He was notoriously mum on any sort of gossip about the people living in the house. And while Amelia thought they'd become friends of sorts, she was annoyed for the whole twenty minutes she'd attempted to question him. She finally gave up, knowing it was futile the moment he crossed his arms over his chest and stared back at her with an unamused expression.

"You're only making it more difficult for me to help you," she insisted.

"And why would we be needing your help, Miss Grant? It's man's business you're interfering with. And Mr. Riley isn't likely to be happy you're after so many answers I'm not able to give."

"It was your contact, Brian, watching my brother."

"What are you going on about now?"

"I want to speak with him."

Huxley laughed. It was her turn to cross her arms over her chest, and she glared at him until he looked at her straight on, not a remnant of a smile on his pockmarked face.

"I'm very serious about the matter, Huxley. And if you don't arrange for me to meet this young man, I'll have no choice but to pester you day in and day out. I know and understand my brother better than any of you. If he did the slightest thing that was unlike him, I'll know." She looked at her nails, letting that sink into Huxley's head.

Mrs. Coleman came into the room before Huxley could respond. "Your carriage is here, Miss Grant."

She gazed at the ormolu clock over the fireplace. She'd be early if she left now, which meant she could talk to Victoria prior to Nick's arrival. The timing was perfect.

"Will you at least think about it, Huxley?"

He gave her one succinct nod and held out her pelisse. "I will accompany you to the tea shop. When you're in Miss Victoria's company, I'll be off to take care of a few things."

As they walked out to the carriage, she asked, "Whatever happened to that wharfinger who was stealing wool?"

"That's what I need to take care of when I'm done with you."

"Mr. Riley doesn't want to be present for that?"

"He'll see him lashed, but he doesn't need to be there for the man's arrest."

Huxley opened the carriage door and gave her a hand up. When he rolled the stairs back up, she said, "I thought you were going to see me to the shop?"

"Oh, I will, miss. Just not in there where you can barrage a poor old man with endless questions."

She bit down on her lip to hold back her laugh. "Are you sure? It's awfully cold out."

"Never been surer." He shut the door and climbed up the side of the carriage to sit with the driver.

CHAPTER THIRTEEN

Amelia was given a seat at a table by herself in a secondary room, separated from the rest of the patrons at Victoria's Tea Emporium—a room, it seemed, where Victoria conducted meetings that were more private in nature and where men were invited to join her. The young woman who oversaw the teahouse said she'd notify her mistress immediately of Amelia's early arrival. While the woman's demeanor was less than friendly, she'd at least had tea brought to the table while Amelia waited.

The teahouse was like a grand greenhouse without all the plants and flowers on display. The ceilings had to be twenty feet high, the vaulted white beams adding to the delicate way the room was laid out. There were thirty-odd tables, most filled with customers. Everything was white and cream in the decor. The only dash of color was in the orchids placed at the center of each round table and the potted palms at every pillar around the perimeter of the room.

The more lively addition of color was the massive red-and-yellow macaw caged near the entrance of the room that

joined the teahouse to the department store. He whistled and
purred, saying the odd silly thing that made patrons laugh.

A wall of windows that faced the street allowed patrons
to watch the passers-by if they so wished. It was as grand a
teahouse as she'd ever seen or been in.

She was saved from wondering if Victoria would delay her
appearance until Nick arrived, when the very woman strolled
into the room as if the world were at her fingertips and hadn't
been really alive until she walked through it. Her dress was
the most beautiful color Amelia had ever seen, a light blue
that was an icy shade no less beautiful than an aquamarine.
Her perfectly styled blonde hair was woven with pearl studs
and pins, as though she was Venus fresh from the clamshell.
There were so many frills and layers of lace that she looked
like a Tissot painting come to life.

Amelia watched as Victoria stopped and talked to a few of
the customers, laughing and chatting in a friendly way, before
she arrived in the private room. They were closed off from the
rest of the teahouse but surrounded in glass and white iron
coated in gilt.

Amelia stood, flattening her hands nervously over her
pink day dress, one that had been purchased from Victoria's
department store and handpicked by this woman she disliked
on principle alone. Amelia dipped her head in greeting. "Miss
Newgate. A pleasure to see you again."

"Spare me your small talk, Miss Grant. It's unfortunate
that we are in the position we are in at all."

"And what position is that?" She hadn't quite expected
their meeting to start on a bad note. She'd hoped to at least
come to like this woman, since Nick insisted he and she were

friends and that status seemed unlikely to change. Not that they would start as friends; she only hoped to work her way up to that point...over a very lengthy time.

"The one where you're making a damnable effort to attract Nick and trap him in some sort of arrangement. I know your type, Miss Grant. You think your virginity is so precious and that offering it up will guarantee you a position as his wife. Nick is not the marrying type, and I dislike anyone taking advantage of the people I care about."

"That couldn't be further from the truth," Amelia said, her cheeks flaming with the assessment of her character, because she had indeed given her virginity to Nick but not to hold that over him and force him to stay with her.

When she didn't seem inclined to respond further, Victoria asked, "Speaking of the man of our lives, where is Nick?"

She wanted to correct her. Nick wasn't Victoria's anything. "He had last-minute errands and said he would meet us here."

"Typical."

"He's been incredibly busy."

Victoria held up her hand to call one of the women on staff over to their private booth. "Aren't we all? I'm not sure if you noticed when you were here last, but there's not a day that I don't have two hundred people through my store and another eighty at the teahouse. I specifically asked that Nick join me for tea to discuss some private business. Your being here changes that."

Amelia chose to ignore that last comment. "Then why did you ask Nick to come at all, if you're too busy to see a friend? You could have made arrangements to visit the house at any time."

"I don't object to spending time with him, Miss Grant. It's only your company I disdain."

"I have given you no reason to dislike me."

What could she say to this woman so she would at least tolerate her presence? While she wished she'd stayed home and badgered Huxley all afternoon, she knew that the woman sitting in front of her would use all of her wiles to tempt Nick. That wasn't to say Amelia didn't trust him, she just couldn't say the same about Victoria. Amelia had never known she could be jealous of anyone.

"Are you sure about that?" Victoria said as another tea serving arrived. Dishes of cake and finger sandwiches were set out between them.

As soon as the server closed the door, Amelia said, "If you're truly a friend of Nick's, you'll let him live his life exactly as he sees fit."

"I intend to, just as soon as I find a way to cut you out of the picture." Victoria's green cat-like eyes flashed in challenge.

Why did this woman care to thwart Amelia's very new and very *secret* relationship with Nick? "I'd advise against it." Amelia stood when she spotted Nick heading in their direction. He couldn't have come sooner and *too soon* at the same time. There were a lot of things she wanted to say to Victoria, and she wasn't sure she'd have another chance beyond today.

"I'm a determined woman, Miss Grant. And I have a tendency to get what I want."

"He broke off with you. Doesn't that tell you everything you need to know?"

"I didn't say I wanted him back in my bed. No, I've found another to fill that role, though he's not nearly as rough as our Nick can get."

Amelia felt her face flame. Not so much with embarrassment as with a rage unlike anything she'd ever felt in her entire life.

"I miss that about him," Victoria continued, as casually as though they were discussing the weather. "But I certainly don't want the likes of you sinking your teeth in and biting off more than you deserve."

"If you were really his friend, you wouldn't be saying any of this to me."

Victoria chuckled and turned just as Nick opened the door. Victoria practically threw herself at him, kissing both his cheeks in greeting as if she were French.

Amelia wanted to haul the woman away by her perfect hair and push her down in the seat farthest from where Nick pulled his chair out. Victoria took his choice as an opportunity to sit next to him. Amelia could do nothing; their relationship had to remain a secret. Though why she bothered when this woman seemed to know exactly what was going on…had Nick told Victoria about them?

"I thought you were coming alone, Nicky. To catch up on old times since we haven't seen each other for an age." Victoria pouted out her bottom lip and gave it a seductive lick before picking up an almond cookie and sucking it like she was sucking…

Amelia dropped her gaze and focused on the tea in front of her. She didn't think Victoria acted like that to draw Nick's attention but more to rile up Amelia. And she would not give Victoria the satisfaction of knowing just how much it affected her.

Taking a breath and raising her gaze only to Nick, Amelia smiled and said, "Victoria was just telling me how much she misses your company, but your schedules rarely allow you to spend time together."

That came out more jealous-sounding than she'd intended. The words couldn't be taken back, and she refused to apologize for her tone.

Nick sat back in his chair, narrowing his eyes in her direction, his question clear. She'd have to tell him that she and Victoria would never be friends, and it was unlikely they'd ever get on amicably. The one burning question she had for him was why he had to remain friends with his old lover at all. She understood that the woman was a friend of his sister's, but that didn't make him obligated to see her again.

"What was your purpose in wanting to see Nick, Miss Newgate?" Amelia asked. "If it was merely to pass an hour, I'd be more than happy to wander around the store and let you have some time alone." Amelia looked right at Nick, hoping he read her discomfort with this situation. That he would declare they needed to leave immediately and say he'd forgotten about a double-booked engagement—anything to get them out of here.

"So that's how it is," Nick said. His steely gaze locked on Victoria. "I thought I was here to discuss Hart's upcoming birthday celebration."

"You can't blame me for wanting to see you again. You haven't visited me in more than a month." The first thread of discomfort filtered into Victoria's thin excuse of an explanation. Amelia would have smiled, were she not seething with resentment.

"Victoria, for the last time, we are friends. Nothing more."

"I'm well aware of that. Don't be a ninny." Victoria leaned forward, showing off her ample décolletage in the square cutout of her dress as she touched his arm. Her hand lingered there.

Amelia pushed out her chair. The sound of the feet skidding across the wood floor broke Victoria and Nick's moment, and she hated that it had taken something external to separate them. She couldn't witness another second of whatever was going on between them. They had unfinished business they needed to sort out, and all she could do was leave them to it.

Nick tried to grab Amelia's hand as she stormed past, but she slipped out the door and through the teahouse. She didn't skulk in the carriage as she wanted to; instead, she made her way into the department store and wandered around to look at all the beautiful wares available for purchase. Not that she would buy anything. She just needed space from that woman.

Victoria and Nick had shared a moment, as if Amelia weren't sitting in the same room with them. That might have been her overactive imagination making her see things that weren't real, but the feeling of jealousy grew in the pit of her stomach and gnawed on her from the inside, making her feel ill.

While her intention in joining Nick for tea was to ensure Victoria didn't try to win Nick back, she knew, after his comment, that she had nothing to worry about. Or at least she hoped she didn't have anything to regret in leaving them alone.

"**W**hat in hell was that, Victoria?" Nick pushed out his chair, having every intention of following Amelia. She was hurt. He had seen that in her expression before he'd even sat down.

"Some women are unpredictable when their emotions are overwrought. She'll be well enough in time. I can send someone to follow her if you like."

"You have one minute to give me a good reason to stay."

"I'm trying to protect you." She reached out to touch his arm in that familiar way of hers.

He pulled back, looking at her hand as though it were a stinger. She was not at liberty to touch him. "Don't. You have never had a reason to protect me from anything. What is it *you*, of all people, can guard me from?"

"I see what she's doing to you." Victoria's eyes were clouded with genuine concern. She was one of the best actresses he knew. "I'm worried you'll fall into her carefully devised trap."

Nick wanted to laugh at the assessment. Nick was the one trying to trap Amelia, not the other way around. "And how do you think that's possible? As you said, I haven't seen you in well over a month, Victoria. And I will not allow Miss Grant to be trifled with."

Victoria fell back in her chair, a slight slouch hunching her shoulders forward. "I didn't want to believe it possible when we met at the Langtry for dinner."

"You'll have to be more specific than that."

"You've fallen in love with her. That's the only reason I can think why you've been avoiding me."

"We go back too far for me to lie to you about something like this, Vic. So the truth is, you're right. But if you think for one minute I'll let you interfere, you are sadly mistaken." He stood from the table, done with this conversation. Done with Victoria, if she didn't see the grave mistake she'd made today.

She wrapped her hand around his forearm. "Humor me, Nick. How long have we known each other?"

"A decade, give or take."

"And in that time, I have never known you to fall for any woman. Whoever this Miss Grant is, she's trouble."

Nick gave her a droll look. "You can't be serious."

"I am. I talked to Sera. She said you'd brought your new mistress around to the school."

Nick clenched his teeth so hard that his jaw cracked. "I'll be sure to correct her."

Victoria nibbled on her lip and batted her lashes. She knew better than to try that kind of tactic on him. He crossed his arms over his chest, eager to leave but needing to know what his sister had said so he could correct her assumptions immediately.

"She might not have put it that way exactly."

"Victoria, my patience is running thin…"

"I let her know that I had met your lady friend."

"Let us get one thing straight. Amelia is not a *lady friend*. And you will treat her with the respect she deserves."

"You've lost your head with her." Victoria's voice was slowly rising; her frustration in this argument was not endearing Nick to her cause.

"I know precisely where my head is. The only thing you risk is cutting off our friendship if you insist on treating her poorly."

"We had a conversation, nothing more."

"Don't come around, Victoria. Don't send notes. Don't talk to me until you can apologize to Amelia."

"That's not fair."

"Life generally isn't. Though that's not something I should need to remind you."

He left her standing in the middle of her private room. Eyes were focused on their glass enclosure, and while patrons likely hadn't heard their exchange, they would be well aware that there was a new rift between them. Something for the gossip columns.

Nick stopped at the front counter. "In which direction did the woman wearing the blush-pink dress head?"

"Through the shop, sir."

He headed into the department store, not sure where Amelia would have gone. If she was merely browsing the counters, he'd find her eventually. Surely she wouldn't leave without him. Ladies' Wear was on the third floor, so he'd check there last, as men weren't supposed to be up there. The first floor was antiquities, porcelain, and silver. The second floor was jewelry. He found her walking between two rows of glass cases, with a salesman two steps behind, should she need assistance.

All Nick knew was that he was happy to have found her. Victoria didn't know the danger Amelia was in, so he couldn't blame her completely for the episode that drove Amelia away. But he was happy to see her safe.

Nick nodded the salesman over. He came quickly, Amelia was not even aware she'd been followed around. "I'll signal to you if the lady wants anything."

The man was younger than he originally thought, maybe eighteen. His face still had spots. "Yes, sir," he said enthusiastically.

Nick walked between the rows of glass cases and made his way to Amelia's side. She paused over a series of lockets—gold, silver, a plethora at her fingertips.

"Do you see something you like?"

She jumped, her shoulders hitting his chest as she let out a small squeal of surprise. She pressed her hand to her chest and inhaled deeply. "Nick. You scared the devil out of me."

He caged his arms around her and leaned close enough that he could talk quietly in her ear. Their conversation was for them alone. People could assume what they wanted with his blatant fawning; he didn't care. There was one thing of which Nick was sure: Amelia was his. And everyone in this shop would see and know that. And anything that was his was not to be trifled with.

"Not my intention to scare you."

"What are you doing up here?"

"Apologizing." Nick ran his fingers over the glass display case mere inches from her hand. He wanted to take it up and press a kiss to the inside of her wrist, but the shop was too busy for such an open display of intimacy. "Perhaps a gift is in order."

Amelia ducked her head, shaking it. "No," she said, so quietly he almost didn't catch it.

"Why not?"

"I was only reminiscing." She pointed to a rather plain silver locket in the case with minimal detail stamped in the face. "This one reminded me of one I once had."

"Ah. Did you have something you wanted to put in the locket? I'm happy to make the purchase."

Her white-gloved fingers trailed a seductive path along the edge of the case. "The day we met, mine was stolen, along with my money. I never cared about the money; it wasn't rightfully mine, but the locket was a gift from my parents. I wasn't wearing it because the chain was broken."

"Then let me buy you another. It's the least I can do after Victoria's abhorrent behavior."

She turned her cheek enough to show him her faint smile of appreciation. "It's not the locket that held value but what lay inside. And your friend Victoria is a topic for another time…when there are fewer ears present, I think."

"I can agree to that for now." Nick motioned to the room around them. Jewels, hairpieces, even diadems filled every case. "I want you to pick something else. Anything."

"That's kind of you, but no thank you. I was passing the time in here, waiting for your meeting with Victoria to end. I don't need anything."

"Humor me."

She blushed a pretty shade of pink. "It's too much, Nick. Buying me a present now will prove your friend right."

"I don't care what Victoria thinks."

She pinched her mouth on a smile. "Please, let's go if you're finished."

"I'll cede this once, but only because *I'm* embarrassed by the way Victoria treated you."

Amelia would be lying if she said she wasn't feeling a little defeated by the events of the afternoon. The only thing that made her feel better was that Nick had followed her shortly after she'd departed the teahouse. It might be petty, but it proved that Nick cared more about her than Victoria in that particular instance.

Then there was the guilt she felt. She'd been the cause of their rift. She'd been the one to let Victoria pick a fight with her when Amelia had ample time to fix the direction of their conversation.

Nick had dropped her off at the house and come in long enough to give her a kiss good-bye and apologize once again for his friend's cruel treatment. The second Huxley had arrived, Nick had left for what remained of the afternoon. Amelia wasn't sure where he'd gone, as he had only one appointment in his book, at four, but that was neither here nor there; she had a lot of paperwork she needed to sort through and that would be difficult with Nick hovering over her shoulder.

He came home just as she was closing the study door. Huxley was talking to him, so she remained straight-faced and aloof, as though she hadn't been waiting to see Nick all evening.

They both looked up when the door clicked shut behind her. "Would you like me to open up the study again?" she asked. "I just turned down all the lighting for the night."

"I have some letters to send out before I retire," Nick said.

She ducked her head for the benefit of Huxley, who was still standing there, and backed into the study to turn on the lamps and light the candles.

"It's nearly ten," Nick said as he stepped into the room and shut the door behind him. "I thought you would be in bed by the time I was home."

"I wanted to wait for your return. I had to tell you that I was partially to blame for the disastrous tea with Miss Newgate this afternoon." When he opened his mouth to dispute that, she put up her hand. "Let me finish before you tell me

I had nothing to do with it. I did. The reason I agreed to go with you today was because I hate that you're friends with her, Nick. It eats me up inside, knowing that she had you first, she knew you first. And I was afraid she'd try to tempt you back into her bed."

The last bit she sort of mumbled through because it was difficult to admit that out loud—no matter how many times she'd gone over this speech in her head. "That woman being a part of your life is the only thing that has ever struck a jealous chord in me, Nick. I could have been the better person today and turned the conversation around, but I chose to pick at her comments. *I* was part of the problem and cause in escalating the sour note you came in on. That's not to say I leave her blameless; she has plenty to be blamed for."

Nick cupped her cheek and gave her one of his rare smiles. "I don't expect you to get along with her, Amelia. But Victoria and I go back too far for me to cut her completely out of my life. The one thing that I can promise you, however, is that I'll never find my way back to her bed, nor she mine."

Hearing him say that eased a lot of her troubles.

"And I don't know how we'll work it out going forward, but eventually, I promise to try. Everything is too new between us for you to ask that of me right now. So please give me time to adjust to her. And here…" Amelia held out a linen envelope. "It arrived a few hours ago."

As tempting as it was to burn whatever contents were inside, she knew it was Victoria apologizing for her own bad behavior this afternoon.

He took it and set it on his desk. A small part of her wondered if he wanted to hide whatever contents were contained within the pages of that letter. But the much bigger part of her was saying that he put it down because right now was about them.

"Am I forgiven?" she asked, turning her cheek into his palm and stepping close enough that their bodies brushed ever so lightly from breast and chest and stomach to hip.

Nick's hand wrapped around her waist, and he maneuvered them toward his desk. "I don't know. What do you think would make a good peace offering for all the trouble you've caused today?"

There was a teasing quality to his voice that had her smiling, though she tried to keep her expression serious and play along.

"You didn't lock the door," she pointed out.

"I'm aware. How about we live dangerously tonight?"

She raised one eyebrow at that. "I see. And how does living dangerously look?"

He hitched her up on the edge of his desk and hiked her skirts out of the way so her stockings were visible all the way up to the garter. He bent over her, saying, "Something like this."

Opening the slit in her drawers, his hands slid under her buttocks to tilt her pelvis up so he could lick the seam of her sex. After a swipe that had her cream flowing liberally, he blew a stream of air over her. Amelia fell back on her elbows, spreading her legs wider, wanting to pull his head closer.

Books, paper, and pencils jabbed into her buttocks, as did the bustle fastened around her waist, but she didn't have the wherewithal to concentrate on anything aside from Nick's tongue lashing out and tasting between the folds of her labia, over and over again.

He sucked at her clitoris, flicking his tongue around the swollen nub and making her cry out. Her hands tangled in his hair and pulled him in tight to her body, where he continued the onslaught of pleasure with his tongue. When she started to thrash, her body desperate to be closer to him, to feel him harder against her, he came over her, shoving his trousers down his hips.

His cock sprang out and rubbed along the wet folds of her sex. He rubbed the head of it around her clitoris. "Do you like that?"

She bit her lip to keep her noises to a minimum but nodded heartily. "Kiss me," she cried out. She needed his mouth on her, to smother the sounds she couldn't keep from making when he tortured her with pleasure.

He pushed the head of his rod inside her and nothing more. He wanted her to beg, and she wasn't above doing just that.

"Please," she cried, louder this time, a breathless noise building in her chest as she tilted her hips, trying to lodge him in deeper. "I need you to kiss me."

One of his elbows came down beside her shoulder, his weight finally crushing her just right. "How about here?" he asked, biting her chin and licking a seductive line across her jaw.

She shook her head and placed the arches of her feet on the edge of the desk, forcing him deeper still. The sounds that passed her lips grew in volume. Lost in them, she was less worried about being heard. "Kiss my mouth. Let me taste myself on your tongue."

He gave her exactly that. His tongue was like a weapon all its own as he lashed it against hers, giving her that musky taste. When she sucked on his tongue, he gave her the rest of himself, battering into her sheath with a need so great that the huge mahogany desk groaned beneath them.

His thrusts were shallow, and his hips gyrated and twisted until the folds of her sex were opened up like a flower, the bud abraded by the coarseness of the hair at the base of his manhood.

They kissed so deeply that their teeth hit, and his beard scraped against her face, burning her skin as it rubbed harder and harder over her, his tongue mimicking the motions of his cock.

Impatiently, he ripped at the buttons on her bodice, trying to open the front to get to her breasts. But their bodies moved too frantically together for him to concentrate on doing more than pop a few of them off, making them clink against the floor as they rolled away.

The corner of a book jabbed her in the head, and Amelia pushed it out of the way, making it fall to the floor with a loud thud. Her legs were wrapped around his hips, holding him as close as she could in their clothed state.

Threading her hands through his hair, she held his head, kneading her fingers into his scalp with every sweep of his tongue against hers. She would never get enough of this man. Every forbidden taste didn't sate the craving she had for him; every touch made her burn for more.

That tingling awareness in her nether region started with a pulse in her clitoris and moved through her veins like water through roots, building and building until her whole body let go. When her orgasm hit, a rush of wetness came out of her, soaking them both and making slick, wet noises as Nick tore his mouth from hers and fucked her so hard and furiously that he shouted when he came a moment after her.

His seed added to the slickness between her thighs, making her feel as though she'd...urinated on herself. On him. Oh, good Lord. What had she just done?

She tried to push him away, ashamed and mortified. His lazy, sated gaze was focused on her face; the grin he wore was half cocky, half victorious.

"Nick, please, get off." Her face was flaming and her ears were hot.

"I know you especially enjoyed that, so why are you shy all of a sudden."

"The door is unlocked." It was the only excuse she could come up with fast.

"That didn't bother you a minute ago."

He flexed his hips forward, lodging his penis deeper inside her, despite his hardness having diminished slightly.

She cringed to hear the squish of wetness between them. "We have to clean up."

Nick wrapped his hand around her throat, rubbing his thumb along one side. "You have no reason to be embarrassed, Amelia."

"I...something..." Something had come out of her that shouldn't have. And she couldn't say it, put words to it. It was that devastatingly humiliating. "Fine, I'm embarrassed. Now, will you get off me so that I might clean up?"

He pressed a rather chaste kiss against her mouth and got off her. The grin on his face was starting to irritate her. And it didn't leave his face once as he righted his clothing, though they were rumpled, and it would be obvious they'd been up to something.

"What has you so…jovial," she asked as she took his arm so he could assist her off the desk.

As she stood, she was suddenly aware that her drawers were soaked. Wetness covered her core, her inner thighs, even the bottom of her buttocks and anus. The faster she escaped him, the faster she could clean up.

Nick apparently had other ideas in mind, because he came at her, caught her up in his arms, and headed for the door. She fought to get down. "You can't be serious. Everyone in the household is still awake."

"They won't bother us."

"Nick," she admonished, "you have to put me down."

He was nearing the door. She could fight to get out of his hold, but then they'd likely both end up on the floor.

"I already admitted that I am embarrassed, and your hauling me out of here like some barbarian crusader is not helping matters. I seemed to have had…" An issue? How did one describe a bodily function delicately?

"I'll make you do it again," he said as he hitched her up higher in his arms and pulled down the door handle. "In fact, it's my mission tonight. I will conquer your body so thoroughly that my whole bed will be soaked with your juices."

"What in the world are you talking about?"

He grinned. "Shush now. You don't want to draw anyone's attention to us as I steal you off to my bedroom like a Viking marauder."

She pinched her lips tight. It was no use arguing with him once the door flung open without a care of its hitting the wall it flew against. She inwardly cringed. Thankfully, not one member of the household was to be found.

When they were in Nick's room, he set her down just inside the door. "I'll draw you a bath."

She could do no more than look at him wide-eyed, feeling heat crawl up her whole body.

He leaned in and pressed a kiss to her lips. "You're thinking right now that you pissed while I fucked you."

His words did nothing to calm her, and she felt herself panicking. Her breath pushed in and out of her lungs so rapidly that she suddenly felt...faint. Nick backed her up against the door. "Far from it, love. You gave me a gift instead. A different kind of orgasm. I intend to repeat that performance, or die trying. So a bath is in order, because there will be no sleep until I accomplish my new mission."

Thankfully, there was no repeat of the episode that had happened in the study. But that didn't stop Nick from trying repeatedly to replicate the outcome.

They didn't sleep. Maybe an hour between bouts of lovemaking, but other than that, eight in the morning came too soon for both of them.

Amelia felt better about where she stood with Nick going forward, but everything could still go to hell before they could make something of their newfound appreciation and honesty with each other. And that scared her more than anything.

CHAPTER FOURTEEN

Amelia had opted to go with Nick to gaol. He was to bear witness to the punishment of the wharfinger for stealing from him, something he'd agreed to do instead of a public lashing that would ruin the man's future prospects of finding work, should he be recognized.

She wasn't sure what to expect; she'd never been inside a prison. But she wanted to be there with Nick to gather a better understanding of what he faced when someone tried to profit on the side and steal from him when he was a generous employer. He'd told her she couldn't go a hundred times, but she'd finally worn him down and made him change his mind. She had to take the good with the bad, she'd told him. And she wanted to understand some of the uglier side of his business. See firsthand what he had to deal with.

Huxley hadn't been thrilled about her attending either. He had told her it was no place for a woman, which was typical of Huxley. When she'd pointed out that she had visited the city's dead house to identify her brother's body, they'd lost the argument, and it had been the end of the conversation. Though she couldn't say she was a victor in this.

She did have an ulterior motive for coming. Nick told her his past was too dark to reveal the truth about his scars. What better way to understand what he'd gone through than to watch the details of today unfold. If she could do that without flinching, how could Nick continue to hold himself back from her?

That she thought the prison yard would be a sight better than the dead house was the only shock she got on arriving.

The surgeon of the prison discussed sentencing with Nick and Huxley for the wharfinger's crime. Amelia sat on a bench on the inside of a tall stone wall, looking around her. The place was abysmal and gray, almost as lifeless as the dead house had been.

She couldn't hear what Nick said to the surgeon, but she sat a stone's throw from the man who had stolen a good percentage of the profits for the past four years. It was a place where the public would sit to witness lashings. The man accused of the crime was filthy—though in a cleaner state than the rest of the prison. His shirt was untucked and smeared with dirt, his hands shackled and chained to the wall. He was older, in his midfifties by her estimation. He had a gray beard and balding head. His eyes were dull and empty.

She wondered if this was the sight of a man who had given up. A man who had nothing left to live for. She couldn't help the twinge of sympathy she felt for him.

He called out to her. "Psst."

She focused on his brown eyes, ready to listen—she knew not why—to what he had to say. All she knew about this man was that he had a problem with gin and whores and didn't seem to have any family to support.

"Ne'er be seein' you 'round here 'fore."

Should she answer? She could politely ignore the man, but seeing as he was in line for a lot of painful lashings, she said, "You've committed a grave crime, sir."

"Mebel. Theys calls me. Mebel, miz." He smiled, showing her why his accent was hard to make out...at least half his teeth were missing, the rest rotting in his mouth.

"So why did you do it, Mebel? Hasn't Mr. Riley treated you well and given you a fair wage for the work you do?"

"Don't know no other way. Lost me wife eight years past, me child not long after. Thought it was easier an' all."

"You could have talked to Huxley. He might have helped."

"Didn't want no help. I'd done too many wrongs by then."

"What do you think your punishment will be?"

"Lashings is what I'm set for. They whip thieves here. Make sure they're too broken to be bothered doin' much but get lost in drink to dull the pain afterwards."

"You said you lost your wife?" Amelia felt something crack inside her. She couldn't help it; he was genuine, and there was no lie to his words, though she could be mistaken in her assessment.

"I did. Was in a workhouse. Didn't see her much, as men weren't allowed. Conditions were poor for living, and she got herself sick. Consumption is what the doc told me; daughter followed her to the grave a week later."

And that was when her heart did break for this man she didn't know. Despite the wrongdoings, he was nothing more than a lost soul.

Nick came over before she could say more to the wharfinger. She stood as Nick drew near, placing a hand on his arm. "What will happen to Mebel?"

"I saw you talking to him, Amelia. You can't be so forgiving of his crimes after talking to him for even a few minutes."

"Did you know his wife died?"

"I did. He worked his way up from warehouse laborer to wharfinger. Don't think I haven't given him the opportunity to fix his circumstance. He went behind my back and stole product from my inventory to feed his addictions. I might have looked the other way, had his intentions been noble. But they weren't. He's a criminal and unlikely to change his ways."

Amelia turned away from both men and gulped in a steady breath of air, hoping for fortitude for what she'd agreed to witness. She didn't want to give Nick any reason to regret allowing her to attend.

"I didn't want to bring you here," he reminded her, "but you insisted. You also promised not to interfere."

"I'm not meaning to interfere." His words seemed to give her enough strength to stand taller and face his steady gaze with her own. "What will his punishment be?"

"Forty lashes."

Her breath audibly caught. "He won't survive it. You can't possible agree to that."

"It's the surgeon's suggestion."

"Well, make another. You don't need this man's death on your hands. Surely you have contacts here as you do with the bobbies. Won't someone take another suggestion? Can't you at least spare his life?"

Nick squeezed her arm before leaving her to join the surgeon and Huxley again. They talked for another ten minutes before he was at her side again, taking her arm and letting her lean against him.

"Ten lashings," was all he said to her. "He'll be shipped to Australia next week to live out the remainder of his life."

"I thought they stopped sending convicts over…" But who was she to argue? It was better than the first choice of punishment.

"Only officially."

"Thank you. You have a heart of gold."

"You won't want to thank me after the lashings. I need to stay to witness the punishment. Huxley can take you back to the carriage if you've seen enough."

"No, I will stay."

"The surgeon doesn't want you here, Amelia. Women don't generally witness such things—sometimes the wives of the convicts but no one else."

"Then tell him I'm not just any woman. I won't leave, Nick."

He nodded succinctly in agreement and signaled to the surgeon that he was ready.

She just hoped she hadn't made the wrong choice. Nick had been lashed when he was only eleven, and there were far more than ten scars etched into his back. She wanted to know just how bad it had been for him. And while witnessing someone else's pain seemed intrusive, she felt it was the only way to understand Nick, as he didn't want to talk about what had happened to him.

The lashings were far worse than she could ever have imagined. The blood, the pain, the curdling scream Mebel let out by the time the fourth lash hit his back. Her stomach roiled with each draw of blood. There was so much blood. It ran in a stream and covered the man's trousers and the gray stones beneath him.

At one point—maybe by the sixth lash—she turned around and threw up on the cobblestone. Nick placed his hand at the base of her back and rubbed it in small circles. He didn't say anything, nor did Huxley, though a dark look came to Nick's eyes, and she could tell he wanted her gone from there. She wasn't sure how she watched the rest of it unfold and thought maybe at one point that Nick had put his hand around her waist to keep her upright.

That had happened to Nick. Some man who had wanted to feel superior had done that to Nick when he was only a boy.

As they left gaol, Nick took her hand in his and stopped in front of the carriage. "I'm sorry. I should have insisted you leave or at least have taken you out of there at the first sign of sickness."

She shook her head. "I needed to see what it was like." She closed her eyes, wishing the lash of a whip on skin didn't look so…awful. There really was no other word for it. She would never be able to scrub that image from her mind. And while she might not picture Mebel, she did picture a younger version of Nick, suffering through that same cruelty.

"Perhaps you'll be able to clear your head when we are in Highgate."

They were set to leave in two days. She nodded, though she wasn't sure anything could clear her head of those images. "Will he be all right?"

"He will. A doctor will tend to his wounds before he's shipped off."

"Did you arrange that for my benefit?" She was talking about the doctor, because one hadn't been standing by when they were in there.

"In a sense."

"I would have preferred you'd done it for you."

"I did it for us, Amelia. I did it because I saw your heart breaking the longer you talked with him. I did it because I was stupid enough to agree with your being here today. This isn't a place for women."

"Women are whipped with the same regularity."

"Not women like you." He opened the carriage door. "This isn't up for debate. Just know that Mebel will live out the rest of his days—short or long; it's up to him at this point."

"Thank you." Amelia looked around them. There were too many present for her to kiss him as she wanted to do, so she climbed into the carriage and tried not to picture Nick, bloody and broken, in chains and unable to help himself.

Nick studied her carefully. "Tell me why you wanted to be here."

"To understand." Perhaps she should have lied, but the truth felt right.

"I need you to be more specific."

"You won't talk about it. You won't tell me what would make a grown man lash out at a child."

"You cannot compare the two."

"Yes. I can. Are you going to deny that you didn't go through something similar?"

"No. But I was young, and I was strong. I healed fast enough."

"It doesn't excuse the behavior of an adult taking a lash to you. There is no reason good enough to do that to a child."

Nick pulled her close, tipping her head down so he could kiss the top. "Everything you do makes me love you more."

"And I you. I just hope nothing gets in the way of our happiness."

"I'll keep you safe, Amelia."

But could he? Shauley was still a threat, and the inspector who had practically interrogated her hadn't shown himself in days.

They would be leaving for Highgate soon, and Nick hadn't been able to find Inspector Laurie. When Nick had shown up at the constabulary headquarters, he'd been told that Inspector Laurie hadn't been seen in days. Not since the day he'd last been at Nick's house. Nick chose not to reveal that tidbit.

"Nick," Hart said as he came through the study door.

Nick stood hastily, shutting the door behind his friend. They would have a few minutes alone before Amelia came up from luncheon. And he didn't want her hearing this conversation.

"What has you dithering like an old maid?" Hart asked as he took a seat in one of the leather chairs.

Nick sat across from him. "Word got back to me that Shauley was to be arrested for indecency and sodomy."

"You knew how to play that one." Hart laughed a little, though the sound held no humor. "Bastard was caught with his pants down."

"He's disappeared. Along with the inspector who accused me of murdering Amelia's brother."

"The two are obviously working together."

"I made that conclusion already," Nick snapped. He rubbed at his eyes, hating that he had no control over either man.

Hart's usually carefree expression was wiped from his face as he leaned forward in the chair, elbows on his knees. "Then how can I help you?"

"I'm leaving for Highgate tomorrow. I need the bastards flushed out from whatever hole they're hiding in."

"I'm not sure I can promise that."

"Hart, you run half this town. I don't trust anyone else with this."

"Huxley?"

Nick shook his head. "He's watching my sister's house until she joins us in Highgate at the end of the week."

"I can put extra eyes on her."

Nick nodded, grateful to his friend. Before they could discuss the issues further, the latch turned on the study door, and Amelia entered, hesitating when she realized Nick had company.

"And the most beautiful woman in the world couldn't have arrived at a better time." Hart stood and walked toward Amelia. He took her hand and kissed it with an exaggerated flourish. "You are looking lovely as usual, Miss Grant."

Amelia blushed. "Good afternoon, Hart. Can I have tea brought up?"

"No. I just came from lunch nearby. I had a few minutes, so thought I'd stop in for a quick visit. I have to be heading out or I'll miss my next appointment."

"I'm sorry to have missed your company," Amelia said with a sweet smile that Nick wished was reserved solely for him.

He got up from his chair and walked Hart out.

"I'll write of any developments while you're in Highgate," Hart promised.

"Just keep those extra eyes on Sera."

"It's done. We'll talk when you're back." Hart put his hat on and skipped down the front stairs of Nick's townhouse, whistling a ditty as he went.

Nick rubbed at his eyes again. Something felt wrong about the situation unfolding. That he had no control only angered him more than the thought of Shauley and Laurie wandering freely when both needed to be questioned about their involvement with Lord Berwick. He wished he were so lucky that they'd disappear, now that their plan to frame him for Lord Berwick's murder had failed. This wasn't something he would discuss with Amelia, as he didn't want to unnecessarily worry her. He might not be a praying man, but he'd pray that nothing happened to Amelia by keeping her in the dark on this. He couldn't think of one good reason to enlighten her to the recent developments that would only worry her. And Highgate was a chance to escape the city and enjoy some time alone with each other.

CHAPTER FIFTEEN

Highgate. They'd finally arrived. It was too far into the fall months to call it a nice country visit. Amelia breathed in the clean air. The grass was dull and faded and whipping around fiercely in the bitterly cold wind that seemed to have arrived the moment they'd left the townhouse. The road was long and narrow and the trees sparse, but the farther they rode out of the city, the denser the trees became.

They were just far enough from the city that the stench of coal didn't weigh down the air. It was refreshing to breath in country air again. She hadn't been outside of London since the summer months, and that felt like an age ago. They headed straight to the manor house, since the inn wasn't expecting them for another two hours.

"It's lovely here, Nick. Though I can't say the same for the house." An ominous monstrosity stared back at them as they stood in the front drive. "Are you sure this is suitable for a school?"

Now that she'd seen it, she was skeptical. Nick let out one of his rare laughs. Come to think of it, his laughs were not so rare these days. At least not when he was spending time in her company.

"It'll do. Let me take you through; maybe I can change your mind. It's rather charming on the inside."

Nick took her hand and led her up the graveled path lined with tall grasses and weeds. There was a fountain in the center of the drive, long dried and holding nothing more than dirt.

To say the house was in a state of disrepair was an understatement. The stone was weather-worn and dimpled, and many of the windows were cracked or missing in too many places to begin counting on the first and second levels, though the dormers on the third level appeared to be in decent shape. The sloped roof didn't look to be keeping the rain out, and the building leaned a little to one side and looked as though a strong gale might cause it to tip over.

Thick vines of ivy raced along the wall on the east side, all the way up to the turreted top, where the parapet was collapsed in on one side. The ivy claimed the building in a wildness that matched the unkempt grounds. There was an addition off one side that looked like it might be in a better state of standing than the rest of the house.

The steps flanking the front entrance were pitted and cracked enough that Amelia had to watch her footing so her heels didn't get caught. There was a lock on the outside of the big wooden doors, which looked like they could keep out an army.

Nick pulled a key from his pocket and stuck it in the padlock. "Good thing I brought this along. I don't think we'll want to leave the house open for travelers when we aren't here."

"Is it safe to go inside?" Her question was skeptical. Safe was a relative term, considering the house looked like it might fall at any time.

"Safe enough. Don't worry. I was here a few months back when Lord Murray showed interest in selling. The floors squeak more than they should, the plaster is peeling from the walls, but there were no structural issues."

"That's not reassuring." She looked up at the house. At one time it had been grand and beautiful, and she imagined it had hosted the most beautiful balls and soirées. That time seemed long gone. "I can see why he wanted rid of this property. No one could possibly live here with the state it's in."

"His lordship closed up this house fifteen years ago. I think he ran out of funds to keep it running and to do repairs as they came up. Easier to lock it up and forget about it than pay servants you can't afford to keep on."

The door creaked open, the sound portentous as dead air washed over them. Amelia actually held her breath for the count of five before pulling out a handkerchief to cover her nose. "I'm beginning to think you've paid too much for it. I've seen the drawings and plans, but I just don't see how you'll save this place."

"You need just a little faith. I have one of the best architects lined up to take the job."

They stepped into the foyer, and Amelia tightened her hand around his, telling herself that she didn't do it because she was afraid...well, maybe a smidgen, but that fear stemmed more for their safety than having something jump out at them. Nick let her go to retrieve a lamp hanging on the wall. He pulled out a match from his pocket to light it. He'd come prepared.

The soft glow had shadows dancing on the high vaulted ceiling. Amelia tilted her head back to look at the architecture. It was beautiful. No other word could describe the sight that met her eyes. There was a painting up there, but she couldn't quite make out the finer details. It looked like a frieze of angels dancing through the air. Something black fell from the ceiling and swooped toward her face. She ducked with a scream, her hands covering her head.

"It's just bats," Nick said. "We were liable to find something." He pulled her to his side again, tucking her close as he swatted at another little black beast flying toward them. He swung the lamp around in an arch, and the winged creatures flew out the front door and into the daylight. Amelia's heart raced, and she felt like they were in a gothic novel, about to find danger around every corner.

"I've never been the fainting type, but this changes everything," Amelia admitted, her voice shaky.

Nick chuckled. "Don't faint on me yet. If I drop this lamp, the place is likely to go up like a box of kindling."

She pushed at his shoulder as she stood, keeping her head down just in case. "That's not funny."

"Only the truth. Now, are you ready to explore?"

In a smaller voice, she asked, "How many more bats do you think we're likely to see?"

"This is the tallest point of the house. We'll be safer on the second floor."

With a groan, she walked farther inside and kept her head ducked in case the flying rats took another dive at them. She never quite let go of Nick's sleeve as she headed toward the stairs. It was just one set that swept up and around in a spiral to the second level, which was shut off by a series of doors.

Placing her hand on the intricate wood balustrade, she pulled away before she made it up two steps; it was covered in a heavy layer of dust and grime. She tried to wipe it off her hand but made a mess of her gloves, so she ignored it and took Nick's arm to keep her balance.

"Why would anyone let such a beautiful house lay in waste?"

"Money. It always comes back to money."

"That makes it all the more sad. He should have sold it sooner."

"I think he was hopeful that his financial situation would improve with time. This house has a better purpose than a private home for Lord Murray. One that will be for the betterment of the community."

She laughed at that; she couldn't help herself. "I don't think they'll see it that way, for some reason."

"Probably not, but I have you at my side to help convince any disconcerted resident. Lady Burley is also a marvel. You two will set the town to rights, with my sister advocating for the education of children who need a good place to learn."

"You're so sure of our ability when we haven't met any of the townsfolk."

He pulled her into his arms, one of his hands holding the lamp aloft so they could see each other clearly. "I am. Are you ready to venture upstairs? Shall we see what we will find behind the first door?"

She smiled at him, though she wasn't sure he could see her in the shadows the lamp cast around them, so she squeezed his arm. "Yes, but I think it wise to shine the light ahead of us first...to ensure there aren't any more surprises. I'm trusting you completely with my safely, as I'm not sure about the durability of these floors."

Nick jumped on the spot and laughed when she let out a squeal and held on to him tighter. Creatures stirred in the rafters of the great room, and somewhere deep in the house, something moved about as though it had been awaken from a long slumber.

Amelia was terrified that they would run into some other type of vermin. "You're absolutely diabolical. I'll not step another foot into this house if you do that again."

His expression suddenly turned serious. "You have my word, Miss Grant. I'll be a perfect gentleman." He held out his arm, as though they were set to stroll a garden path.

"Come on," she said pulling him up the stairs after her; really, she was anxious to be away from whatever moved beneath the floors. And she certainly didn't want to be here when night fell. Call her superstitious from her country upbringing, but bats in the house were not something she was willing to face when the sun went down.

She nearly tripped on the last few steps, but Nick caught her around the waist and lifted her the rest of the way up. She took the second door, because it seemed silly to choose the first for some reason.

Throwing it open, they found a grand sitting room. White sheets were draped over a Spartan amount of furniture, all pushed against the walls.

She pulled away from Nick and walked toward the center. The ceiling was painted in gold leaf, and the walls were a faint blue, like a robin's egg that she'd once seen in an encyclopedia. Where paintings once hung on the walls there was a notable difference in the brightness of paint beneath, untouched from sunlight.

"This room is absolutely massive." She spun around, studying it like she was on the dance floor in a grand ballroom. "It will be a great hall for assemblies."

Heavy curtains were drawn against the windows to keep out the exterior temperature and light, making the air stagnant. She pulled one blue velvet curtain back to let in the dreary day so she could get a better view of their surroundings and promptly coughed as dust flew up around her. She waved it away from her nose and turned from the window.

"I probably should leave things as they are." Cracking her eyes open, she saw the way Nick stared at her, and she blushed. That look was a mixture of amusement and ten kinds of naughty, all covered up in a delicious package she wanted to unwrap and indulge in all day long.

She frowned at that thought. That was the last thing that should be on her mind as they toured the dusty old manor and discussed future plans of the property.

"What do you find so amusing?" she asked.

"You." He was walking toward her. There really wasn't anywhere to go, so he backed her up against the wall. The plaster crunched under her as she pressed her shoulders against it.

"Nick." She put her hand out, stopping him from coming even an inch closer. "We can't do this here."

"Why not? There's no one but the two of us. And the sight of you has me starved for a taste."

Amelia's eyes widened. "That doesn't make it right."

His hand was hard and thorough as it rubbed over one of her bound breasts and then the other. "If I take down a few of these buttons"—he traced the ones that marched up the center of her bodice—"and lift up your skirts enough that you can wrap your legs around my waist...there's no one to hear us for miles."

She flattened her hands against his chest. She intended to push him away, but the hard ridges of muscle begged to be traced.

"We can't," she said, but her words belied her actions.

"We can." His hand pressed hers over his pectoral, and she could feel his heart pounding heavily beneath her touch. "Let our first impression of this place be a good one. There are a lot of memories for me here that I prefer to bury."

"What do you mean?"

"Buying this place was only the first step in cleansing my past. And what better way to wipe the slate clean than to bury myself in you until we are so mad with lust that every time we cross the threshold of this house, it's this moment we remember."

It was hard to argue his point. Tracing her hand over his jaw, she bit her tongue in asking what those bad memories were. It wasn't the time or place to ask for that kind of confession when he was giving her so much, just telling her that. She stored the information away for later, when they were at the inn.

"And what of the driver waiting for us outside?" she asked.

"I'll swallow your cries before they reach his ears. Though I don't think he'll hear a sound with the wind stirring the trees outside." It seemed he didn't need to convince her because he was already pressing his groin against hers, mimicking motions they'd make if there weren't clothes hindering them.

Amelia's breath hitched and caught as he proceeded to release the buttons on her bodice. She didn't stop him. And admittedly, she didn't want to.

Nick carefully regarded her expression the whole time. His fingers dipped between her bare skin and the corset so he could pinch and roll her nipples one at a time. Her eyes fell closed, and her mouth parted as a breath hurried out of her in a rush. Her head fell back against the wall. She was sure bits of plaster stuck in her hat, but she was past caring.

The only thing that mattered was standing in front of her, and he was desperate to fill that aching spot between her legs. Who was she to argue with that?

"I crave you constantly," she murmured. She sucked in her bottom lip, biting it. Wishing he was the one nipping her.

"And I you. I get a raging cockstand in the most inconvenient places."

She giggled. And then covered her mouth with her gloved hand. She had never giggled in her whole life.

"That's a sound I want to hear again."

"It's outrageous and something reserved for young women. I hardly fit either of those descriptions."

"It makes my cock twitch."

A wordless sound passed her lips as his head lowered, and he open-mouth kissed the top mounds of her breasts. Her nipples ached for the suction of his mouth, but her breasts were impossible to free in this dress.

"Should we wait to do this on our return to the inn? I'm sure they can prepare our room earlier than we requested."

He hiked up her skirts and stared her right in the eye. "Definitely not. I'll have my fill of you before we leave this room."

A second after that declaration, he dropped to his knees and disappeared beneath her voluminous skirts. His hands were rough as he pushed her knees apart and his mouth found her mons. His tongue sucked on the lips of her sex, making her groan out loud. She had nothing to hold on to with him beneath her skirts, so she pressed her shoulders against the crumbling plaster wall.

He grabbed one of her legs and hitched it over his shoulder, opening the folds of her sex more. She'd forgone drawers at his insistence; now she knew why. One of her hands cupped his head through her skirts. She couldn't get a good hold on him, but it was enough to keep her balanced against the wall as his tongue lashed against her clitoris. His fingers drove deep into her sheath, taking her hard and fast. When she thought she couldn't take anymore, he moved his fingers to her other entrance, drawing her moisture there, and then stuck one finger deep inside.

A scream built in her throat, and the only way she could stop it was to bite down hard on her lip. She drew blood at the same moment her orgasm tore through her body and left her limp in Nick's arms. He was quite literally the only thing holding her up. He kissed her a few times before pulling the skirts over his head and standing before her.

She rubbed her finger along his beard. "Why, Mr. Riley, I do think you've spilled something on yourself."

He pulled out a handkerchief and handed it to her. "Will you do me the honor?"

She took it and cleaned the evidence of her pleasure from his face. When he tucked the linen back into his pocket and grabbed her hand to pull her farther along in the house, she jerked him to a stop. "You didn't find pleasure of your own."

"Oh, I most certainly did."

"Why am I not inclined to believe that?"

He kissed her hard on the mouth and then grabbed her hand. "Come along; let's finish exploring before it's dark."

"Nick…" She couldn't actually say the words for what she wanted to do, so she looked down at his crotch. He was evidently still in a state of arousal. "Let me reciprocate," she said.

"As much as that would please me, I don't want you down on your knees in this place."

She looked at him oddly. What a strange thing to say. "You were on your knees."

"That's different." He dragged her through a door and into a series of other rooms. All were bare, the echo of their voices making this house an eerie place.

They finished the rest of the tour in under an hour. She'd been right in thinking some parts of the house were newer and required less work, but overall the place needed to be redone, top to bottom.

When they were back in the carriage, Amelia didn't let Nick say no to her again. She had him out and in her hand before he could even think to object. Once her mouth was around his cock, his hands assisted in the bob of her head. Because of the proximity of the driver, Nick was forced to remain quiet, not something he was good at. Amelia smiled, making her teeth lightly scrape the underside of him.

He came in her mouth as he reared off the seat, desperate to be in her deeper. When she sat up across from him, she gave him a grin. The look in his eyes was dark and had her shivering. He still craved her. He still wanted her.

"How long before our dinner reservations at the inn?" he asked.

She reached for the watch in his vest pocket, flipped it open, and read the time.

"About three hours."

"Good."

Thank God she'd had enough sense to ask for adjoining rooms. No one would know that she wasn't, in fact, sleeping in her room.

CHAPTER SIXTEEN

Dinner, it turned out, became a private affair that they could have brought up to their room without having to fully dress. Landon had sent a note to say his carriage was stuck in mud and that they wouldn't arrive in Highgate until the evening hours. They didn't expect to see one another until the following day.

Which meant she and Nick had time alone. Away from the worries of the household discovering them and away from the scrutiny of his friends. It also gave her an opportunity to pry into his past.

"When we were at the house, you said you wanted to remember happier things here." She licked the clotted cream from the top of her pastry. "Did you live at Caldon Manor at some point?"

Nick watched her tongue moving over the cream. "I didn't live there."

"Then why does it hold bad memories?"

"I know some of the people who live in this town. And if you don't stop licking at that, I'm going to see what that tastes like on you."

Her eyes widened, and she put the pastry down. She actually wanted him focused on her questions, not on intimacy—that would come later. Preferably when all her questions were answered, but he seemed to be deflecting her before she'd really started.

"You're going to have to be more forthcoming than that, Nick. I don't want to pry, but you leave me with more questions than answers. Sooner or later, you're going to have to tell me what it is your trying so hard to keep a secret."

His hand trailed up her leg. He was trying very hard to distract her. "I'm not trying to keep secrets, Amelia. You know I'm private about my past."

"That's very much the same thing. How can I ever expect to know you fully if you want to hold back the things that make you the person you are?"

"The things in my past might have shaped me along the way, but they did not make me the person sitting before you."

She didn't agree with that but refused to give in to his need to argue.

"Does Victoria know what happened in your past?" she asked, clearly challenging him.

"Victoria has seen and done things that would leave you shocked and with an entirely different view of her."

"I doubt that. I can't picture myself ever liking one of your old lovers."

"When you put it that way…"

Nick dipped his finger into the cream she'd been licking a moment ago. "Now, about that cream."

She scooted away from him and waved her finger back in forth. "Give me one answer first."

He came toward her, a determined glare hooding his eyes. She slid back for every one of his crawls forward, never letting him get as close as he wanted. He stopped and sat on his haunches, the cream still on the tip of his finger.

"One?" he said, the thread of uncertainty in his voice undeniable.

"Just one."

"Then ask me again what you want to know. Just don't ask me about Highgate."

"Why were you whipped as a boy? Was it your mother?"

Nick shook his head. "That was two questions."

"One derives from the other."

"My mother never raised a hand against me. As for the other, that happened at the all-boys school I attended."

The place, he didn't need to remind her, where he'd been sent with Shauley, only to have unspeakable things happen to him. Why hadn't she guessed that was where he'd been whipped?

"I did not please the vicar when given instructions. He thought he could beat the willfulness out of me."

"I'm so sorry." She really hadn't expected that as an answer. Reaching for his hand, she brought it up to her mouth and kissed it.

"It was a long time ago, Amelia. But now you know why I don't like talking about it."

"I almost regret asking."

He'd appeased her curiosity for now. But she wondered how much more she could learn about him before they left Highgate.

"Don't be sorry." He waggled his finger. "Now, again, I must ask about this cream."

She tried to swat his hand away as he came over her, forcing her back onto the mountain of pillows they'd tossed onto the floor for their makeshift indoor picnic.

They were both laughing as Nick smeared the cream down her sternum. Their laughter died when he shoved the chemise from her shoulder and kissed it, following her collarbone across and then working his way over the line of cream. He didn't stop there; he smeared it over her nipples and then sucked her like a babe.

Nick did show her all the places that cream could be put and licked up. They were both a sticky mess by the time dessert was done. The pillows hadn't fared much better. After a shared bath, they eventually found their way to his bed.

Nick sat up with a start. He covered his eyes, feeling a megrim, feeling like he'd sweated through another nightmare. He reached for Amelia, but she wasn't next to him in the bed. Cracking his eyes open, he got a good look around the room.

Amelia wasn't with him at all.

The bedside lamp was turned over and broken, the glass shards littered on the floor. A table was knocked over, and the washbasin had crashed to the floor at some point, as bits of porcelain and water were washed across the floor.

It took a while to realize that the incessant pounding was not his head but someone at the door. Nick stumbled across the room, aware he was naked only when he threw open the door and the wife of the inn's proprietor screamed at his appearance. Her husband tugged her behind his robust form.

Nick's head was spinning, and it took everything in him to stay on his feet. His shoulder crashed into the doorframe as he tried to get a clear view of the man standing in front of him.

"A man came in here, sir. You were making a racket. Had to call the local magistrate when you didn't stop the noise."

"I'm sorry…what racket?" He didn't remember a single event since he and Amelia had crawled into bed, too exhausted to even bother with the blanket. He did remember helping Amelia into her chemise; she'd insisted on wearing it in the event that someone came to the door and she had to run back into her adjoining room.

He recalled that much. After that…

"We've been banging on the door a good twenty minutes. Thought we were going to have to break it down. You've turned over the room, Mr. Riley. You'll have to pay for the damage."

Nick turned back to his chamber, trying to focus on the mess. He spotted his trousers on the floor and stumbled over to the chair to pull them on. Hand against his head, he tried to recall what had happened. His hand came away wet; when he focused on his hand again, it was to see blood smeared across it.

"Shit," he cursed aloud.

He closed his eyes and tried to recall the last thing he remembered. He and Amelia had gone to bed. He hadn't fallen asleep for quite some time, too worried the memories of this town would drag him under, into a nightmare that would wake the whole inn. But he hadn't dreamed.

There was a different kind of fog clouding his head, not from the remnants of a nightmare but from the blow he'd received.

"Twenty minutes, you say?" Nick looked up to the man still standing in his door. The proprietor's wife had left.

"I don't need trouble here," the man said.

Nick rubbed his hand through his hair, feeling a bump at the back of his head. Had he fallen? No...something had hit him.

"My companion?" Nick asked.

At least four other people were in the hall, looking into Nick's room. He glared at them, though he couldn't stare long, as his vision was going in and out.

"Saw her thrown into the back of a carriage. That's why we sent our boy to get the magistrate. Don't think she was awake, as the burly man holding her carried her over his shoulder without much fuss from her. My wife saw him; got a good look at his face, she did."

"Did your wife recognize him?"

"Can't say she did." The proprietor bent down to retrieve Nick's shirt. "I got daughters, sir. You need to be dressed. There's other women staying here too, and I don't need my inn's reputation tarnished more so from tonight's events. You've caused quite the ruckus."

"I'm sorry. I'm having trouble recalling what happened." Nick shook his head as though that would clear his mind, but it didn't.

"Nick!" Landon came charging into the room, his sleeping cap still on and his shirt unbuttoned. He'd dressed in a hurry. He stopped in his tracks and glanced around at the damage to Nick's room. "What in hell happened here?"

"Asked myself the same thing. I think someone took Amelia."

"Miss Grant?" Landon asked. Nick nodded. There would be no delicate way to explain why Amelia had been in his room. He didn't even try or pretend that it was of an innocent nature. It was what it was and if anyone had a problem with that, he didn't mind giving them a goose egg to rival his own.

"Fetch the proprietor's wife, Landon. I need a description of the man who took her."

"You didn't see anything?"

He shook his head. Now that the fog was clearing from his mind, rage started to take its place. Who would dare? He could think of only two people, one of whom knew he'd be in Highgate shortly after the sale.

"Now listen here," the proprietor said. "You can't go running things how you see fit. I have a business to attend here, and you're scaring off my patrons."

"I will pay for everyone's room tonight, as well as a late evening repast, to give them time to settle from the excitement."

The man's mouth snapped shut. "How do I know you're going to be good for that kind of money, sir?"

"If I wasn't, would I have bought the old Caldon Manor in Highgate?"

"You're the man who bought it? The buildings in town too?"

"I did. Now will you let my friend and associate retrieve your wife? I have some questions to ask her."

"I'll get her myself."

Landon came into the room, tucking his shirt into his trousers and properly buttoning it. "Do you know who did this?"

"I suspect, but until it's confirmed, I don't know where to look."

"Why would they take Amelia? Does she have information they need? Is it to do with the purchase of Murray's lands?"

Nick scrubbed his hand over his eyes.

"To get back at me." To make him suffer for ever succeeding. This was all on Shauley.

The proprietor's wife stepped into the room. "Sir, my husband said you needed a description of the man I saw abscond your secretary."

"Yes." Nick stood, perhaps too quickly, because Landon had to catch him around the waist so he didn't totter right over onto the floor.

"There was two, you see…" And Nick did see, as she gave him the description of a man who could only be the inspector.

Even better, he suspected exactly where they'd taken Amelia.

"Landon, procure some horses. I need to see if the magistrate is here yet. We have some business to take care of."

This was something he should have done years ago. As for the inspector, he would enjoy gutting the man if given the opportunity. No one threatened the people under his protection, especially Amelia.

One minute she'd been curled up next to Nick in bed, the next…even her brain couldn't figure out the finer details. She remembered a sack being put over her head and trying to grab onto something with which to hit her kidnapper, but she had only succeeded in knocking over the washstand as she was thrown out of the room she shared with Nick. Then she was dragged over ground with rocks and gravel before she was thrown over someone's brawny shoulders, just before being tossed into a carriage. She'd blacked out after that and had only come to when the inspector slapped her across the face, leaving her cheek stinging even now.

Amelia faced her kidnapper like a crazed woman. Her hair was half tumbled out of its braid and felt like a tangle of knots over her shoulders. Her chemise was torn in too many places to bother taking inventory.

Her arm hurt where the inspector had grabbed hold of her and hadn't bothered to let go until he'd tied a dirty rope around her wrists and arms and hung her on some sort of hook suspended from the low ceiling. The cabin was a single room. It housed a small cooking hearth on one side and a bed on the other. Shelving hung on the wall, with minimal supplies by the door. Other than that, she didn't see anything that would tell her where she was.

"What do you want from me?" she asked, her voice hoarse from having cried for the past half hour, if not longer.

"Can't you figure it out?" he said, leaning back in a wooden chair, studying her like one might a prized mare.

Bile rose in her throat. She knew that look. She had seen it in other men's eyes. The men her brother had allowed to touch her.

"Did you know my brother?"

He tsked at her question.

She was pulling at straws, but how else would she figure out just what kind of trouble she was in, if she couldn't at least figure out what this man's connection was to her life.

"What do you want?" she repeated with more force. She didn't understand what this man had against her. Or what his purpose was. Did he intend to kill her? "Were you responsible for my brother's death? Did you kill him?"

"You've got too many questions. In case you didn't notice, I'm not answering them. Maybe if you ask the right questions, I'll give you a break."

"Where's Nick?" she asked, suddenly realizing he might have been hurt...or worse. Oh, God, if he had met the same fate as her brother, she didn't know how she would survive that news.

"Don't worry about him. You worry about you. Now, what do you think it is I want from you?"

"I don't know," she sobbed. "Please. Let me go. I'll give you whatever I can. Just let me go."

"You disappoint me, Amelia. Here I thought we were old friends."

"Did you kill my brother?" she asked again. She needed the answer. Needed something that might explain why she was here.

"As much as I would have liked to do, I can't take the credit. That was arranged by a mutual friend."

Amelia tugged at the rope burning her wrists, trying to work her hands through the loops, but she only accomplished burning her skin with every twist.

"I wouldn't bother trying to get out of those knots. You'll only hurt yourself more."

She didn't care if she had to break her hand to get free; she would do whatever she needed to find a way out of this situation.

"Who is our mutual friend, *Inspector?*" She was beginning to think he was not an inspector, but an imposter who had come into her and Nick's lives to ferret out information on them.

"You wound me, dearest." He came at her again, his large frame bearing down on her like a bull taking charge. He slapped her across the face, making her ears ring. "You will address me as Inspector Laurie."

"Are you really an inspector?"

"Of course I am. How else could I go about town wearing my uniform?"

"Why do you want to hurt me?" Amelia's lips quivered, but she held back the sobs that wanted to escape.

"Here I thought you were smarter than you let on." He stood so close that she could feel the heat coming off him in sickening waves. And that closeness made her want to vomit all over him. She held back, swallowed against the bile rising in her throat, knowing that if she lost control that would surely drive him over the edge he was walking with sanity.

"Any friend of yours is no friend of mine," Amelia spit out.

He turned her head to the side to examine her face. She noticed she'd left claw marks over the side of his cheek.

"He's not going to like that your face is damaged." The inspector looked down at the rest of her body. She wasn't blind to the fact that she wore only a chemise. Thankfully, he didn't touch her.

"Please, you don't want to hurt me. Let me go. I won't tell anyone I was here."

"You say that as if *here* will be found."

She had to believe that Nick would find her. That was, if he was alive. Tears welled up in her eyes. Now she was sick with worry. Sick at not knowing what had happened and feeling helpless in her current situation. If there was one thing she hated in life, it was being made to feel helpless. She needed to focus on escaping. Focus on how she could help herself, not worry herself sick.

"Where are we?"

The inspector tsked again. "That's a surprise."

"Do you plan on killing me?"

"No, I plan on getting paid for bringing you to the man who wants to get back at Nick."

So the inspector was easily bought. Hadn't Nick told her something to that effect? She stored that information away for later—if he could be bought, who was to say Nick couldn't purchase this man's temporary loyalty for more money?

"Why was my brother killed?"

"A means to an end. It was supposed to look like Riley did it. The situation and timing were perfect. But I misjudged him. Want to know how?"

She nodded, trying to keep him talking as she twisted her hands in the rope.

"Didn't realize Riley was so well connected with the bobbies. Called an investigation into my actions, he did, and my work. Had to run, you know. I need to get back at him for that. I had a good thing set up in London. Was making decent pay as an inspector and even better pay keeping thugs off the streets, and from causing trouble for the businesses."

It seemed she was asking the right questions now, for he was giving her information that might solve the mystery of why she'd been kidnapped.

"How did my brother die?"

"Picked a fight and started a brawl at a whorehouse. I had no hand in killing him. Not directly, anyway. We had men inside that made sure he didn't survive the beating he got."

"What was your purpose in trying to pin my brother's murder on Mr. Riley?"

"Riley had an old debt yet to be paid."

"I'm sure he has the funds to pay any debts outstanding."

His gaze snapped to hers. She stopped moving immediately, not wanting to draw attention to the fact that she was trying to free herself.

"So innocent, yet not. How long have you been Riley's mistress? You played it well, pretending to be his secretary. You almost had me fooled."

It wouldn't do her any good, arguing with him, so she didn't respond to his question and instead asked, "Will you please let me down? I can't feel my hands."

He shook his head. "Wasn't born yesterday, Miss Somerset. I know you'll run. Or at least attempt it, and I don't want to hurt you. Not yet. Not unless you make me."

Amelia looked around the sparse room. "You can tie me to the bedpost. Please, I can't feel my arms." Which was partially true. But more than anything, she needed to put herself in a better position.

"I'm as good as dead if you get away now."

"I promise not to run," she easily lied. Tears flooded her eyes again, making her seem all the more sincere. "Please tell me what will happen to me?"

"Don't much care. My pay on this job is enough to start over in another city."

"Then explain to me why this man wants to get back at Nick."

"Not really any of my business. I just do the job I'm given, take my pay, and move on to the next job. Though if you think about it, it's obvious that getting back at Riley has something to do with this chunk of land."

The inspector had given her two valuable pieces of information.

First, he had confirmed that a *man* wanted to get back at Nick. That could only be Shauley. The second had been the way he'd indicated the cabin as part of the lands. So this must be the groundskeeper's house she'd seen on the property drawings. That put her a mile down the road and in the woods from the house, not that there was anything back at the house that could help her. But it also put her a couple miles from the town and the inn, so she'd have to run east as soon as she found a way out of here.

"This is all Mr. Shauley's doing, isn't it?"

A proud smile lifted the inspector's lips, though it was a bit too frightening to call a smile. "See? I knew you were smart enough to eventually figure it out."

"How can he have the funds to pay you for kidnapping me? Mr. Riley can pay you a decent sum more."

"Don't be so sure."

"Then why didn't he buy the manor house if he didn't want Mr. Riley to have it?"

The inspector shrugged as though that wasn't a matter for him to worry about.

Could that be the only grudge Shauley had against Nick? The manor house seemed so trivial and worthless as a reason

to murder and now kidnapping. This obviously
to res   ething to do with their childhood. With the school
had ttended.

hat are Shauley's plans for me? Surely he told you
hing."

Didn't bother to ask. Don't really care. You're pretty enough
all, but not my type, and certainly not Shauley's type."

The thunder of what sounded like a hundred horses
shook the little cabin. The windows rattled and the old wood
door shook in its hinges. The inspector stood and pulled out
a pistol that had been hanging over the back of the chair. He
pointed it at her temple, and Amelia thought for a second he
was going to pull the trigger.

"Not a sound," he said. "Or I'll be handing you over with
a bullet lodged in your head."

She nodded and sealed her lips, biting back a sob that
wanted to escape her. She wasn't sure whether or not he would
kill her; and that wasn't a chance she was willing to risk.

The inspector went over to the window and pulled back
the dark burlap that covered the glass so he could look outside. He cursed and closed it quickly, obviously needing to
seal off the evidence of light from the cabin. He leaned over
the rustic table and blew out the lamp, just to be sure there
was nothing but darkness in the cramped room.

Amelia felt the cold steel of the pistol head against her
arm and bit her lip to keep her trembling still. As she promised, she didn't make a sound. But she did send a prayer up
that it was Nick on the other side of that door.

The horses came to a stop, and she could hear their snorts
and neighs.

The only sound on the inside of the cabin was her ~~ored~~
breathing. The inspector was like a ghost when he ~~ired~~
away from her. She didn't hear him moving about. T
was only the one door, so whoever was on the other side v
either going to come in, or the inspector would attempt v
go out.

When the door flew open, it was Shauley standing at the
threshold.

"What in hell is she doing trussed up there?" Shauley
demanded from the inspector.

"Didn't have anywhere else to tie her off."

"She's not a bloody horse, though I'm sure she plays the
brood mare well."

Amelia wanted to scream as Shauley charged toward her
with his knife out. She closed her eyes when he was a handspan from her and was surprised to find herself falling to the
hard floor. He'd cut the loops that had held her to the hook
dangling from the ceiling. She curled her feet under her and
pushed herself into a kneeling position. All that mattered
now was that she had a better chance of running, and she
would find whatever advantage she could.

Shauley turned a chair around and sat astride it. "Give
me the pistol," he said to the inspector, who handed it to him
without dispute. Shauley pointed the crude piece of metal at
her head. "I want nothing more than to shoot you, but I'm
afraid you'll make better collateral alive."

"And what do you need collateral for?"

"Safe passage. I know one man who can give that to me."

"Why did you go to the trouble of kidnapping me, then?"

"It's the easiest way to get his cooperation, don't you think?" She wanted to argue, but he was right. "Did you know Nick tried to have me arrested in London?"

"I can't understand why, unless it's for the murder of my brother." She couldn't guard her tongue any longer. If was going to kill her, he'd have done it already. And she believed she was worth more alive than dead to him.

Shauley stood and cuffed her across the face with the back of his hand. Amelia tasted blood in her mouth. "You're very bold for having no say in this matter. I said I needed you alive, but that doesn't mean I can't hand you over bloody and broken."

Amelia pinched her lips closed and turned away from both men. Now it was a matter of waiting for them to strike a deal. She hoped that was soon, because she couldn't stay in this cabin with either of these men for much longer.

The magistrate wanted to call off their search, as the conditions were not ideal for the horses, and traipsing through the woods in full night was likely to cause someone harm. But Nick pushed onward, refusing to give up on Amelia. He'd promised to keep her safe, but tonight he'd failed her.

After checking the manor house, and finding nothing, they had headed back to the village strip and looked in every place near the main road that Shauley and Inspector Laurie could have hidden. They even tried locating the carriage the innkeeper's wife had described. They'd met nothing but dead ends, and there had been no sign of Amelia.

She'd been gone for hours at this point. And he didn't know if he should extend his search beyond Highgate. Landon rode up next to him. His friend had stayed at his side all evening and didn't complain about being out when the first rays of the sun shot through the sky.

"What do you want to do?" Landon asked.

They were walking the horses back toward the inn, though Nick doubted he'd stop searching. He was just trying to work out Shauley's plan. "We didn't leave any stone unturned. I don't know where they could have taken her."

"I was so sure he'd be at the manor house."

"Do you want to head back there? Check it one more time? It's possible he was hiding in plain sight, but we missed him in the dark." Landon motioned toward the lighting sky. "The day ahead is on our side."

Nick rubbed his hand through his hair, wincing when he brushed against the cut at the back. He looked at his friend long and hard. "The manor was the only place that made sense to take her."

"Care to enlighten me as to why?"

"It was a place from my childhood." A place the instructors of the school had brought them to commit their sins when the earl wasn't in residence.

"Shauley and I attended school in Highgate. We used to skip our instructions and hide...I'll be damned. He's at the fucking cabin." Nick mounted his horse and tightened his thighs around the animal, propelling it forward at a quicker pace. He shouted back to his party, "He's at the Caldon Manor cabin."

Why in hell hadn't he thought to look there in the first place? Landon was right; Shauley was hiding in plain sight.

No one questioned him. And though many of the men were tired and their horses were growing weary, they didn't hesitate to follow his lead. Nick rode at a breakneck pace; his only worry was getting to Amelia before anything happened to her.

Amelia's head was throbbing, and her eyes felt like they'd had sand thrown at them. She could barely keep awake, and she felt herself nod off, only to jolt awake the next second. She wasn't sure how long she'd been at the cabin, but she could see the sky lighting up outside through the thin curtain that covered the small window.

The inspector had left a while ago, though she couldn't say precisely how long because she was too focused on trying to keep awake. If she fell asleep, they could move her. And then she'd be at a greater disadvantage, should she have an opportunity to escape. She knocked her head back on the wall, trying to keep it up and keep alert where she was crouched in the corner of the cabin.

Shauley was ignoring her, reading a newspaper at the table situated in the middle of the room. He hadn't said much to her since he'd first arrived, but she held out hope that he didn't intend to hurt her more than he already had.

She wished the inspector were here; he was slightly easier to talk to, and if she didn't start talking, she was apt to fall asleep where she was crouched. Amelia rubbed her eyes with the side of her hands, which were still bound. She wasn't sure she had the strength to stand on her own, but she might have to do so if the gritty feeling in her eyes didn't cease.

"Is the inspector off to make a bargain with Mr. Riley?" Her mouth was dry, and her voice gravelly.

"You're not at liberty to ask anything of me," Shauley said without lifting his head from his paper.

"Why do you hate Nick so much? He told me you were once friends, but friends don't turn on each other."

Shauley spun around on his chair and studied her a moment. "Told you, did he?"

"He did. And about the depravities at the school." She wasn't sure if she'd said too much, but she needed to stay awake and talking was the only thing keeping her mind active. "He won't make a deal with you. Not after the trouble you've caused us."

Shauley stood and came toward her faster than she expected. She tried to shrink away from him, but he didn't hit her. He ripped a strip of her chemise from the hem and held her legs down by kneeling on her when she tried to kick him away.

"I've had about all I can take of you." Shauley held up the strip of her chemise and wrapped it around her mouth before she realized what he was doing. She tried to scream, but it was muffled with the cloth stuffed in her mouth and wrapped around her head where he knotted it.

"Much better," he said and went back to his paper.

Amelia was back to trying to stay awake. Her head bobbed every time she nearly lost her battle with her body.

She swore she heard horses in the distance. She'd heard them last night too, but they hadn't come close to the cabin.

When Shauley stood to peer out the window, she knew her ears weren't fooling her. She pushed her knees under her and pressed her back against the wall to try to stand. If she could make a run for the door and throw it open—she tested her hands, hoping they could grasp the knob and turn it—she might be spotted.

Shauley picked up the pistol from the table and stared in her direction. "Stand, and I won't hesitate to shoot you."

She slid back down the wall, tears tracking down her face.

"If you're not in the same spot I left you when I get back, I'll make sure you can't walk. And I promise you, a broken limb or two is going to feel a lot worse than the bump we gave you on your head."

Shauley slipped out the front door, leaving her alone. All Amelia could think was that the threat of a broken leg was better than ending up somewhere unfamiliar. A place that was farther from Nick. She pushed herself up against the wall. Pins and needles ran up and down her numb legs, so she waited a minute as the feeling came back to them. This might be her only opportunity to get free.

Though they tried to be quiet as they approached the cabin, Nick knew it was impossible not to hear the dozen horses that were surrounding and filling the woods. They'd found the carriage used to kidnap Amelia, but no horses, which meant they'd either mounted up and taken Amelia to a new location, or...

He told himself for the millionth time that hurting her would serve no purpose to either man. They'd taken her for ransom; that much was obvious. And that meant they needed to ensure her safety to some degree.

Shauley wasn't a stupid man; he would have had a contingency plan in place, had his plan gone to shit with the murder of Lord Berwick, and it had.

The closer they got to the cabin, the more anxious he grew. He drew the pistol he kept on him when he traveled but had never found reason to use. Today might be an exception.

Nick dismounted a hundred meters or so from the cabin, wanting to blend in with the forest so he could approach undetected. The closer he got, he told himself, the easier it would be to get to Amelia and take her to safety.

Shots rang around the woods, and Nick was forced to take shelter behind a tree. Someone yelled; another of Nick's party shouted, "In the tree line." The report of shots going off sent hundreds of birds to the sky, almost blackening the morning. Nick took the distraction as an opportunity and sprinted toward the cabin entrance, pistol at the ready.

When the door flew open, Amelia let out a muffled scream and fell forward into his arms. "Amelia. Thank God," he found himself uttering as he caught her.

The crack of twigs behind him had him spinning around, taking aim. The inspector held a rifle, and Nick didn't hesitate for a second as he yanked Amelia down to the ground behind him and shot Laurie through the chest. A moment of surprise shaded the inspector's face before he fell to the ground, his chest moving up and down in a whistling breath. Landon broke into the clearing just then with three other men, surrounding the downed inspector. Nick nodded to his friend and turned back to his only concern. Amelia.

He'd found her. She was safe. Her face was bruised and there was blood in her hair, but she was alive. And Nick felt a stab of tears in his eyes.

He dropped his pistol and stripped out of his jacket. He wrapped it around Amelia as he cut through the rope binding her wrists and carefully untied the knot of cloth at the back of her head. She sobbed and buried her head in his chest. He rubbed her back, letting her cry out her relief and fear. Giving him enough time to compose himself before he had to face the rest of the men who had assisted him.

When she stopped shaking, he helped her put her arms through the sleeves in the jacket and buttoned it up in the front.

Once she had calmed, she tried to stand but couldn't seem to get her legs under her. Nick lifted her in his arms and carried her toward his horse. He sat her up in the saddle and pulled himself up behind her, keeping her body cradled tight against his, her legs over to one side so she could wrap her arms tightly around his middle.

Though it wasn't full light, he could still see there were at least eight men milling around, half of them already on their horses. The still form of the inspector lay sprawled out on the ground, a pool of blood growing and spreading from his motionless body. No one said anything, or maybe they did but Nick's only concern now was getting Amelia to safety.

He took the horse at a careful pace so as not to jostle her. She cried into his shirt. Neither said a word as they headed back to the inn. It was enough just to have found each other.

CHAPTER SEVENTEEN

Amelia pushed Nick away. He was inspecting the goose egg in her hairline for the tenth time in the past hour. He hadn't stopped fussing over her since they'd arrived back in his room at the inn.

"Please, I've been poked and prodded with doctor's instruments for the past hour. I just want to sleep."

"The doctor said otherwise," Nick reminded her.

"That doesn't mean I'm not tired. I can at least rest for a while. I just want to forget everything that happened."

Though she doubted she would ever forget the scene that had unfolded as Nick opened the door to the cabin. He'd shot the inspector without hesitation. He'd killed man in front of her without a second thought. She couldn't say if the inspector planned to negotiate something with Nick or pull the trigger on his own gun. Still, it had to have been a hard decision for Nick to make.

"That you were ever put in that position tells me I have let my guard down when it should be highest in this town, of all places." Nick pulled her closer, her body lying half on top of his as she stretched out on the bed beside him.

She played with a button on his shirt. "Did you find Shauley?" she asked. Fear snaked through her body as she asked that. There was no denying that there was something mentally wrong with that man for him to have done all he'd done to her and Nick.

"We didn't. But he'll have everyone in the country looking for him after today. He's a wanted man, and I'm willing to put a price on his head if that keeps him from coming after you again."

When Nick had carried her over to his horse, she had been surprised to see just how many riders had been aiding Nick through the night. Amelia planned to thank every single one of the volunteers who Nick had pulled together as soon as she was rested and able to form coherent sentences. If it hadn't been for them, if it hadn't been for Nick...

It didn't bear thinking.

Nick tilted her chin up, making her look at him. "You're not falling asleep on me, are you?"

"No, thinking."

"Might I ask what about?"

"What did Shauley think to gain in kidnapping me? Why did he kill my brother? Jeremy wasn't anyone I admired or respected, but that his death was avoidable makes me feel as if I was the one who killed him."

"You have nothing to feel guilty about. If you want to blame anyone for what unfolded, blame me."

Amelia sat up so she could better look Nick in the eye. "I could never blame you. You came into my life like a knight on a white steed, and you haven't let me down since."

He swiped his thumb across her cheek, wiping her tears away. But more tears fell, covering her face. "Do you know how perfect you are? How much you mean to me?" he asked.

She shook her head, still not able to talk, not without sobbing.

"Without you in my life, I have nothing to live for."

"Don't say that," she choked out. "You've built an empire. You have helped so many people, and so many others count on you. Don't say that."

He took her hands in his, kissing each finger before kissing the abrasions on her wrists where the rope had burned into her skin.

"What will happen if Shauley is caught?"

Nick let out a long sigh. "He'll be tried, found guilty, and hanged for his crimes."

"I don't know what to say, other than I'm sorry, Nick. I know you haven't been friends with him in a long time, but having once trusted, it must be difficult to believe him capable of what he's done."

"I'm not sorry. Shauley and I haven't been friends for twenty years," he said. "Make no mistake; I would have killed Shauley myself, had I found him before finding you." A dark look clouded his eyes for only a moment before he focused his full attention on her. "I'd rather talk about us," he said, his tone changing.

She looked at him curiously. "Us?" Was there something wrong? "What is it?"

"There are thirty people staying at this inn. It's the only one in a ten-mile radius on the main road."

She tucked her chin closer to her chest, unable to meet his gaze. "They've already labeled me a harlot, haven't they?"

He remained silent.

"It makes our working together impossible, Nick. No one will take me seriously after this. What must your friends think of me?"

"Landon will stand by me, no matter my decisions. He'll stand ready as your friend too."

"How can he? How can Lady Burley? They'll judge me from the events of tonight."

"Marry me. Let us prove the world wrong. Stand at my side as my wife."

She looked up at him, eyes wide, shocked by the proposition and at a complete loss for words or how to respond. "Surely you don't mean that."

"I do." He was in earnest. "Let everyone know of our devotion. Let them remove prejudices and labels they've already assigned to our relationship."

She wanted to say yes. She did. But was he only asking out of pity for the situation they now found themselves in? What if the only reason he was offering was in sympathy and regret for their having been found out? Maybe that's what scared her most—that it wasn't a genuine offer but asked out of guilt.

She rubbed her hands over her eyes. This shouldn't be a difficult decision, but it was exactly that. Didn't every young woman want the man she loved to propose marriage?

To make a commitment for the future?

"Are you sure that's what you want?" she asked. Why was she denying him?

A frown creased his brow. "What makes you think I haven't thought this through?"

She opened her mouth to respond but found herself still at a loss for words.

"Would you be offering this, had we not been discovered?"

"It's no lie that I never imagined myself the marrying type."

"And what is the 'marrying type'?" She almost laughed that such a type existed in his mind, but she was too on edge with what he might say, so she bit her lip and waited for his response.

"I've had a difficult life. I've watched the people I love live through some terrible situations. There are things I have done for which polite society would label me a monster."

"If we marry, you have to be open and honest in all things." That was a condition on which she wouldn't budge.

"I'm willing to live with that."

"All things, Nick. I cannot have it any other way. We either have all of each other or nothing."

"I agree to your terms."

"There isn't anything you don't know about me," she countered.

"I know." He chuckled. "But when we leave this room tomorrow, I plan on telling everyone that you are my fiancée."

She felt something grow in her belly and expand outward. Excitement. She suddenly felt alive, and any bit of tiredness left from her ordeal was washed away. She pulled herself up and sat over his thighs, wrapping her arms around his shoulders.

"I will marry you, Nicholas Riley. As long as you don't hide your heart from me."

The last thing she expected was for a smile to light up his whole face. She pressed her hand against his beard and kissed him on the mouth.

When she pulled away, he said, "Amelia, I will give you that and so much more."

Start from the beginning and see where it all started!
Continue reading for an excerpt from

DESIRE ME NOW

An Excerpt from

DESIRE ME NOW

She needed to get out of this house—and fast. Sliding out of the bed, trying to make as little noise as possible, she knelt on the cold plank floor and pulled out the sack she'd stowed under the bed. Retrieving what clothes she had, she rolled them up tight and stuffed them into the bag.

At the washbasin, she gathered the last bit of soap she'd taken from her home in Berwick and the silver brush that had been her mother's. She had no other possessions, except a small oil painting of her parents in a broken silver locket, given to her on her tenth birthday and torn from her neck during one of her brother's rages on her eighteenth birthday.

Pulling up a loose floorboard, she retrieved her draw-string reticule with the money she'd stolen from her brother. It wasn't a lot of money, but it had been enough to get her to London and pay for lodgings for a month, if she had needed that long to find a job. The money would be put to good use now.

She packed only what she'd come with, as she didn't want her employer accusing her of thievery. Hopefully, if she left quietly, Sir Ian wouldn't pursue her, as she knew something of the determination of men when they were denied what they wanted.

With her sack tied and slung over one shoulder, and her shawl and mantle over her dress to keep her possessions safe, she tiptoed down the servants' stairs and escaped out the back gate near the stable house. The cool air bit at her cheeks, so she quickened her stride, hoping that would keep her warm.

Once she was on the main streets, Amelia kept her head down so no one would see the tears flooding her eyes. It hit her suddenly that she'd left behind her last hope for a decent job.

Had she known how abhorrent her employer was, she'd have turned down the opportunity to teach his children. Sir Ian hadn't wanted a proper governess for his young boys; he'd wanted a mistress living under his own roof. A woman he could visit in the cover of night, when his ill, bedridden wife was none the wiser.

She covered her mouth with her lace-gloved hand, feeling sick to her stomach. All she could do now was go back to the agency that had placed her and hope to find new employment.

Where would she go if they turned her away?

She picked up her stride, even though she'd developed a stitch in her side that made breathing difficult. She had only been in London for three weeks. Not enough time to make friends or learn her way around. She didn't even know where she could find decent, safe lodgings. She supposed there was enough money to put herself on a train and go back home to her brother.

No. Never that.

She refused to lower herself to that type of desperation. She would find another job. In fact, she would demand a new placement from the agency. She was well educated and the daughter of a once-prominent earl, which made her valuable and an asset for any job requiring someone intelligent and capable.

The only problem was that she'd told no one in London of her true identity.

Someone jostled her shoulder, spinning her from the path she walked.

"Pardon, ma'am," he said, grasping her under the arm to right her footing.

Before she could turn and offer her gratitude, he was just another bobbing hat on the street. Reaching for her reticule to pull out her handkerchief, she came up empty-handed.

"That thief!" she shouted and then slapped her hand over her mouth.

Those around her called up the alarm. She pointed in the direction she was sure the thief had gone, but there wasn't a suspicious soul to be seen.

Amelia started pushing through the crowded street, apologizing along the way when she knocked into a few pedestrians. She grew frantic and inhaled in great gulps, trying to get air into her lungs and to keep at bay the panic that was threatening to rob her of her ability to think rationally.

Eventually, her feet slowed as the cramping in her side worsened. She could barely see beyond the tears falling from her eyes. Her face was damp, and she had nothing to wipe it clean except the sleeve of her day dress. She was unfit to go to the agency, but what other choice did she have?

Despair robbed her of the last of her breath, and she was forced to stop her pursuit.

Bracing one arm against an old stone building, she breathed in and out until she was calm. The last of her tears had dried on her face and made her cheeks stiff.

She should give up, crawl back to her brother, and beg for his eternal forgiveness. There were few viable choices left to her. She couldn't stay out in the streets. Awful things happened to women who had no place to go. Things far worse than what she had escaped, though in a moment of clarity, she might refute that statement.

Walking around to the side of the building where she'd stopped, she threw up the dinner she'd eaten the previous night. Feeling dizzy and unwell, she drew on the last of her courage, straightened her shoulders, and somehow found the strength to continue walking.

She needed to find new employment and accommodations without delay. The agency had been a room full of women; they would understand the situation she'd found herself in. They would help her.

Light-headed, she walked toward Fleet Street, where the agency was tucked neatly behind a printing house. While the day had started rather dreary and dull in so many senses, the odd peek of sunshine cut through the coal-heavy air and pressed against her face. The sun warming her skin gave her a glimmer of optimism.

When the sun disappeared behind the clouds again, she focused on her surroundings and caught sight of a group of urchins, recognizing the tallest of the bunch immediately.

"You little swindler. Give me back what is mine," she cried out loud and clear.

The boy, who had been counting the contents in her reticule, pocketed her money and took off at a full run. His pace was quick and light-footed, and she was sure he took one step to her three, though she still tried to catch up to him.

Shaken, with a cramp in her side and the dizzy feeling growing worse through her body, Amelia refused to give in. When the urchin dodged across a street heavy with traffic, she knew there was no time for hesitation. She needed that money back.

Before she made it halfway across the road, the urchin was lost among the carts. Tears welled in her eyes again, blurring her vision. Someone yelled for her to get off the road; someone else emphasized his point with obscenities she didn't fully comprehend.

Though nearly to the other side, she didn't move quite fast enough for the two-seat open carriage clipping down the street much more swiftly than the other carts.

"Move, you bloody fool," the driver bellowed.

His speeding horses, black as pitch, headed toward her like the devil on her heels. She hiked up her skirts and ran but tripped over the stone curb and tumbled hard to her knees, twisting her foot on the way down. The pain of the impact caused black spots to dot across her vision. As she tried to gain her footing, she collapsed back onto her bruised, pained knees and cried.

A strong arm supported her under her elbow and hauled her to her feet, but it was apparent to them both that she couldn't stand on her own. When the stranger knelt before her, all she saw was his tall beaver hat as he put one arm around her back and shoulders and the other under her legs. That was all the warning he gave before he lifted her into his arms and walked up the lawn as if she weighed nothing.

"Thank you," she said weakly, her heated face pressed into his finely made wool jacket. His cologne was subtle and masculine with undertones of amber and citrus. She inhaled the scent deeper, wanting that comforting smell to wrap around her, wishing it would let her forget just how her day had unfolded.

Instead of releasing her when they were away from the road, he continued walking up the slight incline of the grassy field. A flush washed over her face as she stuttered for words of admonishment that anyone might see this gentleman carrying a poor, injured woman in his arms. She didn't actually want him to put her down, but common decency demanded it of her.

Gazing at the face under his well-made top hat stopped any further protestations. She dropped her gaze and stared at his striped necktie tucked neatly into a charcoal vest.

"You need not carry me. I can find my way," she said, but her request lacked any conviction.

The sun shone through the clouds once more, shining directly in her eyes and allowing her to pull away from the power that radiated from his gaze.

His short, close-clipped beard emphasized the strong line of his jaw. Black hair fanned out a little under his hat, longer than fashionable but suiting to the rough edge this man carried.

She could tell that his mouth, though pinched, was full, the bow on top well defined. The type of lips young ladies tittered and wrote poems about.

"I just witnessed you hike up your skirts well past your shins to run across one of the busiest streets in London." His voice was gruff, with a sensual quality that warmed her right to the very core.

Just as she thought her blush couldn't get worse, she felt her ears burning from the blunt observation of what he'd witnessed.

Amelia cleared her throat, realizing she'd been staring at him too long. "I am sorry you had to witness that."

He settled her down on a slated wood bench under the shade of an ancient burled oak tree. "It's arguable that you did that in a careful manner," he said.

The gentleman removed his leather gloves, set them on the bench beside her, and went down on his knees to stretch out her foot to look at the injury she'd done herself.

She tucked her feet under the bench, away from his searching hands. They were in the open, and anyone could see his familiarity. "I only need to rest a minute. I wish I could repay you for your troubles, but I have nothing of value..."

When he looked at her—really looked at her—she was struck speechless by the sincerity of his regard. His eyes were gray like flint and as hard as steel. *Unusual and beautiful,* she thought. But it wasn't the color that had her at a loss for words. It was the intensity behind his gaze that made her feel that she was the only person in the world he was focused on; almost like nothing but the two of them existed on this tiny patch of grass in the middle of the bustling city.

This perfect man before her, who clearly didn't have to worry about putting a roof over his head or bread on the table, held a maelstrom of emotions in his cool, assessing gaze. She trusted what she saw in his eyes, trusted a man for the first time in she didn't know how long.

She wanted to reach toward his face but grasped the edge of the bench tightly instead.

Just how dire her situation was hit her so hard, she swayed where she sat. Her money was gone, her only picture of her parents taken with it.

And then she cried.

She didn't mean to. She didn't even think she had the energy left for such an outpouring. But she couldn't stop now that the dam had broken on her emotions. Histrionics didn't seem to put her rescuer off, because he only huffed a helpless breath and waited for her to calm herself, which she tried to do in great gulping breaths.

"Let me get you to a doctor." His voice was deep and commanding. He would never have to raise his voice to draw the attention of those around him. It was the kind of voice to which one was naturally drawn, and it stirred something deep inside her.

She shook her head at his offer.

She needed to loosen whatever spell he had over her.

She felt the command of his stare but did not turn her face up to his again.

"Let me see you to a doctor to ensure it is nothing more than a turned ankle," he offered, his voice full of sincerity.

She shook her head again. She tried to explain about the agency, but none of what she said came out coherently, and her tears fell harder.

Before she could attempt saying anything more, her rescuer lifted her in his arms once again and strode toward the street.

About the Author

———————————————

Deciding that life had far more to offer than a nine-to-five job, bickering children, and housework of any kind (unless she's on a deadline, when everything is magically spotless), **TIFFANY CLARE** opened up her laptop to write stories she could get lost in. Tiffany writes sexy historical romances set in the Victorian era. She lives in Toronto with her husband, two kids, and two dogs, and you can find out more about her and her books at www.tiffanyclare.com.

Discover great authors, exclusive offers, and more at hc.com.

Give in to your Impulses. . .
Continue reading for excerpts from
our newest Avon Impulse books.
Available now wherever e-books are sold.

CLOSE TO HEART
By T.J. Kline

THE MADDENING LORD MONTWOOD
THE RAKES OF FALLOW HALL SERIES
By Vivienne Lorret

CHAOS
By Jamie Shaw

THE BRIDE WORE DENIM
A SEVEN BRIDES FOR SEVEN COWBOYS NOVEL
By Lizbeth Selvig

An Excerpt from

CLOSE TO HEART
by T. J. Kline

It only took an instant for actress Alyssa Cole's
world to come crashing down . . . but Heart Fire
Ranch is a place of new beginnings, even for
those who find their way there by accident.

Justin stared at the woman across from him. As familiar as she looked, he couldn't put his finger on where he might have seen her before. Alyssa wasn't from around here, that much was certain. There weren't many women in town who could afford a designer purse, impractical boots, and a luxury vehicle more suited to city jaunts than the winter mountain terrain. But there was something else, some memory niggling at the back of his mind, teasing him, just out of reach.

Her waifish appearance reminded him of a fashion model. She was certainly lovely enough to be one, but the idea didn't suit the woman standing in front of him. Justin assumed models would be accustomed to taking criticism and judgment, and this woman looked as if she'd crumble if he so much as raised his voice.

That was it, he realized. Behind her sadness, he recognized fear. Justin felt the uncontrollable instinct to protect Alyssa swell in his chest. She might not be his responsibility, but he couldn't stop the desire to help her any more than he could have let the dog die. When she glanced up at him again, his mouth opened without acknowledgment from his brain.

"D'you know anything about accounting or running an office? You did pretty well with these guys. You could work here for a while, at least until you get your car fixed or figure something out, since my regular help doesn't seem inclined to answer her phone."

"I guess, but I couldn't let you fire her . . ."

What the hell are you doing? He knew she came from money, since she wore a huge wedding ring. Hell, that ring alone should have been enough reason for him to keep his mouth shut, since she was another man's wife, but his lips continued to move.

Justin laughed out loud, but he wasn't sure whether it was at himself for his stupidity or her comment. "I can't fire her; she's my cousin. But maybe this would be a wake-up call to be more responsible."

Alyssa gave him a slight smile before ducking her head again. He didn't miss the fact that she wasn't able to meet his eyes for more than a few seconds.

"My sister has a ranch with a few guest cabins. I can see if she has one empty. I'm sure she'll let you stay as long as you need to."

Her eyes jumped back up to meet his. He could easily read the gratitude, and a hopeful light flickered to life in her eyes. But there was more—a wariness he couldn't explain and that had no reason to be there.

"Why are you being so nice? You don't know me."

Justin shrugged, as if car crashes and late-night emergency puppy deliveries were commonplace for him. "It's the right thing to do."

The light in her eyes darkened immediately and she frowned, not saying anything more. He reached for the runt, still in front of the oxygen and barely moving. "I don't know if this little guy is going to make it," he warned, slipping the dropper into the puppy's mouth. He wasn't surprised when the puppy didn't even try to suck. It wasn't a good sign.

"We have to help him," she insisted, her voice firm as she set the puppy she was feeding back into the squirming pile of little bodies.

Justin looked up at the determination he heard in her voice, the antithesis of the resignation he'd seen there only moments before. His gaze crashed into hers, and he felt an instant throb of desire. He cursed the reaction, especially since she was right, he *didn't* know her or her story.

"*We?* Does this mean you're staying?" The corner of his mouth tipped upward in anticipation of spending some time with her, finding out how a woman like her ended up in the middle of nowhere like this.

Easy, boy. You're allowed to help and that's all. That ring on her finger and that belly say she's committed to someone else.

Yeah, well, that sadness in her eyes and the fact that she's alone say something completely different, he internally argued with himself. Justin wondered what happened to his "no romantic entanglement" resolution and how quickly this woman was able to make him reconsider it. But he couldn't just leave a damsel in distress to figure things out on her own. His father had taught him better than that.

An Excerpt from

THE MADDENING
LORD MONTWOOD
The Rakes of Fallow Hall Series
by Vivienne Lorret

Lucan Montwood is the last man Frances Thorne
should ever trust. A gambler and a rake, he's
known for causing more trouble than he solves.
So when he offers his protection after Frances's
home and job are taken from her, she's more than a
little wary. After all, she knows Lord Montwood's
clever smile can disarm even the most guarded
heart. If she's not mindful, Frances may fall
prey to the most dangerous game of all—love.

"You've abducted me?" A pulse fluttered at her throat. It came from fear, of course, and alarm. It most certainly did not flutter out of a misguided wanton thrill. At her age, she knew better. Or rather, she *should* know better.

That grin remained unchanged. "Not at all. Rest assured, you are free to leave here at any time—"

"Then I will leave at once."

"As soon as you've heard my warning."

It did not take long for a wave of exasperation to fill her and then exit her lungs on a sigh. "This is in regard to Lord Whitelock again. Will you ever tire of this subject? You have already said that you believe him to be a snake in disguise. I have already said that I don't agree. There is nothing more to say unless you have proof."

"And yet you require no proof to hold ill will against me," he challenged with a lift of his brow. "You have damned me with the same swift judgment that you have elevated Whitelock to sainthood."

What rubbish. "I did not set out to find the good in his lordship. The fact of his goodness came to me naturally, by way of his reputation. Even his servants cannot praise him enough. They are forever grateful for his benevolence. And I can find no fault in a man who would offer a position to a woman who'd been fired by her former employer and whose own father was taken to gaol."

"Perhaps he wants your gratitude," Lucan said, his tone edged with warning as he prowled nearer. "This entire series of events that has put you within his reach reeks of manipulation. You are too sensible to ignore how conveniently these circumstances have turned out in his favor."

"Yet I suppose I'm meant to ignore the *convenience* in which you've abducted me?"

He laughed. The low, alluring sound had no place in the light of day. It belonged to the shadows that lurked in dark alcoves and to the secret desires that a woman of seven and twenty never dare reveal.

"It was damnably hard to get you here," he said with such arrogance that she was assured her desires would remain secret forever. "You have no idea how much liquor Whitelock's driver can hold. It took an age for him to pass out."

Incredulous, she shook her head. "Are you blind to your own manipulations? It has not escaped my notice that you reacted *without* surprise to the news of my recent events. I can only assume that you are also aware of my father's current predicament."

"I have been to Fleet to see him." Lucan's expression lost all humor. "He has asked me to watch over you. So that is what I am doing."

What a bold liar Lucan was—and looking her in the eye all the while, no less. "*If* that is true," she scoffed, "you then interpreted his request as '*Please, sir, abduct my daughter*'? I find it more likely that he would have asked you to pay his debts to gain his freedom."

"He declined my offer."

She let out a laugh. "That is highly suspect. I do not think you are speaking a single word of truth."

"You are putting your faith in the wrong man." Something akin to irritation flashed in his gaze, like a warning shot. He took another step. "Perhaps those spectacles require new lenses. They certainly aren't aiding your sight."

"I wear these spectacles for reading, I'll have you know. Otherwise, my vision is fine," she countered, ignoring the heady static charge in the air between them. "I prefer to wear them instead of risking their misplacement."

"You wear them like a shield of armor."

The man irked her to no end. "Preposterous. I've no need for a shield of any sort. I cannot help it if you are intimidated by my spectacles *and* by my ability to see right through you."

He stepped even closer. An unknown force, hot and barely leashed, crackled in the ever-shrinking space. She watched as he slid the blank parchment toward him before withdrawing the quill from the stand. Ignoring her, he dipped the end into the ink and wrote something on the page.

Undeterred, she continued her harangue. "Though you may doubt it, I can spot those *snakes*—as you like to refer to members of your own sex—quite easily. I can come to an understanding of a man's character within moments of introduction. I am even able to anticipate"—Lucan handed the parchment to her. She accepted it and absently scanned the page—"his actions."

Suddenly, she stopped and read it again. *"As soon as you've finished reading this, I am going to kiss you."*

While she was still blinking at the words, Lucan claimed her mouth.

An Excerpt from

CHAOS

by Jamie Shaw

Jamie Shaw's rock stars are back, and a girl from
Shawn's past has just joined the band. But will a
month cooped up on a tour bus rekindle an old
flame . . . or destroy the band as they know it?

"That was a hundred years ago, Kale!" I shout at my closed bedroom door as I wiggle into a pair of skintight jeans. I hop backward, backward, backward—until I'm nearly tripping over the combat boots lying in the middle of my childhood room.

"So why are you going to this audition?"

I barely manage to do a quick twist-and-turn to land on my bed instead of my ass, my furrowed brow directed at the ceiling as I finish yanking my pants up. "Because!"

Unsatisfied, Kale growls at me from the other side of my closed door. "Is it because you still like him?"

"I don't even KNOW him!" I shout at a white swirl on the ceiling, kicking my legs out and fighting against the taut denim as I stride to my closed door. I grab the knob and throw it open. "And he probably doesn't even remember me!"

Kale's scowl is replaced by a big set of widening eyes as he takes in my outfit—tight, black, shredded-to-hell jeans paired with a loose black tank top that doesn't do much to cover the lacy bra I'm wearing. The black fabric matches my wristbands and the parts of my hair that aren't highlighted blue. I turn away from Kale to grab my boots.

"*That* is what you're wearing?"

I snatch up the boots and do a showman's twirl before plopping down on the edge of my bed. "I look hot, don't I?"

Kale's face contorts like the time I convinced him a Sour Patch Kid was just a Swedish Fish coated in sugar. "You're my *sister*."

"But I'm hot," I counter with a confident smirk, and Kale huffs out a breath as I finish tying my boots.

"You're lucky Mason isn't home. He'd never let you leave the house."

Freaking Mason. I roll my eyes.

I've been back home for only a few months—since December, when I decided that getting a bachelor's degree in music theory wasn't worth an extra year of nothing but general education requirements—but I'm already ready to do a kamikaze leap out of the nest again. Having a hyperactive roommate was nothing compared to my overprotective parents and even more overprotective older brothers.

"Well, Mason isn't home. And neither is Mom or Dad. So are you going to tell me how I look or not?" I stand back up and prop my hands on my hips, wishing my brother and I still stood eye to eye.

Sounding thoroughly unhappy about it, Kale says, "You look amazing."

A smile cracks across my face a moment before I grab my guitar case from where it's propped against the wall. As I walk through the house, Kale trails after me.

"What's the point in dressing up for him?" he asks with the echo of our footsteps following us down the hall.

"Who says it's for him?"

"Kit," Kale complains, and I stop walking. At the top of the stairs, I turn and face him.

"Kale, you know this is what I want to do with my life. I've wanted to be in a big-name band since middle school. And Shawn is an amazing guitarist. And so is Joel. And Adam is an amazing singer, and Mike is an amazing drummer . . . This is my chance to be *amazing*. Can't you just be supportive?"

My twin braces his hands on my shoulders, and I have to wonder if it's to comfort me or because he's considering pushing me down the stairs. "You know I support you," he says. "Just . . ." He twists his lip between his teeth, chewing it cherry red before releasing it. "Do you have to be amazing with *him*? He's an asshole."

"Maybe he's a different person now," I reason, but Kale's dark eyes remain skeptical as ever.

"Maybe he's not."

"Even if he isn't, *I'm* a different person now. I'm not the same nerd I was in high school."

I start down the stairs, but Kale stays on my heels, yapping at me like a nippy dog. "You're wearing the same boots."

"These boots are killer," I say—which should be obvious, but apparently needs to be said.

"Just do me a favor?"

At the front door, I turn around and begin backing onto the porch. "What favor?"

"If he hurts you again, use those boots to get revenge where it counts."

An Excerpt from

THE BRIDE WORE DENIM
A Seven Brides for Seven Cowboys Novel
by Lizbeth Selvig

When Harper Lee Crockett returns home
to Paradise Ranch, Wyoming, the last thing
she expects is to fall head-over-heels in lust
for Cole, childhood neighbor and her older
sister's long-time boyfriend. The spirited and
artistic Crockett sister has finally learned to
resist her craziest impulses, but this latest trip
home and Cole's rough and tough appeal might
be too much for her fading self-control.

Thank God for the chickens. They knew how to liven up a funeral.

Harper Crockett crouched against the rain-soaked wall of her father's extravagant chicken coop and laughed until she cried. This time, however, the tears weren't for the man who'd built the Henhouse Hilton—as she and her sisters had christened the porch-fronted coop that rivaled most human homes—they were for the eight multi-colored, escaped fowl that careened around the yard like over-caffeinated bees.

The very idea of a chicken stampede on one of Wyoming's largest cattle ranches was enough to ease her sorrow, even today.

She glanced toward the back porch of her parent's huge log home several hundred yards away to make sure she was still alone, and she wiped the tears and the rain from her eyes. "I know you probably aren't liking this, Dad," she said, aiming her words at the sopping chickens. "Chaos instead of order."

Chaos had never been acceptable to Samuel Crockett.

A *bock-bocking* Welsummer rooster, gorgeous with its burnt orange and blue body and iridescent green tail, powered past, close enough for an ambush. Harper sprang from her position and nabbed the affronted bird around its thick, shiny body. "Gotcha," she said as its feathers soaked her sweater. "Back to the pen for you."

The rest of the chickens squawked in alarm at the apprehension and arrest of one of their own. They scattered again scolding and flapping.

Yeah, she thought as she deposited the rooster back in the chicken yard, her father had no choice now but to glower at the bedlam from heaven. He was the one who'd left the darn birds behind.

As the hens fussed, Harper assessed the little flock made up of her father's favorite breeds—all chosen for their easygoing temperaments: friendly, buff-colored cochins; smart, docile, black and white Plymouth rocks; and sweet, shy black Australorps. Oh, what freedom and gang mentality could do—they'd turned into a band of egg-laying gangsters helping each other escape the law.

And despite there being seven chickens still left to corral, Harper reveled in sharing their attempted run for freedom with nobody. She brushed ineffectually at the mud on her soggy blue and brown broom skirt—hippie clothing, in the words of her sisters—and the stains on her favorite, crocheted summer sweater. It would have been much smarter to run back to the house and recruit help. Any number of kids bored with funereal reminiscing would have gladly volunteered. Her sisters—Joely and the triplets, if not Amelia—might have as well. The wrangling would have been done in minutes.

Something about facing this alone, however, fed her need to dredge any good memories she could from the day. She'd chased an awful lot of chickens throughout her youth. The memories served, and she didn't want to share them.

Another lucky grab garnered her a little Australorp who was returned, protesting, to the yard. Glancing around once more to check the empty, rainy yard, Harper squatted back under the eaves of the pretty, yellow chicken mansion and let the half dozen chickens settle. These were not her mother's birds. These were her father's "girls"—creatures who'd sometimes received more warmth than the human females he'd raised.

Good memories tried to flee in the wake of her petty thoughts, and she grabbed them back. Of course her father had loved his daughters. He'd just never been good at showing it. There'd been plenty of good times.

Rain pittered in a slow, steady rhythm over the lawn and against the coop's gingerbread scrollwork. It pattered into the genuine, petunia-filled, window boxes on their actual multi-paned windows. Inside, the chickens enjoyed oak-trimmed nesting boxes, two flights of ladders, and chicken-themed artwork. Behind their over-the-top manse stretched half an acre of safely-fenced running yard trimmed with white picket fencing. Why the idiot birds were shunning such luxury to go AWOL out here in the rain was beyond Harper—even if they had found the gate improperly latched.

Wiping rain from her face again, she concentrated like a cat stalking canaries and made three more successful lunges. Chicken wrangling was rarely about mad chasing and much more about patience. She smiled evilly at the remaining three criminals who now eyed her with concern.

"Give yourselves up, you dirty birds," she called. "Your day on the lam is finished."

She swooped toward a fluffy Cochin, a chicken breed

normally known for its lazy friendliness, and the fat creature shocked her by feinting and then dodging. For the first time in this hunt, Harper missed her chicken. A resulting belly-flop onto the grass forced a startled grunt from her throat, and she slid four inches through a puddle. Before she could let loose the mild curse that bubbled up to her tongue, the mortifying sound of clapping echoed through the rain.

"I definitely give that a nine-point-five."

A hot flash of awareness blazed through her stomach, leaving behind unwanted flutters. She closed her eyes, fighting back embarrassment, and she hadn't yet found her voice when a large, sinewy male hand appeared in front of her, accompanied by rich, baritone laughter. She groaned and reached for his fingers.

"Hello, Cole," she said, resignation forcing her vocal chords to work as she let him help her gently but unceremoniously to her feet.

Cole Wainwright stood before her, the knot of his tie pulled three inches down his white shirt front, the two buttons above it spread open. That left the tanned, corded skin of his neck at Harper's eye level, and she swallowed. His brown-black hair was spiked and mussed, as if he'd just awoken, and his eyes sparkled in the rain like blue diamonds. She took a step back.

"Hullo, you," he replied.